IDOLATRY:
A ROMANCE.

IDOLATRY: A ROMANCE.

JULIAN HAWTHORNE.

WILDSIDE PRESS

IDOLATRY: A ROMANCE

This edition published 2005 by Wildside Press, LLC.
www.wildsidepress.com

DEDICATION

To ROBERT CARTER, Esq.

Not the intrinsic merits of this story embolden me to inscribe it
to you, my dear friend, but the fact that you, more than any other man,
are responsible for its writing. Your advice and encouragement first led
me to book-making; so it is only fair that you should partake of whatever obloquy (or honor) the practice may bring upon me.

The ensuing pages may incline you to suspect their author of a
repugnance to unvarnished truth; but,—without prejudice to Othello,—
since varnish brings out in wood veins of beauty invisible before the
application, why not also in the sober facts of life? When the transparent artifice has been penetrated, the familiar substance underneath
will be greeted none the less kindly; nay, the observer will perhaps
regard the disguise as an oblique compliment to his powers of insight,
and his attention may thus be better secured than had the subject worn
its everyday dress. Seriously, the most matter-of-fact life has moods
when the light of romance seems to gild its earthen chimney-pots into
fairy minarets; and, were the storyteller but sure of laying his hands
upon the true gold, perhaps the more his story had of it, the better.

Here, however, comes in the grand difficulty; fact nor fancy is
often reproduced in true colors; and while attempting justly to combine life's elements, the writer has to beware that they be not mere
cheap imitations thereof. Not seldom does it happen that what he prof-
fers as genuine arcana of imagination and philosophy affects the reader
as a dose of Hieroglyphics and Balderdash. Nevertheless, the first duty
of the fiction-monger—no less than of the photographic artist doomed
to produce successful portraits of children-in-arms—is, to be amusing;
to shrink at no shifts which shall beguile the patient into procrasti-
nating escape until the moment be gone by. The gentle reader will not
too sternly set his face against such artifices, but, so they go not the
length of fantastically presenting phenomena inexplicable upon any
common-sense hypothesis, he will rather lend himself to his own
beguilement. The performance once over, let him, if so inclined, strip
the feathers from the flights of imagination, and wash the color from
the incidents; if aught save the driest and most ordinary matters of fact
reward his researches, then let him be offended!

De te fabula does not apply here, my dear friend; for you will show
me more indulgence than I have skill to demand. And should you find

matter of interest in this book, yours, rather than the author's, will be the merit. As the beauty of nature is from the eye that looks upon her, so would the story be dull and barren, save for the life and color of the reader's sympathy.

Yours most sincerely,
Julian Hawthorne.

I.

The Enchanted Ring.

One of the most imposing buildings in Boston twenty years ago was a granite hotel, whose western windows looked upon a graveyard. Passing up a flight of steps, and beneath a portico of dignified granite columns, and so through an embarrassing pair of swinging-doors to the roomy vestibule,—you would there pause a moment to spit upon the black-and-white tessellated pavement. Having thus asserted your title to Puritan ancestry, and to the best accommodations the house afforded, you would approach the desk and write your name in the hotel register. This done, you would be apt to run your eye over the last dozen arrivals, on the chance of lighting upon the autograph of some acquaintance, to be shunned or sought according to circumstances.

Let us suppose, for the story's sake, that such was the gentle reader's behavior on a certain night during the latter part of May, in the year eighteen hundred and fifty-three. If now he will turn to the ninety-ninth page of the register above mentioned, he will remark that the last name thereon written is, "Doctor Hiero Glyphic. Room 27." The natural inference is that, unless so odd a name be an assumed one, Doctor Glyphic occupies that room. Passing on to page one hundred, he will find the first entry reads as follows "Balder Helwyse, Cosmopolis. Room 29."

In no trifling mood do we call attention to these two names, and, above all, to their relative position in the book. Had they both appeared upon the same page, this romance might never have been written. On such seemingly frail pegs hang consequences the most weighty. Because Doctor Glyphic preferred the humble foot of the ninety-ninth page to the trouble of turning to a leading position on the one hundredth; because Mr. Helwyse, having begun the one hundredth page, was too incurious to find out who was his next-door neighbor on the ninety-ninth, ensued unparalleled adventures, and this account of them.

Our present purpose, by the reader's leave, and in his company, is to violate Doctor Hiero Glyphic's retirement, as he lies asleep in bed. Nor shall we stop at his bedside; we mean to penetrate deep into the darksome caves of his memory, and to drag forth thence sundry odd-looking secrets, which shall blink and look strangely in the light of discovery;—little thought their keeper that our eyes should ever behold them! Yet will he not resent our, intrusion; it is twenty years ago,—and he lies asleep.

Two o'clock sounds from the neighboring steeple of the Old South Church, as we noiselessly enter the chamber,—noiselessly, for the hush of the past is about us. We scarcely distinguish anything at first; the moon has set on the other side of the hotel, and perhaps, too, some of the dimness of those twenty intervening years affects our eyesight. By degrees, however, objects begin to define themselves; the bed shows doubtfully white, and that dark blot upon the pillow must be the face of our sleeping man. It is turned towards the window; the mouth is open; probably the good Doctor is snoring, albeit, across this distance of time, the sound fails to reach us.

The room is as bare, square, and characterless as other hotel rooms; nevertheless, its occupant may have left a hint or two of himself about, which would be of use to us. There are no trunks or other luggage; evidently he will be on his way again tomorrow. The window is shut, although the night is warm and clear. The door is carefully locked. The Doctor's garments, which appear to be of rather a jaunty and knowing cut, are lying disorderly about, on chair, table, or floor. He carries no watch; but under his pillow we see protruding the corner of a great leathern pocketbook, which might contain a fortune in banknotes.

A couple of chairs are drawn up to the bedside, upon one of which stands a blown-out candle; the other supports an oblong, coffin-shaped box, narrower at one end than at the other, and painted black. Too small for a coffin, however; no human corpse, at least, is contained in it. But the frame that lies so quiet and motionless here, thrills, when awaked to life, with a soul only less marvellous than man's. In short, the coffin is a violin-case, and the mysterious frame the violin. The Doctor must have been fiddling overnight, after getting into bed; to the dissatisfaction, perhaps, of his neighbor on the other side of the partition.

Little else in the room is worthy notice, unless it be the pocket-comb which has escaped from the Doctor's waistcoat, and the shaving materials (also pocketable) upon the wash-stand. Apparently our friend does not stand upon much toilet ceremony. The room has nothing more of significance to say to us; so now we come to the room's occupant. Our eyes have got enough accustomed to the imperfect light to discern what manner of man he may be.

Barely middle-aged; or, at a second glance, he might be fifteen to twenty-five years older. His face retains the form of youth, yet wears a subtle shadow which we feel might be consistent even with extreme old age. The forehead is wide and low, supported by regular eyebrows; the face beneath long and narrow, of a dark and dry complexion. In sleep, open-mouthed, the expression is rather inane; though we can readily imagine the waking face to be not devoid of a certain intensity and comeliness of aspect, marred, however, by an air of guarded anxiety which is apparent even now.

We prattle of the dead past, and use to fancy that peace must dwell there, if nothing else. Only in the past, say we, is security from jostle, danger, and disturbance; who would live at his ease must number his days backwards; no charm so potent as the years, if read from right to left. Living in the past, prophecy and memory are at one; care for the future can harass no man. Throw overboard that Jonah, Time, and the winds of fortune shall cease to buffet us. And more to the same effect.

And yet it is not so. The past, if more real than the future, is no less so than the present; the pain of a broken heart or head is never annihilated, but becomes part and parcel of eternity. This uneasy snorer here, for instance: his earthly troubles have been over years ago, yet, as our fancy sees him, he is none the calmer or the happier for that. Observe him, how he mumbles inarticulately, and makes strengthless clutchings at the blanket with his long, slender fingers.

But we delay too long over the external man, seeing that our avowed business is with the internal. A sleeping man is truly a helpless creature. They say that, if you take his hand in yours and ask him questions, he has no other choice than to answer—or to awake. The Doctor—as we know by virtue of the prophetic advantages just remarked upon—will stay asleep for some hours yet. Or, if you are clairvoyant, you have but to fall in a trance, and lay a hand on his forehead, and you may read off his thoughts,—provided he does his thinking in his head. But the world is growing too wise, nowadays, to put faith in old woman's nonsense like this. Again, there is—or used to be—an odd theory that all matter is a sort of photographic plate, whereon is registered, had we but eyes to read it, the complete history of itself. What an invaluable pair of eyes were that! In vain, arraigned before them, would the criminal deny his guilt, the lover the soft impeachment. The whole scene would stand forth, photographed in fatal minuteness and indelibility upon face, hands, coat-sleeve, shirt-bosom. Mankind would be its own book of life, written in the primal hieroglyphic character,—the language understood by all. Vocal conversation would become obsolete, unless among a few superior persons able to discuss abstract ideas.

We speak of these things only to smile at them; far be it from us to insult the reader's understanding by asking him to regard them seriously. But story-tellers labor under one disadvantage which is peculiar to their profession,—the necessity of omniscience. This tends to make them top arbitrary, leads them to disregard the modesty of nature and the harmonies of reason in their methods. They will pretend to know things which they never could have seen or heard of, and for the truth of which they bring forward no evidence; thus forcing the reader to reject, as lacking proper confirmation, what he would else, from its inherent grace or sprightliness, be happy to accept.

That we shall be free from this reproach is rather our good fortune than our merit. It is by favor of our stars, not by virtue of our own, that we turn not aside from the plain path of truth to the byways of super-naturalism and improbability. Yet we refrain with difficulty from a breath of self-praise; there is a proud and solid satisfaction in holding an unassailable position could we but catch the world's eye, we would meet it calmly!

Let us hasten to introduce our talisman. You may see it at this very moment, encircling the third finger of Doctor Glyphic's left hand; in fact, it is neither more nor less than a quaint diamond ring. The stone, though not surprisingly large, is surpassingly pure and brilliant; as its keen, delicate ray sparkles on the eye, one marvels whence, in the dead of night, it got together so much celestial fire. Observe the setting; the design is unique. Two fairy serpents—one golden, the other fashioned from black meteoric iron—are intertwined along their entire length, forming the hoop of the ring. Their heads approach the diamond from opposite sides, and each makes a mighty bite at it with his tiny jaws, studded with sharp little teeth. Thus their contest holds the stone firmly in place. The whole forms a pretty symbol of the human soul, battled for by the good and the evil principles. But the diamond seems, in its entirety, to be an awkward mouthful for either. The snakes are wrought with marvellous dexterity and finish; each separate scale is dis-tinguishable upon their glistening bodies, the wrinkling of the skin in the coils, the sparkling points of eyes, and the minute nostrils. Such works of art are not made nowadays; the ring is an antique,—a relic of an age when skill was out of all proportion to liberty,—a very distant time indeed. To deserve such a setting, the stone must have exceptional qualities. Let us take a closer look at it.

Fortunately, its own lustre makes it visible in every part; the minuteness of our scrutiny need be limited only by our power of eye. It is cut with many facets,—twenty-seven, if you choose to count them; perhaps (though we little credit such fantasies) some mystic signifi-cance may be intended in this number. Concentrating now our atten-tion upon any single facet, we see—either inscribed upon its surface, or showing through from the interior of the stone—a sort of monogram, or intricately designed character, not unlike the mysterious Chinese letters on tea-chests. Every facet has a similar figure, though no two are identical. But the central, the twenty-seventh facet, which is larger than the others, has an important peculiarity. Looking upon it, we find therein, concentrated and commingled, the other twenty-six characters; which, separately unintelligible, form, when thus united, a simple and consistent narrative, equivalent in extent to many hundred printed pages, and having for subject nothing less than the complete history of the ring itself.

Some small portion of this narrative—that, namely, which relates more particularly to the present wearer of the ring—we will glance at; the rest must be silence, although, going back as it does to the earliest records of the human race, many an interesting page must be skipped perforce.

The advantages to a historian of a medium such as this are too patent to need pointing out. Pretension and conjecture will be avoided, because unnecessary. The most trifling thought or deed of any person connected with the history of the ring is laid open to direct inspection. Were there more such talismans as this, the profession of authorship would become no less easy than delightful, and criticism would sting itself to death, in despair of better prey. So far as is known, however, the enchanted ring is unique of its kind, and, such as it is, is not likely to become common property.

II.

Out of Egypt.

But the small hours of the morning are slipping away; we must construe our hieroglyphics without further palaver. The sleeper lies upon his side, his left hand resting near his face upon the pillow. Were he to move it ever so little during our examination, the history of years might be thrown into confusion. Nevertheless, we shall hope to touch upon all the more important points, and in some cases to go into details.

Concentrating our attention upon the central facet, its clear ray strikes the imagination, and forthwith transports us to a distant age and climate. The air is full of lazy warmth. A full-fed river, glassing the hot blue sky, slides in long curves through a low-lying, illimitable plain. The rich earth, green with mighty crops, everywhere exhales upward the quivering heat of her breath. An indolent, dark-skinned race, turbaned and scantly clothed, move through the meadows, splash in the river, and rest beneath the palm-trees, which meet in graceful clusters here and there, as if striving to get beneath one another's shadow. Dirty villages swarm and babble on the river's brink.

Were there leisure to listen, the diamond could readily relate the whole history of this famous valley. For the stone was fashioned to its present shape while the thought that formed the Pyramids was yet unborn, and while the limestone and granite whereof they are built lay in their silent beds, dreaming, perchance, of airy days before the deluge, long ere the heated vapors stiffened into stone. Some great patriarch of early days, founder of a race called by his name, picked up this diamond in the southern desert, and gave it its present form; perhaps, also, breathed into it the marvellous historical gift which it retains to this day. Who was that primal man? how sounded his voice? were his eyes terrible, or mild? Seems, as we speak, we glimpse his majestic figure, and the grandeur of his face and cloudy beard.

He passed away, but the enchanted stone remained, and has sparkled along the splendid march of successive dynasties, and has reflected men and cities which to us are nameless, or but a half deciphered name. It has seen the mystic ceremonies of Egyptian priests, and counts their boasted wisdom as a twice-told tale. It has watched the unceasing toil of innumerable slaves, piling up through many ardent years the idle tombs of kings. It has beheld vast winding lengths of processions darken and glitter across the plain, slowly devoured by the shining city, or issuing from her gates like a monstrous birth.

But whither wander we? Standing in this hotel of modern Boston, we must confine our inquiries to a far later epoch than the Pharaohs'. Step aside, and let the old history sweep past, like the turbid and eddying current of the mysterious Nile; forbearing to launch our skiff earlier than at the beginning of the present century.

The middle of June, eighteen hundred and sixteen: the river is just beginning to rise, and the thirsty land spreads wide her lap to receive him. Some miles to the north slumbers Cairo in white heat, its outline jagged with minarets and bulbous domes. Southward, the shaded Pyramids print their everlasting outlines against the tremulous distance; old as they are, it seems as though a puff of the Khamsin might dissolve them away. Near at hand is a noisy, naked crowd of men and boys, plunging and swimming in the water, or sitting and standing along the bank. They are watching and discussing the slow approach up stream of a large boat with a broad lateen-sail, and a strange flag fluttering from the mast-head. Rumor says that this boat contains a company of strangers from beyond the sea; men who do not wear turbans, whose dress is close-fitting, and covers them from head to foot,—even the legs. They come to learn wisdom and civilization from the Pyramids, and among the ruins of Memphis.

A hundred yards below this shouting, curious crowd, stands, waist-deep in the Nile, a slender-limbed boy, about ten years old. He belongs to a superior caste, and holds himself above the common rabble. Being perfectly naked, a careless eye might, however, rank him with the rest, were it not for the talisman which he wears suspended to a fine gold chain round his neck; a curiously designed diamond ring, the inheritance of a long line of priestly ancestors. The boy's face is certainly full of intelligence, and the features are finely moulded for so young a lad.

He also is watching the upward progress of the lateen-sail; has heard, moreover, the report concerning those on board. He wonders where is the country from which they come. Is it the land the storks fly to, of which mother (before the plague carried both her and father to a stranger land still) used to tell such wonderful stories? Does the world really extend far beyond the valley? Is the world all valley and river, with now and then some hills, like those away up beyond Memphis? Are there other cities beside Cairo, and that one which he has heard of but never seen,—Alexandria? Wonders why the strangers dress in tight-fitting clothes, with leg-coverings, and without turbans! Would like to find out about all these things,—about all things knowable beside these, if any there be. Would like to go back with the strangers to their country, when they return, and so become the wisest and most powerful of his race; wiser even than those fabulously learned priestly instructors of his, who are so strict with him. Perhaps he might find all his forefathers there, and his kind mother, who used to tell him stories.

Bah! how the sun blisters down on head and shoulders: will take a dive and a swim,—a short swim only, not far from shore; for was not the priest telling of a boy caught by a great crocodile, only, a few days ago, and never seen since? But there is no crocodile near today; and, besides, will not his precious talisman keep him from all harm?

The subtile Nile catches him softly in his cool arms, dandles him, kisses Him, flatters him, wooes him imperceptibly onwards. Now he is far from shore, and the multitudinous feet of the current are hurrying him away. The slow-moving boat is much nearer than it was a minute ago,—seems to be rasping towards him, in spite of the laziness of the impelling breeze. The boy, as yet unconscious of his peril, now glances shorewards, and sees the banks wheel past. The crowd of bathers is already far beyond hearing yet, frightened and tired, he wastes his remaining strength in fruitless shouts. Now the deceitful eddies, once so soft and friendly, whirl him down in ruthless exultation. He will never reach the shore, good swimmer though he be!

Hark! what plunged from the bank,—what black thing moves towards him across the water? The crocodile! coming with tears in his eyes, and a long grin of serried teeth. Coming!—the ugly scaly head is always nearer and nearer. The boy screams; but who should hear him? He feels whether the talisman be yet round his neck. He screams again, calling, in half delirium, upon his dead mother. Meanwhile the scaly snout is close upon him.

A many-voiced shout, close at hand; a splashing of poles in the water; a rippling of eddies against a boat's bows! As the boy drifts by, a blue-eyed, yellow-bearded viking swings himself from the halyard, catches him, pulls him aboard with a jerk and a shout, safe! The long grin snaps emptily together behind him. The boy lies on the deck, a vision of people with leg-coverings and other oddities of costume swimming in his eyes; one of them supports his head on his knee, and bends over him a round, good-natured, spectacled face. Above, a beautiful flag, striped and starred with white, blue, and red, flaps indolently against the mast.

Precisely at this point the sleeper stirs his hand slightly, but enough to throw the record of several succeeding years into uncertainty and confusion. Here and there, however, we catch imperfect glimpses of the Egyptian lad, steadily growing up to be a tall young man. He is dressed in European clothes, and lives and moves amid civilized surroundings: Egypt, with her pyramids, palms, and river, we see no more. The priest's son seems now to be immersed in studies; he shows a genius for music and painting, and is diligently storing his mind with other than Egyptian lore. With him, or never far away, we meet a man considerably older than the student,—good-natured, whimsical, round of head and face and insignificant of feature. Towards him does the student observe the profoundest deference, bowing before him, and addressing him as "Master Hiero," or "Master Glyphic." Master Hiero, for his part, calls the Egyptian "Manetho"; from which we might infer his descent from the celebrated historian of that name, but will not insist upon this genealogy. As for the studies, from certain signs we fancy them tending towards theology; the descendant of Egyptian priests is to become a Christian clergyman! Nevertheless, he still wears his talismanic ring. Does he believe it saved him from the crocodile? Does his Christian enlightenment not set him free from such superstition?

So much we piece together from detached glimpses; but now, as the magic ray steadies once more, things become again distinct. Judging from the style and appointments of Master Hiero Glyphic's house, he is a wealthy man, and eccentric as well. It is full of strange incongruities and discords; beauties in abundance, but ill harmonized. One half the house is built like an Egyptian temple, and is enriched with many spoils from the valley of the Nile; and here a secret chamber is set apart for Manetho; its very existence is known to no one save himself and Master Hiero. He spends much of his time here, meditating and working amidst his books and papers, playing on his violin, or leaning idly back in his chair, watching the sunlight, through the horizontal aperture high above, his head, creep stealthily across the opposite wall.

But these saintly and scholarly reveries are disturbed anon. Master Hiero, though a bachelor, has a half sister, a pale, handsome, indolent young woman, with dark hair and eyes, and a rather haughty manner. Helen appears, and thenceforth the household lives and breathes according to her languid bidding. Manetho comes out of his retirement, and dances reverential attendance upon her. He is twenty-five years old, now; tall, slender, and far from ill-looking, with his dark, narrow eyes, wide brows, and tapering face. His manners are gentle, subdued, insinuating, and altogether he seems to please Helen; she condescends to him,—more than condescends, perhaps. Meantime, alas! there is a secret opposition in progress, embodied in the shapely person of that bright-eyed gypsy of a girl whom her mistress Helen calls Salome.

There is no question as to Salome's complete subjection to the attractions of the young embryo clergyman; she pursues him with eyes and heart, and seeing him by Helen's side, she is miserably but dumbly jealous.

How is this matter to end? Manetho's devotion to Helen seems unwavering; yet sometimes it is hard not to suspect a secret understanding between him and Salome. He has ceased to wear his ring, and once we caught a diamond-sparkle from beneath the thick folds of lace which cover Helen's bosom; but, on the other hand, we fear his arm has been round the gypsy's graceful waist, and that she has learnt the secret of the private chamber. Is demure Manetho a flirt, or do his affections and his ambition run counter to each other? Helen would bring him the riches of this world,—but what should a clergyman care for such vanities?—while Salome, to our thinking, is far the prettier, livelier, and more attractive woman of the two. Brother Hiero, whimsical and preoccupied, sees nothing of what is going on. He is an antiquary,—an Egyptologist, and thereto his soul is wedded. He has no eyes nor ears for the loves of other people for one another.

Provoking! The uneasy sleeper has moved again, and disorganized, beyond remedy, the events of a whole year. Judging from such fragments as reach us, it must have been a momentous epoch in our history. From the beginning, a handsome, stalwart, blue-eyed man, with a great beard like a sheaf of straw, shoulders upon the scene, and thenceforth becomes inextricably mixed up with dark-eyed Helen. We recognize in him an old acquaintance; he was on the lateen-sailed boat that went up the Nile; it was he who swung himself from the vessel's side, and pulled Manetho out of the jaws of death,—a fact, by the way, of which Manetho remained ignorant until his dying day. With this new arrival, Helen's supremacy in the household ends. Thor—so they call him—involuntarily commands her, and so her subjects. Against him, the Reverend Manetho has not the ghost of a chance. To his credit is it that he conceals whatever emotions of disappointment or jealousy he might be supposed to feel, and is no less winning towards Thor than towards the rest of the world. But is it possible that the talisman still hides in Helen's bosom? Does the conflict which it symbolizes beset her heart?

The enchanted mirror is still again, and a curious scene is reflected from it. A large and lofty room, windowless, lit by flaring lamps hung at intervals round the walls; the panels contain carvings in bas-relief of Egyptian emblems and devices; columns surround the central space, their capitals carved with the lotos-flower, their bases planted amidst papyrus leaves. A border of hieroglyphic inscription encircles the walls, just beneath the ceiling. In each corner of the room rests a red granite sarcophagus, and between each pair of pillars stands a mummy in its wooden case. At that end farthest from the low-browed doorway—which is guarded by two great figures of Isis and Osiris, sitting impassive, with hands on knees—is raised an altar of black marble, on which burns some incense. The perfumed smoke, wavering upwards, mingles with that of the lamps beneath the high ceiling. The prevailing color is ruddy Indian-red, relieved by deep blue and black, while brighter tints show here and there. Blocks of polished stone pave the floor, and dimly reflect the lights.

In front of the altar stands a ministerial figure,—none other than Manetho, who must have taken orders,—and joins together, in holy matrimony, the yellow-bearded Thor and the dark-haired Helen. Master Hiero, his round, snub-nosed face red with fussy emotion, gives the bride away; while Salome, dressed in white and looking very pretty and ladylike, does service as bridesmaid,—such is her mistress's whim. She seems in even better spirits than the pale bride, and her black eyes scarcely wander from the minister's rapt countenance.

But a few hours later, when bride and groom are gone, Salome,—who, on some plausible pretext of her own, has been allowed to remain with brother Hiero until her mistress returns from the wedding-tour,—Salome appears in the secret chamber, where the Reverend Manetho sits with his head between his hands. We will not look too closely at this interview. There are words fierce and tender, tears and pleadings, feverish caresses, incoherent promises, distrustful bargains; and it is late before they part. Salome passes out through the great tomblike hall, where all the lamps save one are burnt out; and the young minister remains to pursue his holy meditations alone.

We are too discreet to meddle with the honeymoon; but, passing over some eight months, behold the husband and wife returned, to plume their wings ere taking the final flight. Another strange scene attracts us here.

The dusk of a summer evening. Helen, with a more languid step and air than before marriage, saunters along a path through the trees, some distance from the house. She is clad in loose-flowing drapery, and has thrown a white shawl over her head and shoulders. Reaching a bench of rustic woodwork, she drops wearily down upon it.

Manetho comes out all at once, and stands before her; he seems to have darkened together from the shadow of the surrounding trees. Perhaps a little startled at his so abrupt appearance, she opens her eyes with a wondering haughtiness; but, at the same time, the light pressure of the enchanted ring against her bosom feels like a dull sting, and her heart beats uncomfortably. He begins to speak in his usual tone of softest deference; he sits down by her, and now she is paler, glances anxiously up the path for her delaying husband, and the hand that lifts her handkerchief to her lips trembles a little. Is it at his words? or at their tone? or at what she sees lurking behind his dusky eyes, curdling beneath his thin, dark skin, quivering down to the tips of his long, slender fingers?

All in a moment he bursts forth, without warning, without restraint, the fire of the Egyptian sun boiling in his blood and blazing in his passion. He seizes her soft white wrist,—then her waist; he presses against his, her bosom,—what a throbbing!—her cheek to his,—how aghast! He pours hot words in torrents into her ears,—all that his fretting heart has hoarded up and brooded over these months and years! all,—sparing her not a thought, not a passionate word. She tries to repel him, to escape, to scream for help; but he looks down her eyes with his own, holds her fast, and she gasps for breath. So the serpent coils about the dove, and stamps his image upon her bewildered brain.

Verily, the Reverend Manetho has much forgotten himself. The issue might have been disastrous, had not Helen, in the crisis of the affair, lost consciousness, and fallen a dead weight in his arms. He laid her gently on the bench, fumbled for a moment in the bosom of her dress, and drew out the diamond ring. Just then is heard the solid step of Thor, striding and whistling along the path. Manetho snaps the golden chain, and vanishes with his talisman; and he is the first to appear, full of sympathy and concern, when the distracted husband shouts for help.

Next morning, two little struggling human beings are blinking and crying in a darkened room, and there is no mother to give them milk, and cherish them in her bosom. There sits the father, almost as still and cold as what was his wife. She did not speak to him, nor seem to know him, to the last. He will never know the truth; Manetho comes and goes, and reads the burial-service, unsuspected and unpunished. But Salome follows him away from the grave, and some words pass between them. The man is no longer what he was. He turns suddenly upon her and strikes out with savage force; the diamond on his finger bites into the flesh of the gypsy's breast; she will carry the scar of that brutal blow as long as she lives. So he drove his only lover away, and looked upon her bright, handsome face no more.

Here Doctor Glyphic—or whoever this sleeping man may be—turns heavily upon his face, drawing his hand, with the blood-stained ring, out of sight. We are glad to leave him to his bad dreams; the air oppresses us. Come, 't is time we were off. The eastern horizon bows before the sun, the air colors delicate pink, and the very tombstones in the graveyard blush for sympathy. The sparrows have been awake for a half hour past, and, up aloft, the clouds, which wander ceaselessly over the face of the earth, alighting only on lonely mountaintops, are tinted into rainbow-quarries by the glorious spectacle.

III.

A May Morning.

King Arthur, in his Bohemian days, carried an adamantine shield, the gift of some fairy relative. Not only was it impenetrable, but, so intolerable was its lustre, it overthrew all foes before the lance's point could reach them. Observing this, the chivalric monarch had a cover made for it, which he never removed save in the face of superhuman odds.

Here is an analogy. The imaginative reader may look upon our enchanted facet-mirror as too glaringly simple and direct a source of facts to suit the needs of a professed romance. Be there left, he would say, some room for fancy, and even for conjecture. Let the author seem occasionally to consult with his companion, gracefully to defer to his judgment. Bare statement, the parade of indisputable evidence, is well enough in law, but appears ungentle in a work of fiction.

How just is this mild censure! how gladly are its demands conceded! Let dogmatism retire, and blossom, flowers of fancy, on your yielding stems! Henceforward the reader is our confidential counsellor. We will pretend that our means of information are no better than other writers'. We will uniformly revel in speculation, and dally with imaginative delights; and only when hard pressed for the true path will we snatch off the veil, and let forth for a moment a redeeming ray.

In this generous mood, we pass through the partition between No. 27 and No. 29. In the matter of bedchambers—even hotel bedchambers —there can be great diversity. That we were in just now was close and unwholesome, and wore an air of feverishness and disorder. Here, on the contrary, the air is fresh and brisk, for the breeze from Boston harbor—slightly flavored, it is true, by its journey across the northern part of the city—has been blowing into the room all night long. Here are some trunks and carpetbags, well bepasted with the names of foreign towns and countries, famous and infamous. One of the trunks is a bathing-tub, fitted with a cover—an agreeable promise of refreshment amidst the dust and weariness of travel. A Russia-leather travelling-bag lies open on the table, disgorging an abundant armament of brushes and combs and various toilet niceties. Mr. Helwyse must be a dandy.

Cheek by jowl with the haversack lies a cylindrical case of the same kind of leather, with a strap attached, to sling over the shoulder.

This, perhaps, contains a telescope. It would not be worth mentioning, save that our prophetic vision sees it coming into use by and by. Not to analyze too closely, everything in this room speaks of life, health, and movement. In spite of smallness, bareness, and angularity, it is fit for a May morning to enter, and expand to full-grown day.

It is now about half past four, and the crisp new sunshine, just above ground, has clambered over the windowsill, taken a flying leap across the narrow floor, and is chuckling full in the agreeable face asleep upon the pillow. The face, feeling the warmth, and conscious, through its closed eyelids, of the light, presently stretches its eyebrows, then blinks, and finally yawns,—Ah—h! Thirty-two even, white teeth, in perfect order; a great, red, healthy tongue, and a round, mellow roar, the parting remonstrance of the sleepy god, taking flight for the day. Thereupon a voice, fetched from some profounder source than the back of the head,—

"Steward! bring me my—Oh! A landlubber again, am I!"

Mr. Balder Helwyse now sits up in bed, his hair and beard,—which are extraordinarily luxuriant, and will be treated at greater length hereafter,—his hair and beard in the wildest confusion. He stares about him with a pair of well-opened dark eyes, which contrast strangely with his fair Northern complexion. Next comes a spasmodic stretching of arms and legs, a whisking of bedclothes, and a solid thump of two feet upon the floor. Another survey of the room, ending with a deep breathing in of the fresh air and an appreciative smack of the lips.

"O nose, eyes, ears, and all my other godlike senses and faculties! what a sensation is this of Mother Earth at sunrise! Better, seems to me, than ocean, beloved of my Scandinavian forefathers. Hear those birds! look at those divine trees, and the tall moist grass round them! By my head! living is a glorious business!—What, ho! slave, empty me here that bathtub, and then ring the bell."

The slave—a handsome, handy fellow, unusually docile, inseparable from his master, whose life-long bondsman he was, and so much like him in many ways (owing, perhaps, to the intimacy always subsisting between the two), that he had more than once been confounded with him,—this obedient menial—

No! not even for a moment will we mislead our reader. Are we not sworn confidants? What is he to think, then, of this abrupt introduction, unheralded, unexplained? Be it at once confessed that Mr. Helwyse travelled unattended, that there was no slave or other person of any kind in the room, and that this high-sounding order of his was a mere ebullition of his peculiar humor.

He was a philosopher, and was in the habit of making many of his tenets minister to his amusement, when in his more sportive and genial moods. Not to exhaust his characteristics too early in the story, it need only be observed here that he held body and soul distinct, and so far antagonistic that one or the other must be master; furthermore, that the soul's supremacy was the more desirable. Whether it were also invariable and uncontested, there will be opportunity to find out later. Meantime, this dual condition was productive of not a little harmless entertainment to Mr. Helwyse, at times when persons less happily organized would become victims of ennui. Be the conditions what they might, he was never without a companion, whose ways he knew, and whom he was yet never weary of questioning and studying. No subject so dull that its different aspects, as viewed from soul and from body, would not give it piquancy. No question so trivial that its discussion on material and on spiritual grounds would not lend it importance. Nor was any enjoyment so keen as not to be enhanced by the contrast of its physical with its psychical phase.

Waking up, therefore, on this May morning, and being in a charming humor, he chose to look upon himself as the proprietor of a body-servant, and to give his orders with patrician imperiousness. The obedient menial, then,—to resume the thread,—sprang upon the tub-trunk, whipped off the lid, and discharged the contents upon the bed in a twinkling. This done, he stepped to the bell-rope, and lent it a vigorous jerk, soon answered by a brisk tapping at the door.

"Please, sir, did you ring?"

"Indeed I did, my dear. Are you the pretty chambermaid?"

This bold venture is met by silence, only modified by a low delighted giggle. Presently,—"Did you want anything, sir, please?"

"Ever so many things, my girl; more than my life is long enough to tell! First, though, I want to apologize for addressing you from behind a closed door; but circumstances which I can neither explain nor overcome forbid my opening it. Next, two pails of the best cold water at your earliest convenience. Hurry, now, there's a Hebe!"

"Very good, sir," giggles Hebe, retreating down passage.

It is to be supposed that it was the plebeian body-servant that carried on this unideal conversation, and that the patrician soul had nothing to do with it. The ability to lay the burden of lapses from good taste, and other goods, upon the shoulders of the flesh, is sometimes convenient and comforting.

Balder Helwyse, master and man, turns away from the door, and catches sight of a white-robed, hairy-headed reflection in the looking-glass, the phantom face of which at once expands in a genial expression of mirth; an impalpable arm is outstretched, and the mouth seems thus to speak:

"Stick to your bath, my good fellow, and the evil things of this life shall not get hold of you. Water is like truth,—purifying, transparent; a tonic to those fouled and wearied with the dust and vanity of this transitional phenomenon called the world. Patronize it! be thy acquaintance with it constant and familiar! Remember, my dear Balder, that this slave of thine is the medium through which something better than he (thyself, namely) is filtered to the world, and the world to thee. Go to, then! if the filter be foul, shall not that which is filtered become unclean also?"

Here the rhetorical phantom was interrupted by the sound of a very good violin, touched with unusual skill, in the next room. The phantom vanished, but Mr. Helwyse seated himself softly upon the bed, listening with full enjoyment to every note; his very toes seeming to partake of his appreciation. Music is the mysterious power which makes body and soul—master and man—thrill as one string. The musician played several bars, beautiful in themselves, but unconnected; and ever and anon there sounded a discordant note, like a smirch upon a fair picture. The execution, however, showed a master hand, and the themes betrayed the soul of a true musician, albeit tainted with some subtile deformity.

"Heard him last night, and fell asleep, dreaming of a man with the brain of a devil and an angel's heart.—Drop in on him presently, and have him down to breakfast. If young, shall be our brother,—so long as there's anything in him. If—as I partly suspect—old, and a father, marry his daughter. But no; such a fiddler as he can't be married, unless unhappily." Mr. Helwyse runs his hands dreamily through his tangled mane, and shakes it back. If philosophical, he seems also to be romantic and imaginative, and impressionable by other personalities. It is, to be sure, unfair to judge a man from such unconsidered words as he may let fall during the first half hour after waking up in the morning; were it otherwise, we should infer that, although he might take a genuine interest in whomever he meets, it would be too analytical to last long, except where the vein was a very rich one. He would pick the kernel out of the nut, but, that done, would feel no sentimental interest in the shell. Too much of this! and yet who can help drawing conclusions (and not always incorrectly) from the first sight and sound of a new acquaintance?

There is a knock at the door, and Mr. Helwyse calls out, "Hullo? Ah! the cold water, emblem of truth. Thank you, Hebe; and scamper away as fast as you can, for I'm going to open the door!"

We also will retire, fastidious reader, and employ the leisure interval in packing an imaginary carpetbag for a short journey. Our main business, during the next few days, is with Mr. Helwyse, and since there will be no telling what becomes of him after that, he must be followed up pretty closely. A few days does not seem much for the getting a satisfactory knowledge of a man; nevertheless, an hour, rightly used, may be ample. If he will continue his habit of thinking aloud, will affect situations tending to bring out his leading traits of character; if we may intrude upon him, notebook in hand, in all his moods and crises,—with all this in addition to discretionary use of the magic mirror,—it will be our own fault if Mr. Helwyse be not turned inside out. Properly speaking, there is no mystery about men, but only a great dulness and lethargy in our perceptions of them. The secret of the universe is no more a secret than is the answer to a schoolboy's problem. A mathematician will draw you a triangle and a circle, and show you the trigonometrical science latent therein. But a profounder mathematician would do as much with the equation man!

While Mr. Helwyse is still lingering over his toilet, his neighbor the fiddler, whom he had meant to ask to breakfast, comes out of his room, violin-box in hand, walks along the passageway, and is off down stairs. An odd-looking figure; those stylish clothes become him as little as they would a long-limbed, angular Egyptian statue. Fashion, in some men, is an eccentricity, or rather a violence done to their essential selves. A born fop would have looked as little at home in a toga and sandals, as did this swarthy musician, doctor, priest, or whatever he was, in his fashion-plate costume. Then why did he wear it?

There are other things to be followed up before attending to that question. But the man is gone, and Balder Helwyse has missed this opportunity of making his acquaintance. Had he been an hour earlier,—had any one of us, for that matter, ever been an hour earlier or later,—who can tell how the destinies of the world would be affected! Luckily for our peace of mind, the hypothesis involves an impossibility.

IV.

A Brahman.

Whoever has been in Boston remembers, or has seen, the old Beacon Hill Bank, which stood, not on Beacon Hill, indeed, but in that part of School Street now occupied by the City Hall. You passed down by the dirty old church, on the northeast corner of School and Tremont Streets, which stands trying to hide its ugly face behind a row of columns like sooty fingers, and whose School Street side is quite bare, and has the distracted aspect peculiar to buildings erected on an inclined plane;—passing this, you came in sight of the bank, a darksome, respectable edifice of brick, two stories and a half high, and gambrel-roofed. It stood a little back from the street, much as an antiquated aristocrat might withdraw from the stream of modern life, and fancy himself exclusive. The poor old bank! Its respectable brick walls have contributed a few rubbish-heaps to the new land in the Back Bay, perhaps; and its floors and gambrel-roof have long since vanished up somebody's chimney; only its money—its baser part—still survives and circulates. Aristocracy and exclusivism do not pay.

The bank, perhaps, took its title from the fact that it owed its chief support to the Beacon Hill families,—Boston's aristocracy; and Boston's standard names appeared upon its list of managers. If business led you that way, you mounted the well-worn steps, and entered the rather strict and formal door, over which clung the weather-worn sign,—faded gold lettering upon a rusty black background. Nothing that met your eyes looked new, although everything was scrupulously neat. Opposite the doorway, a wooden flight of stairs mounted to the next floor, where were the offices of some old Puritan lawyers. Leaving the stairs on your left, you passed down a dusky passage, and through a glass door, when behold! the banking-room, with its four grave bald-headed clerks. But you did not come to draw or deposit, your business was with the President. "Mr. MacGentle in?" "That way, sir." You opened a door with "Private" painted in black letters upon its ground-glass panel. Another bald-headed gentleman, with a grim determination about the mouth, rose up from his table and barred your way. This was Mr. Dyke, the breakwater against which the waves of would-be intruders into the inner seclusion often broke themselves in vain; and unless you had a genuine pass, your expedition ended there.

Our pass—for we, too, are to call on Mr. MacGentle—would carry us through solider obstructions than Mr. Dyke; it is the pass of imagination. He does not even raise his head as we brush by him.

But, first, let us inquire who Mr. MacGentle is, besides President of the Beacon Hill Bank. He is a man of refinement and cultivation, a scholar and a reader, has travelled, and, it is said, could handle a pen to better purpose than the signing banknotes. In his earlier years he studied law, and gained a certain degree of distinction in the profession, although (owing, perhaps, to his having entered it with too ideal and high-strung views as to its nature and scope) he never met with what is vulgarly called success. Fortunately for the ideal barrister, an ample private estate made him independent of professional earnings. Later in life, he trod the confines of politics, still, however, enveloping himself in that theoretical, unpractical atmosphere which was his most marked, and, to some people, least comprehensible characteristic. A certain mild halo of statesmanship ever after invested him; not that he had at any time actually borne a share in the government of the nation, but it was understood that he might have done so, had he so chosen, or had his political principles been tough and elastic enough to endure the wear and strain of action. As it was, some of the most renowned men in the Senate were known to have been his intimates at college, and he still met and conversed with them on terms of equality.

Between law, literature, and statesmanship, in all of which pursuits he had acquired respect and goodwill, without actually accomplishing anything, Mr. MacGentle fell, no one knew exactly how, into the presidential chair of the Beacon Hill Bank. As soon as he was there, everybody saw that there he belonged. His social position, his culture, his honorable, albeit intangible record, suited the old bank well. He had an air of subdued wisdom, and people were fond of appealing to his judgment and asking his advice,—perhaps because he never seemed to expect them to follow it when given (as, indeed, they never did). The Board of Directors looked up to him, deferred to him,—nay, believed him to be as necessary to the bank's existence as the entire aggregate of its supporters; but neither the Board nor the President himself ever dreamed of adopting Mr. MacGentle's financial theories in the conduct of the banking business.

Let no one hastily infer that the accomplished gentleman of whom we speak was in any sense a sham. No one could be more true to himself and his professions. But—if we may hazard a conjecture—he never breathed the air that other men breathe; another sun than ours shone for him; the world that met his senses was not our world. His life, in short, was not human life, yet so closely like it that the two might be said to correspond, as a face to its reflection in the mirror; actual contact being in both cases impossible. No doubt the world and he knew of the barrier between them, though neither said so. The former, with its usual happy temperament, was little affected by the separation, smiled good-naturedly upon the latter, and never troubled itself about the difficulties in the way of shaking hands. But Mr. MacGentle, being only a single man, perhaps felt lonely and sad. Either he was a ghost, or the world was. In youth, he may have believed himself to be the only real flesh and blood; but in later years, the terrible weight of the world's majority forced him to the opposite conclusion. And here, at last, he and the world were at one!

Suppose, instead of listening to a personal description of this good old gentleman, we take a look at him with our own eyes. There is no danger of disturbing him, no matter how busy he may be. The inner retreat is very small, and as neat as though an old maid lived in it. The furniture looks as good as new, but is subdued to a tone of sober maturity, and chimes in so well with the general effect that one scarcely notices it. The polished table is mounted in dark morocco; behind the horsehair-covered armchair is a gray marble mantel-piece, overshadowing an open grate with polished bars and fire-utensils in the English style. During the winter months a lump of coal is always burning there; but the flame, even on the coldest days, is too much on its good behavior to give out very decided heat. Over the mantel-piece hangs a crayon copy of Correggio's Reading Magdalen,—the only touch of sentiment in the whole room, and that, perhaps, accidental.

The concrete nature of the President's surroundings is at first perplexing, in view of our theory about his character. But it is evident that the world could never provide him with furniture corresponding to the texture of his mind; and hence he would instinctively lay hold of that which was most commonplace and noncommittal. If he could realize nothing outside himself, he might at least remove whatever would distract him from inward contemplation. There is, however, one article in this little room which we must not omit to notice. It is a looking-glass; and it hangs, of all places in the world, right over Mr. MacGentle's standing-desk, in the embrasure of the window. As often as he looks up he beholds the reflection of his cultured and sad-lined physiognomy, with a glimpse of dusky wall beyond. Is he a vain man? His worst enemy, had he one, would not call him that. Nevertheless, Mr. MacGentle finds a pathetic comfort in this small mirror. No one, not even he, could tell wherefore; but we fancy it to be like that an exile feels, seeing a picture of his birthplace, or hearing a strain of his native music. The mirror shows him something more real, to his sense, than is anything outside of it!

Well, there stands the old gentleman, writing at this desk in the window. All men, they say, bear more or less resemblance to some animal; Mr. MacGentle, rather tall and slender, with his slight stoop, and his black broadcloth frock-coat buttoned closely about his waist, brings to mind a cultivated, grandfatherly greyhound, upon his hind legs. He has thick white hair, with a gentle curl in it, growing all over his finely moulded head. He is close-shaven; his mouth and nose are formed with great delicacy; his eyes, now somewhat faded, yet show an occasional reminiscence of youthful fire. The eyebrows are habitually lifted,—a result, possibly, of the growing infirmity of Mr. MacGentle's vision; but it produces an expression of half plaintive resignation, which is rendered pathetic by the wrinkles across his forehead and the dejected lines about his delicate mouth.

He is dressed with faultless nicety and elegance, though in a fashion now out of date. Perhaps, in graceful recognition of the advance of age, he has adhered to the style in vogue when age first began to weigh upon his shoulders. He gazes mildly out from the embrasure of an upright collar and tall stock; below spreads a wide expanse of spotless shirt-front. His trousers are always gray, except in the heat of summer, when they become snowy white. They are uniformly too long; yet he never dispenses with his straps, nor with the gaiters that crown his gentlemanly shoes.

Although not a stimulating companion, one loves to be where Amos MacGentle is; to watch his quiet movements, and listen to his meditative talk. What he says generally bears the stamp of thought and intellectual capacity, and at first strikes the listener as rare good sense; yet, if reconsidered afterwards, or applied to the practical tests of life, his wisdom is apt to fall mysteriously short. Is Mr. MacGentle aware of this curious fact? There sometimes is a sadly humorous curving of the lips and glimmering in the eyes after he has uttered something especially profound, which almost warrants the suspicion. The lack of accord between the old gentleman and the world has become to him, at last, a dreary sort of jest.

But we might go on forever touching the elusive chords of Mr. MacGentle's being; one cannot help loving him, or, if he be not real enough to love, bestowing upon him such affection as is inspired by some gentle symphony. Unfortunately, he figures but little in the coming pages, and in no active part; such, indeed, were unsuited to him. But it is pleasant to pass through his retired little office on our way to scenes less peaceful and subdued; and we would gladly look forward to seeing him once more, when the heat of the day is over and the sun has gone down.

V.

A New Man With an Old Face.

About an hour before noon on this same twenty-seventh of May, Mr. Dyke heard a voice in the outer room. He had held his position in the house as confidential clerk for nearly or quite twenty-five years, was blessed with a good memory, and was fond of saying that he never forgot a face or a voice. So, as this voice from the outer room reached his ears, he turned one eye up towards the door and muttered, "Heard that before, somewhere!"

The ground-glass panel darkened, and the door was thrown wide open. Upon the threshold stood a young man about six feet in height, of figure rather graceful and harmonious than massive. A black velveteen jacket fitted closely to his shape; he had on a Tyrolese hat; his boots, of thin, pliant leather, reached above the knee. He carried a stout cane, with a handle of chamois-horn; to a couple of straps, crossing each shoulder, were attached a travelling-scrip and a telescope-case.

But neither his attire nor the unusual size and dark brilliancy of his eyes was so noticeable as his hair and beard, which outgrew the bounds of common experience. Beards, to be sure, were far more rare twenty years ago than they have since become. The hair was yellow, with the true hyacinthine curl pervading it. Rejoicing in luxuriant might, it clothed and reclothed the head, and, descending lower, tumbled itself in bold masses on the young man's shoulders. As for the beard, it was well in keeping. Of a purer yellow than the hair, it twisted down in crisp, vigorous waves below the point marked by mankind's third shirt-stud. It was full half as broad as it was long, and lay to the right and left from the centre-line of the face. The owner of this oriflamme looked like a young Scandinavian god.

There seems to be a deeper significance in hair than meets the eye. Sons of Esau, whose beards grow high up on their cheekbones, who are hairy down to their ankles, and to the second joints of their fingers, are generally men of a kindly and charitable nature, strong in what we call the human element. One remembers their stout hand-grip; they look frankly in one's face, and the heart is apt to go out to them more spontaneously than to the smooth-faced Jacobs. Such a man was Samson, whose hair was his strength,—the strength of inborn truth and goodness, whereby he was enabled to smite the lying Philistines. And although they once, by their sophistries, managed to get the better of him for a while, they forgot that good inborn is too vigorous a matter for any mere razor finally to subdue. See, again, what a great beard Saint Paul had, and what an outspoken, vigorous heart! Was it from freak that Greeks and Easterns reverenced beards as symbols of manhood, dignity, and wisdom? or that Christian Fathers thundered against the barber, as a violator of divine law? No one, surely, could accuse that handy, oily, easy little personage of evil intent; but he symbolized the subtle principle which pares away the natural virtue of man, and substitutes an artificial polish, which is hypocrisy. It is to be observed, however, that hair can be representative of natural evil as well as of good. A tangle-headed bush-ranger does not win our sympathies. A Mussulman keeps his beard religiously clean.

Meanwhile the yellow-haired Scandinavian, whom we have already laid under the imputation of being a dandy, stood on the threshold of Mr. Dyke's office, and that gentleman confronted him with a singularly inquisitive stare. The visitor's face was a striking one, but can be described, for the present, only in general terms. He might not be called handsome; yet a very handsome man would be apt to appear insignificant beside him. His features showed strength, and were at the same time cleanly and finely cut. There was freedom in the arch of his eyebrows, and plenty of eye-room beneath them.

He took off his hat to Mr. Dyke, and smiled at him with artless superiority, insomuch that the elderly clerk's sixty years were disconcerted, and the Cerberus seemed to dwindle into the bumpkin! This young fellow, a good deal less than half Mr. Dyke's age, was yet a far older man of the world than he. Not that his appearance suggested the kind of maturity which results from abnormal or distorted development,—on the contrary, he was thoroughly genial and healthful. But that power and assurance of eye and lip, generally bought only at the price of many years' buffetings, given and taken, were here married to the first flush and vigor of young manhood.

"My name is Helwyse; I have come from Europe to see Mr. Amos MacGentle," said the visitor, courteously.

"Helwyse!—Hel—" repeated Mr. Dyke, having seemingly quite forgotten himself. His customary manner to strangers implied that he knew, better than they did, who they were and what they wanted; and that what he knew was not much to their credit. But he could only open his mouth and stare at this Helwyse.

"Mr. MacGentle is an old friend; run in and tell him I'm here, and you will see." The young man put his hand kindly on the elderly clerk's shoulder, much as though the latter were a gaping schoolboy, and directed him gently towards the inner door.

Mr. Dyke regained his voice by an effort, though still lacking complete self-command. "I beg your pardon, Mr. Helwyse, sir,—of course, of course,—it didn't seem possible,—so long, you know,—but I remembered the voice and the face and the name,—I never forget,—but, by George, sir, can you really be—?"

"I see you have a good memory; you are Dyke, aren't you?" And Mr. Helwyse threw back his head and laughed, perhaps at the clerk's bewildered face. At all events, the latter laughed, too, and they both shook hands very heartily.

"Beg pardon again, Mr. Helwyse, I'll speak to the President," said Mr. Dyke, and stepped into the sanctuary of sanctuaries.

Mr. MacGentle was taking a nap. He was seventy years old, and could drop asleep easily. When he slept, however lightly and briefly, he was pretty sure to dream; and if awakened suddenly, his dream would often prolong itself, and mingle with passing events, which would themselves put on the semblance of unreality. On the present occasion the sound of Helwyse's voice had probably crept through the door, and insinuated itself into his dreaming brain.

Mr. Dyke was too much excited to remark the President's condition. He put his mouth close to the old gentleman's ear, and said, in an emphatic and penetrating undertone:

"Here's your old friend Helwyse, who died in Europe two years ago, come back again, *younger than ever!*"

If the confidential clerk expected his superior to echo his own bewilderment, he was disappointed. Mr. MacGentle unclosed his eyes, looked up, and answered rather pettishly:

"What nonsense are you talking about his dying in Europe, Mr. Dyke? He hasn't been in Europe for six years. I was expecting him. Let him come in at once."

But he was already there; and Mr. Dyke slipped out again with consternation written upon his features. Mr. MacGentle found himself with his thin old hand in the young man's warm grasp.

"Helwyse, how do you do?—how do you do? Ah! you look as well as ever. I was just thinking about you. Sit down,—sit down!"

The old President's voice had a strain of melancholy in it, partly the result of chronic asthma, and partly, no doubt, of a melancholic temperament. This strain, being constant, sometimes had a curiously incongruous effect as contrasted with the subject or circumstances in hand. Whether hailing the dawn of the millennium; holding playful converse with a child, making a speech before the Board,—under whatever rhetorical conditions, Mr. MacGentle's intonation was always pitched in the same murmurous and somewhat plaintive key. Moreover, a corresponding immobility of facial expression had grown upon him; so that altogether, though he was the most sympathetic and sensitive of men, a superficial observer might take him to be lacking in the common feelings and impulses of humanity.

Perhaps the incongruity alluded to had not altogether escaped his own notice, and since discord of any kind pained him, he had mended the matter—as best he could—by surrendering himself entirely to his mournful voice; allowing it to master his gestures, choice of language, almost his thoughts. The result was a colorlessness of manner which did great injustice to the gentle and delicate soul behind.

This conjecture might explain why Mr. MacGentle, instead of falling upon his friend's neck and shedding tears of welcome there, only uttered a few commonplace sentences, and then drooped back into his chair. But it throws no light upon his remark that he had been expecting the arrival of a friend who, it would appear, had been dead two years. Helwyse himself may have been puzzled by this; or, being a quick-witted young man, he may have divined its explanation. He looked at his entertainer with critical sympathy not untinged with humor.

"I hope you are as well as I am," said he.

"A little tired this morning, I believe; I never was so strong a man as you, Helwyse. I think I must have passed a bad night. I remember dreaming I was an old man,—an old man with white hair, Helwyse."

"Were you glad to wake up again?" asked the young man, meeting the elder's faded eyes.

"I hardly know whether I'm quite awake yet. And, after all, Thor, I'm not sure that I don't wish the dream might have been true. If I were really an old man, what a long, lonely future I should escape! but as it is—as it is—"

He relapsed into reverie. Ah! Mr. MacGentle, are you again the tall and graceful youth, full of romance and fire, who roamed abroad in quest of adventures with your trusty friend Thor Helwyse, the yellow-bearded Scandinavian? Do you fancy this fresh, unwrinkled face a mate to your own? and is it but the vision of a restless night,—this long-drawn life of dull routine and gradual disappointment and decay? Open those dim eyes of yours, good sir! stir those thin old legs! inflate that sunken chest!—Ha! is that cough imaginary? those trembling muscles,—are they a delusion is that misty glance only a momentary weakness There is no youth left in you, Mr. MacGentle; not so much as would keep a rose in bloom for an hour.

"Have you seen Doctor Glyphic lately?" inquired Helwyse, after a pause.

"Glyphic?—do you know, I was thinking of him just now,—of our first meeting with him in the African desert. You remember!—a couple of Bedouins were carrying him off,—they had captured him on his way to some apocryphal ruin among the sand-heaps. What a grand moment was that when you caught the Sheik round the throat with your umbrella-handle, and pulled him off his horse! and then we mounted poor Glyphic upon it,—mummied cat and all,—and away over the hot sand! What a day was that! what a day was that!"

The speaker's eyes had kindled; for a moment one saw the far flat desert, the struggling knot of men and horses, the stampede of the three across the plain, and the high sun flaming inextinguishable laughter—over all!—and it had happened nigh forty years ago.

"He never forgot that service," resumed Mr. MacGentle, his customary plaintive manner returning. "To that, and to your saving the Egyptian lad,—. Manetho,—you owe your wife Helen: ah! forgive me,—I had forgotten; she is dead,—she is dead."

"I never could understand," remarked Helwyse, aiming to lead the conversation away from gloomy topics, "why the Doctor made so much of Manetho." "That was only a part of the Egyptian mania that possessed him, and began, you know, with his changing his name from Henry to Hiero; and has gone on, until now, I suppose, he actually believes himself to be some old inscription, containing precious secrets, not to be found elsewhere. Before the adventure with the boy, I remember, he had formed the idea of building a miniature Egypt in New Jersey; and Manetho served well as the living human element in it. 'Though I take him to America,' you know he said, 'he shall live in Egypt still. He shall have a temple, and an altar, and Isis and Osiris, and papyri and palm-trees and a crocodile; and when he dies I will embalm him like a Pharaoh.' 'But suppose you die first?' said one of us. 'Then he shall embalm me!' cried Hiero, and I will be the first American mummy.'"

Mr. MacGentle seemed to find a dreamy enjoyment in working this vein of reminiscence. He sat back in his low armchair, his unsubstantial face turned meditatively towards the Magdalen, his hands brought together to support his delicate chin. Helwyse, apprehending that the vein might at last bring the dreamer down to the present day, encouraged him to follow it.

"It must have been a disappointment to the Doctor that his protégé took up the Christian religion, instead of following the faith and observances of his Egyptian ancestors, for the last five thousand years!"

"Why, perhaps it was, Thor, perhaps it was," murmured Mr. MacGentle. "But Manetho never entered the pulpit, you know; it would not have been to his interest to do so; besides that, I believe he is really devoted to Glyphic, believing that it was he who saved him from the crocodile. People are all the time making such absurd mistakes. Manetho is a man who would be unalterable either in gratitude or enmity, although his external manner is so mild. And as to his taking orders, why, as long as he wore an Egyptian robe, and said his prayers in an Egyptian temple, it would be all the same to Glyphic what religion the man professed!"

"Doctor Glyphic is still alive, then?"

The old man looked at the young one with an air half apprehensive, half perplexed, as if scenting the far approach of some undefined difficulty. He passed his white hand over his forehead. "Everything seems out of joint today, Helwyse. Nothing looks or seems natural, except you! What is the matter with me?—what is the matter with me?"

Helwyse sat with both hands twisted in his mighty beard, and one booted leg thrown over the other. He was full of sympathy at the spectacle of poor Amos MacGentle, blindly groping after the phantom of a flower whose bloom and fragrance had vanished so terribly long ago; and yet, for some reason or other he could hardly forbear a smile. When anything is utterly out of place, it is no more pathetic than absurd; moreover, young men are always secretly inclined to laugh at old ones!

"Why should not Glyphic be alive?" resumed Mr. MacGentle. "Why not he, as well as you or I? Aren't we all about of an age?"

Helwyse drew his chair close to his companion's, and took his hand, as if it had been a young girl's. "My dear friend," said he, "you said you felt tired this morning, but you forget how far you've travelled since we last met. Doctor Glyphic, if he be living now, must be more than sixty years old. Your dream of old age was such as many have dreamed before, and not awakened from in this world!"

"Let me think!—let me think!" said the old man; and, Helwyse drawing back, there ensued a silence, varied only by a long and tremulous sigh from his companion; whether of relief or dejection, the visitor could not decide. But when Mr. MacGentle spoke, it was with more assurance. Either from mortification at his illusion, or more probably from imperfect perception of it, he made no reference to what had passed. Old age possesses a kind of composure, arising from dulled sensibilities, which the most self-possessed youth can never rival.

"We heard, through the London branch of our house, that Thor

Helwyse died some two years ago."

"He was drowned in the Baltic Sea. I am his son Balder."

"He was my friend," observed the old man, simply; but the tone he used was a magnet to attract the son's heart. "You look very much like him, only his eyes were blue, and yours, as I now see, are dark; but you might be mistaken for him."

"I sometimes have been," rejoined Balder, with a half smile.

"And you are his son! You are most welcome!" said Mr. Mac-Gentle, with old-fashioned courtesy.

"Forgive me if I have—if anything has occurred to annoy you. I am a very old man, Mr. Balder; so old that sometimes I believe I forget how old I am! And Thor is dead,—drowned,—you say?"

"The Baltic, you know, has been the grave of many of our forefathers; I think my father was glad to follow them. I never saw him in better spirits than during that gale. We were bound to England from Denmark."

"Helen's death saddened him,—I know,—I know; he was never gay after that. But how—how did—?"

"He would keep the deck, though the helmsman had to be lashed to the wheel. I think he never cared to see land again, but he was full of spirits and life. He said this was weather fit for a Viking.

"We were standing by the foremast, holding on by a belaying-pin. The sea came over the side, and struck him overboard. I went after him. Another wave brought me back; but not my father! I was knocked senseless, and when I came to, it was too late."

Helwyse's voice, towards the end of this story, became husky, and Mr. MacGentle's eyes, as he listened, grew dimmer than ever.

"Ah!" said he, "I shall not die so. I shall die away gradually, like a breeze that has been blowing this way and that all day, and falls at sunset, no one knows how. Thor died as became him; and I shall die as becomes me,—as becomes me!" And so, indeed, he did, a few years later; but not unknown nor uncared for.

Balder Helwyse was a philosopher, no doubt; but it was no part of his wisdom to be indifferent to unstrained sympathy. He went on to speak further of his own concerns,—a thing he was little used to do.

It appeared that, from the time he first crossed the Atlantic, being then about four years old, up to the time he had recrossed it, a few weeks ago, he had been journeying to and fro over the Eastern Hemisphere. His father, who, as well as himself, was American by birth, was the descendant of a Danish family of high station and antiquity, and inherited the restless spirit of his ancestors. In the course of his early wanderings he had fallen in with MacGentle, who, though somewhat older than Helwyse, was still a young man; and later these two had encountered Hiero Glyphic. About fifteen years after this it was that Thor appeared at Glyphic's house in New Jersey, and was welcomed by that singular man as a brother; and here he fell in love with Glyphic's sister Helen, and married her. With her he received a large fortune, which the addition of his own made great; and at Glyphic's death Thor or his heirs would inherit the bulk of the estate left by him.

So Thor, being then in the first prime of life, was prepared to settle down and become domestic. But the sudden death of his wife, and the subsequent loss of one of the children she had borne him, drove him once more abroad, with his baby son, never again to take root, or to return. And here Balder's story, as told by him, began. He seemed to have matured very early, and to have taken hold of knowledge in all its branches like a Titan. The precise age at which he had learned all that European schools could teach him, it is not necessary to specify; since it is rather with the nature of his mind than with the list of his accomplishments that we shall have to do. It might be possible, by tracing his connection with French, or German, or English philosophers, to make shrewd guesses at the qualities of his own! creed; but these will perhaps reveal themselves less diffidently under other tests.

The last four or five years of his life Balder had spent in acquiring such culture as schools could not give him. Where he went, what he did and saw, we shall not exercise our power categorically to reveal; remarking only that his means and his social rank left him free to go as high as well as low as he pleased,—to dine with English dukes or with Russian serfs. But a fine chastity inherent in his Northern blood had, whatever were his moral convictions, kept him from the mire; and the sudden death of his father had given him a graver turn than was normal to his years. Meanwhile, the financial crash, which at this time so largely affected Europe, swallowed up the greater part of Balder's fortune; and with the remnant (about a thousand pounds sterling), and a potential independence (in the shape of a learned profession) in his head, he sailed for Boston.

"I knew you were my uncle Hiero's bankers," he added, "and I supposed you would be able to tell me about him. He is my only living relative."

"Why, as to that, I believe it is a long time since the house has had anything to do with his concerns," returned the venerable President, abstractedly gazing at Balder's high boots; "but I'll ask Mr. Dyke. He remembers everything."

That gentleman (who had not passed an easy moment since Mr. Helwyse's arrival) was now called in, and his suspense regarding the mysterious visitor soon relieved. In respect to Doctor Glyphic's affair he was ready and explicit.

"No dollar of his money has been through our hands since winter of Eighteen thirty-five–six, Mr. Helwyse, sir,–winter following your and your respected father's departure for foreign parts," stated Mr. Dyke, straightening his mouth, and planting his fist on his hip.

"Hm–hm!" murmured the President, standing thin and bent before the empty fireplace, a coattail over each arm.

"You have heard nothing of him since then?"

"Nothing, Mr. Helwyse, sir! Reverend Manetho Glyphic—understood to be the Doctor's adopted son—came here and effected the transfer, under authority, of course, of his foster-father's signature. Where the property is at this moment, how invested with what returns, neither the President nor I can inform you, sir."

"Hm–hm!" remarked Mr. MacGentle again. It was a favorite comment of his upon business topics.

"It is possible I may be a very wealthy man," said Balder, when Mr. Dyke had made his resolute bow and withdrawn. "But I hope my uncle is alive. It would be a loss not to have known so eccentric a man. I have a miniature of him which I have often studied, so that I shall know him when we meet. Can he be married, do you think?"

"Why no, Balder; no, I should hardly think so," answered Mr. MacGentle, who, at the departure of his confidential clerk, had relapsed into his unofficial position and manner. "By the way, do *you* contemplate that step?"

"It is said to be an impediment to great enterprises. I could learn little by domestic life that I could not learn better otherwise."

"Hm,–we could not do without woman, you know."

"If I could marry Woman, I would do it," said the young man, unblushingly. "But a single crumb from that great loaf would be of no use to me."

"Ah, you haven't learned to appreciate women! You never knew your mother, Balder; and your sister was lost before she was old enough to be anything to you. By the way, I have always cherished a hope that she might yet be found. Perhaps she may,–perhaps she may."

Balder looked perplexed, till, thinking the old gentleman might be referring to a reunion in a future state, he said:

"You believe that people recognize one another in the next world, Mr. MacGentle?"

"Perhaps,–perhaps; but why not here as well?" murmured the other, in reply; and Balder, suspecting a return of absent-mindedness, yielded the point. He had grown up in the belief that his twin sister had died in her infancy; but his venerable friend appeared to be under a different impression.

"I shall go to New York, and try to find my uncle, or some trace of him," said he. "If I'm unsuccessful, I mean to come back here, and settle as a physician."

"What is your specialty?"

"I'm an eye-doctor. The Boston people are not all clear-eyed, I hope."

"Not all,—I should say not all; perhaps you may be able to help me, to begin with," said Mr. MacGentle, with a gleam of melancholy humor. "I will ask Mr. Dyke about the chances for a practice he knows everything. And, Balder," he added, when the young man rose to go, "let me hear from you, and see you again sometimes, whatever may happen to you in the way of fortune. I'm rather a lonely old man,—a lonely old man, Balder."

"I'll be here again very soon, unless I get married, or commit a murder or some such enormity," rejoined Helwyse, his long mustache curling to, his smile. They shook hands,—the vigorous young god of the sun and the faded old wraith of Brahmanism,—with a friendly look into each other's eyes.

VI.

The Vagaries Of Helwyse.

Balder Helwyse was a man full of natural and healthy instincts: he was not afraid to laugh uproariously when so inclined; nor apt to counterfeit so much as a smile, only because a smile would look well. What showed a rarer audacity,—he had more than once dared to weep! To crush down real emotions formed, in short, no part of his ideal of a man. Not belonging to the Little-pot-soon-hot family, he had, perhaps, never found occasion to go beyond the control of his temper, and blind rage he would in no wise allow himself; but he delighted in antagonisms, and though it came not within his rules to hate any man, he was inclined to cultivate an enemy, as more likely to be instructive than some friends. His love of actual battle was intense: he had punched heads with many a hard-fisted schoolboy in England; he bore the scar of a German *schläger* high up on his forehead; and later, in Paris, he had deliberately invaded the susceptibilities of a French journalist, had followed him to the field of honor, and been there run through the body with a small-sword, to the satisfaction of both parties. He was confined to his bed for a while; but his overflowing spirits healed the wound to the admiration of his doctors.

These examples of self-indulgence have been touched upon only by way of preparing the gentle reader for a shock yet more serious. Helwyse was a disciple of Brillat-Savarin,—in one word, a gourmand! His appetite never failed him, and, he knew how wisely to direct it. He never ate a careless or thoughtless meal, be its elements simple as they might. He knew and was loved by the foremost cooks all over Europe. Never did he allow coarseness or intemperance to mar the refinement of his palate.

"Man," he was accustomed to say, "is but a stomach, and the cook is the pope of stomachs, in whose church are no respectable heretics. Our happiness lies in his saucepan,—at the mercy of his spit. Eating is the appropriation to our needs of the good and truth of life, as existing in material manifestation: the cook is the high-priest of that symbolic ceremony! I, and kings with me, bow before him! But his is a responsibility beneath which Atlas might stagger; he, of all men, must be honest, warm-hearted, quick of sympathy, full of compassion towards his race. Let him rejoice, for the world extols him for its well-being;—yet tremble! lest upon his head fall the curse of its misery!"

This speech was always received with applause; the peroration being delivered with a vast controlled emphasis of eye and voice; and it was followed by the drinking of the cook's health. "The generous virtues," Mr. Helwyse would then go on to say, "arise from the cultivation of the stomach. From man's very earthliness springs the flower of his spiritual virtue. We affect to despise the flesh, as vile and unworthy. What, then, is flesh made of? of nothing?—let who can, prove that! No, it is made of spirit,—of the divine, everlasting substance; it is the wall which holds Heaven in place! If there be anything vile in it, it is of the Devil's infusion, and enters not into the argument."

A man who had expressed such views as these at the most renowned tables of France and England was not likely to forget his principles in the United States. Accordingly, he arose early, as we have seen, on the morning after his arrival, and forced an astonished waiter to marshal him to the kitchen, and introduce him to the cook. The cook of the Granite Hotel at that time was a round, red-lipped Italian, an artist and enthusiast, but whose temper had been much tried by lack of appreciation; and, although his salary was good, he contemplated throwing it over, abandoning the Yankee nation to its fate, and seeking some more congenial field. Balder, who, when the mood was on him, could wield a tongue persuasive as Richard the Third's, talked to this man, and in seven minutes had won his whole heart. The immediate result was a delectable breakfast, but the sequel was a triumph indeed. It seems that the æsthetic Italian had for several days been watching over a brace of plump, truffled partridges. This day they had reached perfection, and were to have been eaten by no less a person than the cook himself. These cherished birds did he now actually offer to make over to his eloquent and sympathetic acquaintance. Balder was deeply moved, and accepted the gift on one condition,—that the donor should share the feast! "When a man serves me up his own heart,—truffled, too,—he must help me eat it," he said, with emotion. The condition imposed was, after faint resistance, agreed to; the other episodes of the bill of fare were decided upon, and the Italian and the Scandinavian were to dine together that afternoon.

It still lacked something of the dinner-hour when Mr. Helwyse came out through the dark passageway of the Beacon Hill Bank, and paused for a few moments on the threshold, looking up and down the street. Against the dark background he made a handsome picture,—tall, gallant, unique. The May sunshine, falling, athwart the face of the gloomy old building, was glad to light up the waves of his beard and hair, and to cast the shadow of his hat-brim over his forehead and eyes.

The picture stays just long enough to fix itself in the memory, and then the young man goes lightly down the worn steps, and is lost along the crowded street. Such as he is now, we shall not see him standing in that dark frame again!

Wherever he went, Balder Helwyse was sure to be stared at; but to this he was admirably indifferent. He never thought of speculating about what people thought of Mr. Helwyse; but to his own approval—something not lightly to be had—he was by no means indifferent. Towards mankind at large he showed a kindly but irreverent charity, which excused imperfection, not so much from a divine principle of love as from scepticism as to man's sufficient motive and faculty to do well. Of himself he was a blunt and sarcastic critic, perhaps because he expected more of himself than of the rest of the world, and fancied that that person only had the ability to be his censor!

If the Christian reader regards this mental attitude as unsound, far be it from us to defend it! It must, nevertheless, be admitted that whoever feels the strong stirring of power in his head and hands will learn its limits from no purely subjective source. The lesson must begin from without, and the only argument will be a deadly struggle. Until then, self-esteem, however veiled beneath self-criticism, cannot but increase. And if the man has had wisdom and strength to abstain from vulgar self-pollution, Satan must intrust his spear to no half fledged devil, but grasp it in his own hand, and join battle in his own person.

Undismayed by this fact, Helwyse reached Washington Street, and followed its westerly meanderings, meaning to spend part of the interval before dinner in exploring Boston. He walked with an easy sideways-swaying of the shoulders, whisking his cane, and smiling to himself as he recalled the points of his interview with the President.

"Just the thing, to make MacGentle tutelary divinity of so elusive a matter as money! Wonder whether the Directors ever thought of that? For all his unreality, though, he has something more real in him than the heaviest Director on the Board!

"How composedly he took me for my father! and when he discovered his mistake, how composedly he welcomed me in my own person! Was that the extreme of senility? or was it a subtile assertion of the fact, that he who keeps in the vanguard of the age in a certain sense contains his father—the past—within himself, and is a distinct person chiefly by virtue of that containing power?

"Why didn't I ask him more about my foster-cousin Manetho? Egyptians are more astute than affectionate. Would he cleave to my poor uncle for these last eighteen years merely for love? Why did he transfer that money so soon after we sailed? Ten to one, he has in his own hands the future as well as the present disposal of Doctor Hiero Glyphic's fortune! The old gentleman has had time to make a hundred wills since the one he showed my father, twenty years ago!

"Well, and what is that to you? Ah, Balder Helwyse, you lazy impostor, you are pining for Egyptian fleshpots! Don't tell me about civility to relatives, and the study of human nature! You are as bad as you accuse your poor cousin of being,—who may be dead, or pastor of a small parish, for all you know. And yet every schoolgirl can prattle of the educational uses of poverty, and of having to make one's own living! I have a good mind to take your thousand pounds sterling out of your pocket and throw them into Charles River,—and then begin at the beginning! By the time I'd learnt what poverty can teach, it would be over,—or I am no true man! Only they who are ashamed of themselves, or afraid of other people, need to start rich."

Nevertheless, he could not do otherwise than hunt up the only relative he had in America. Subsequent events did not convict him of being a mere egotist, swayed only by the current of base success. He did not despise prosperity, but he cared yet more to find out truths about things and men. This is not the story of a fortune-hunter; not, at all events, of a hunter of such fortunes as are made and lost nowadays. But, when one half of a man detects unworthy motives in the other half, it is embarrassing. He acts most wisely, perhaps, who drops discussion, and lets the balance of good and bad, at the given moment, decide. Our compound life makes many compromises, whereby our progress, whether heavenward or hellward, is made slow—and sure!

Here, or hereabouts, Balder lost his way. When thinking hard, he was beside himself; he strode, and tossed his beard, and shouldered inoffensive people aside, and drew his eyebrows together, or smiled. Then, by and by, he would awake to realities, and find himself he knew not where.

This time, it was in an unsavory back-street; some dirty children were playing in the gutters, and a tall, rather flashily dressed man was walking along some distance ahead, carrying something in one hand. Helwyse at first mended his pace to overtake the fellow, and ask the way to the hotel. But he presently changed his purpose, his attention being drawn to the oddity of the other's behavior.

The man was evidently one of those who live much alone, and so contract unconscious habits, against which society offers the only safeguard. He was absorbed in some imaginary dialogue; and so imperfectly could his fleshly veil conceal his mental processes, that he gesticulated everything that passed through his mind. These gestures, though perfectly apparent to a steady observer, were so far kept within bounds as not to get more than momentary notice from the passers-by, who, indeed, found metal more attractive to their gaze in Helwyse.

Now did the man draw his head back and spread out his arms, as in surprise and repudiation; now his shoulders rose high, in deprecation or disclaimer. Now his forefinger cunningly sought the side of his nose; now his fist shook in an imaginary face. At times he would stretch out a pleading arm and neck; the next moment he was an inflexible tyrant, spurning a suppliant. Again he would break into a soundless chuckle; then, raising his hand to his forehead, seem overwhelmed with despair and anguish. Occasionally he would walk some distance quite passively, only glancing furtively about him; but erelong he would forget himself again, and the dialogue would begin anew.

Balder watched the man curiously, but without seeming to perceive the rather grisly similitude between the latter's vagaries and his own.

"What an ugly thing the inside of this person seems to be!" he said. "But then, whose thoughts and emotions would not render him a laughing-stock if they could be seen? If everybody looked, to his fellow, as he really is, or even as he looks to himself, mankind would fly asunder, and think the stars hiding places not remote enough! How many men in the world could walk from one end of the street they live in to the other, talking and acting their inmost thoughts all the way, and retain a bit of anybody's respect or love afterwards? No wonder Heaven is pure, if, our spiritual bodies are only thoughts and feelings! and a Hell where every devil saw his fellow's deformity outwardly manifested would be Hell indeed!

"But that can't be. Angels behold their own loveliness, because doing so makes them lovelier; but no devil could know his own vileness and live. They think their hideousness charming, and, when the darkness is thickest about them, most firmly believe themselves in Heaven. But the light of Heaven would be real darkness to them, for a ray of it would strike them blind!"

Helwyse was too prone to moralizing. It shall not be our cue to quote him, save when to do so may seem to serve an ulterior purpose.

"I would like to hear the story that fellow is so exercised about," muttered his pursuer. "How do I know it doesn't concern me? That violin-box he carries is very much in his way; shall I offer to carry it for him, and, in return, hear his story? If the music soothes his soul as much as the box moderates his gestures—"

Here the man abruptly turned into a doorway, and was gone. On coming up, Helwyse found that the doorway led in through a pair of green folding-doors to some place unseen. The house had an air of villanous respectability,—a gambling-house air, or worse. Did the musician live there? Helwyse paused but a moment, and then walked on; and thus, sagacious reader, the meeting was for the second time put off.

When he reached his hotel, he had only half an hour to dress for dinner in; but he prepared himself faultlessly, chanting a sort of hymn to Appetite the while. "Hunger," quoth he, "is mightiest of magicians; breeds hope, energy, brains; prompts to love and friendship. Hunger gives day and night their meaning, and makes the pulse of time beat; creates society, industry, and rank. Hunger moves man to join in the work of creation,—to harmonize himself with the music of the universe,—to feel ambition, joy, and sorrow. Hunger unites man to nature in the ever-recurring inspiration to food, followed by the ever-alternating ecstasy of digestion. Morning tunes his heart to joy, for the benison of breakfast awaits him. The sun scales heaven to light him to his noonday meal. Evening wooes him supperwards, and night brings timeless sleep, to waft him to another dawn. Eating is earth's first law, and heaven itself could not subsist without it!"

So Balder Helwyse and the cook feasted gloriously that afternoon, in the back pantry, and they solemnly installed the partridges among the constellations!

VII.

A Quarrel.

That same afternoon Mr. MacGentle put his head into the outer office and said, "Mr. Dyke, could I speak with you a moment?"

Mr. Dyke scraped back his chair and went in, with his polished bald head, and square face and figure,—a block of common-sense. He was more common-sensible than usual, that afternoon, because he had so strangely forgotten himself in the morning. Mr. MacGentle was in his usual position for talking with his confidential clerk,—standing up with his back to the fireplace, and his coattails over his arms. Experience had taught him that this attitude was better adapted than any other to sustain the crushing weight of Mr. Dyke's sense. To have conversed with him in a sitting position would have been to lose breath and vitality before the end of five minutes.

"Mr. Helwyse has thoughts of settling in Boston to practise his profession," began the President, gently. "I told him you would be likely to know what the chances are."

"Profession is—what?" demanded Mr. Dyke, settling his fist on his hip.

"O—doctor—physician; eye doctor, he said, I think."

"Eye doctor? Well, Dr. Schlemm won't last the winter; may drop any day. Just the thing for Mr. Helwyse,—Dr. Helwyse." And the subject, being discussed at some length between the two gentlemen, took on a promising aspect. His house was picked out for the new incumbent, his earnings calculated, his success foretold. Two characters so diverse as were the President and his clerk united, it seems, in liking the young physician.

"Married?" asked Mr. Dyke, after a pause.

"Why, no,—no; and he doesn't seem inclined to marry. But he is quite young; perhaps he may, later on in life, Mr. Dyke."

The elderly clerk straightened his mouth. "Matter of taste—and policy. Gives solidity,—position;—and is an expense and a responsibility." Mr. Dyke himself was well known to be the husband of an idolized wife, and the father of a despotic family.

"He never had the advantage of woman's influence in his childhood, you know. His poor mother died in giving him and his sister birth; and the sister was lost,—stolen away, two or three years later. He does not appreciate woman at her true value," murmured MacGentle.

"Stolen away? His sister died in infancy,—so I understood, sir," said the clerk, whose versions of past events were apt to differ from the President's.

But the President—perhaps because he was conscious that his memory regarding things of recent occurrence was treacherous—was abnormally sensitive as to the correctness of his more distant reminiscences.

"O no, she was stolen,—stolen by her nurse, just before Thor Helwyse went to Europe, I think," said he.

"Beg your pardon, sir," said Mr. Dyke, with an iron smile; "died,—burnt to death in her first year,—yes, sir!"

"Mr. Dyke," rejoined MacGentle, dignifiedly, lifting his chin high above his stock, "I have myself seen the little girl, then in her third year, pulling her brother's hair on the nursery floor. She was dark-eyed,—a very lovely child. As to the burning, I now recollect that when the house in Brooklyn took fire, the child was in danger, but was rescued by her nurse, who herself received very severe injuries."

Mr. Dyke heaved a long, deliberate sigh, and allowed his eyes to wander slowly round the room, before replying.

"You are not a family man, Mr. MacGentle, sir! Don't blame you, sir! Your memory, perhaps—But no matter! The nurse who stole the child was, I presume, the same who rescued her from the fire?"

Mr. Dyke perhaps intended to give a delicately ironical emphasis to this question, but his irony was apt to be a rather unwieldy and unmistakable affair. The truth was, he was a little staggered by the President's circumstantial statement; whence his deliberation, and his not entirely pertinent rejoinder about "a family man."

"And why not the same, sir? I ask you, why not the same?" demanded Mr. MacGentle, with slender imperiousness.

But, by this time, Mr. Dyke had thought of a new argument.

"The little girl, I understood you to say, was dark? Since she was the twin sister of one of Mr. Balder Helwyse's complexion, that is odd, Mr. MacGentle,—odd, sir." And the solid family man fixed his sharp brown eyes full upon the unsubstantial bachelor. The latter's delicate nostrils expanded, and a pink flush rose to his faded cheeks. He was now as haughty and superb as a paladin.

"I will discuss business subjects with my subordinates, Mr. Dyke; not other subjects, if you please! This dispute was not begun by me. Let it be carried no further, sir! Twins are not necessarily, nor invariably, of the same complexion. Let nothing more be said, Mr. Dyke. I trust the little girl may yet be found and restored to her family—to—to her brother! I trust she may yet be found, sir!" And he glared at Mr. Dyke aggressively.

"I trust you may live to see it, Mr. MacGentle, sir!" said the confidential clerk, shifting his ground in a truly masterly manner; and before the President could recover, he had bowed and gone out. Ten minutes afterwards MacGentle opened the door, and lo! Dyke himself on the threshold.

"Mr. Dyke!"

"Mr. MacGentle!" in the same breath.

"I—Mr. Dyke, let me apologize for my asperity,—for my rudeness," says MacGentle, stepping forward and holding out his thin white hand, his eyebrows more raised than ever, the corners of his mouth more depressed. "I am sincerely sorry that—that—"

"O sir!" cries the square clerk, grasping the thin hand in both his square palms; "O sir! O sir! No, no!—no, no! I was just coming to beg you—My fault,—my fault, Mr. MacGentle, sir! No, no!"

Thus incoherently ended the quarrel between these two old friends, the dispute being left undecided. But the important point was established that Balder Helwyse was insured a practice in Boston, in case his uncle Glyphic's fortune failed to enrich him.

VIII.

A Collision Imminent.

A large, handsome steamer was the "Empire State," of the line which ran between Newport and New York. She was painted white, had walking-beam engines, and ornamented paddle-boxes, and had been known to run nearly twenty knots in an hour. On the evening of the twenty-seventh of May, in the year of which we write, she left her Newport dock as usual, with a full list of passengers. On getting out of the harbor, she steamed into a bank of solid fog, and only got out of it the next morning, just before passing Hellgate, at the head of East River, New York. On the passage down Long Island Sound she met with an accident. She ran into the schooner Resurrection, which was lying becalmed across her course, carrying away most of the schooner's bowsprit, but doing no serious damage. This, however, was not the worst. On arriving in New York, it was found that one of the passengers was missing! He had fallen overboard during the night, possibly at the time of the collision.

Balder Halwyse was on board. After dining with the cook, and smoking a real Havana cigar (probably the first real one that he had ever been blessed with), he put a package of the same brand in his travelling-bag, bade his entertainer,—who had solemnly engaged to remain in Boston for Mr. Helwyse's sole sake,—bade his fellow-convivialist good by, and took the train to Newport, and from there the "Empire State" for New York.

The darkness was the most impenetrable that the young man had ever seen; Long Island Sound was like a pocket. The passengers—those who did not go to their staterooms at once—sat in the cabin reading, or dozing on the chairs and sofas. A few men stayed out on deck for an hour or two, smoking; but at last they too went in. The darkness was appalling. The officer on the bridge blew his steam fog-whistle every few minutes, and kept his lanterns hung out; but they must have been invisible at sixty yards.

Helwyse kept the deck alone. Apparently he meant to smoke his whole bundle of cigars before turning in. He paced up and down, Napoleonlike in his high boots, until finally he was brought to a stand by the blind night-wall, which no man can either scale or circumvent. Then he leaned on the railing and looked against the darkness. Not a light to be seen in heaven or on earth! The water below whispered and swirled past, torn to soft fragments by the gigantic paddlewheel. Helwyse's beard was wet and his hands sticky with the salt mist.

Ever and anon sounded the fog-whistle, hoarsely, as though the fog had got in its throat; and the pale glare of a lantern, fastened aloft somewhere, lighted up the white issuing steam for a moment. There was no wind; one was conscious of motion, but all sense of direction and position—save to the steersman—was lost. Helwyse could see the red end of his cigar, and very cosey and friendly it looked; but he could see nothing else.

It is said that staid and respectable people, when thoroughly steeped in night, will sometimes break out in wild grimaces and outlandish gesticulations. It is certainly the time when unlawful thoughts and words come to men most readily and naturally. Night brings forth many things that daylight starts from. The real power of darkness lies not in merely baffling the eyesight, but in creating the feeling of darkness in the soul. The chains of light are broken, and we can almost believe our internal night to be as impenetrable to God's eyes as that external, to our own!

By and by Helwyse thought he would find some snug place and sit down. The cabin of the "Empire State" was built on the main deck, abaft the funnel, like a long, low house. Between the stern end of this house and the taffrail was a small space, thickly grown with camp-stools. Helwyse groped his way thither, got hold of a couple of the camp-stools, and arranged himself comfortably with his back against the cabin wall. The waves bubbled invisibly in the wake beneath. After sitting for a while in the dense blackness, Helwyse began to feel as though his whole physical self were shrivelled into a single atom, careering blindly through infinite space!

After all, and really, was he anything more? If he chose to think not, what logic could convince him of the contrary? Visible creation, as any child could tell him, was an illusion,—was not what it seemed to be. But this darkness was no illusion! Why, then, was it not the only reality? and he but an atom, charged with a vital power of so-called senses, that generally deceived him, but sometimes—as now—let him glimpse the truth? The fancy, absurd as it was, had its attraction for the time being. This great living, staring world of men and things is a terrible weight to lug upon one's back. But if man be an invisible atom, what a vast, wild, boundless freedom is his! Infinite space is wide enough to cut any caper in, and no one the wiser.

One would like to converse with a man who had been born and had lived in solitude and darkness. What original views he would have about himself and life! Would he think himself an abstract intelligence, out of space and time? What a riddle his physical sensations would be to him! Or, suppose him to meet with another being brought up in the same way; how they would mystify each other! Would they learn to feel shame, love, hate? or do the passions only grow in sunshine? Would they ever laugh? Would they hatch plots against each other, lie, deceive? Would they have secrets from each other?

But, fancy aside, take a supposable case. Suppose two sinners of our daylight world to meet for the first time, mutually unknown, on a night like this. Invisible, only audible, how might they plunge profound into most naked intimacy,—read aloud to each other the secrets of their deepest hearts! Would the confession lighten their souls, or make them twice as heavy as before? Then, the next morning, they might meet and pass, unrecognizing and unrecognized. But would the knot binding them to each other be any the less real, because neither knew to whom he was tied? Some day, in the midst of friends, in the brightest glare of the sunshine, the tone of a voice would strike them pale and cold.

Somewhat after this fashion, perhaps, did Helwyse commune with himself. He liked to follow the whim of the moment, whither it would lead him. He was romantic; it was one of his agreeablest traits, because spontaneous; and he indulged it the more, as being confident that he had too much solid ballast in the hold to be in danger of upsetting. Tonight, at this point of his mental ramble, he found that his cigar had gone out. Had he been thinking aloud? He believed not, and yet there was no telling; he often did so, unconsciously. Were it so, and were any one listening, that person had him decidedly at advantage!

What put it into his head that some one might be listening? It may have come by pure accident,—if there be such a thing. The idea returned, stealing over his mind like a chilling breath. What if some one had all along been close beside him, with eyes fixed upon him! Helwyse found himself sitting perfectly still, holding his breath to listen. There was no disguising it,—he felt uneasy. He wished his cigar had not gone out. On second thoughts, he wished there had not been any cigar at all, because, if any one were near, the cigar must have pointed out the smoker's precise position. The uneasiness did not lessen, but grew more defined.

It was like the sensation felt when pointed at by a human finger, or stared at persistently. Was there indeed any one near? No sound or movement gave answer, but the odd sensation continued. Helwyse fancied he could now tell whence it came;—from the left, and not far away. He peered earnestly thitherward, but his eyes only swallowed blackness.

Was not this carrying a whim to a foolish length? If he thought he had a companion, why not speak, and end the doubt? But the dense silence, darkness, uncertainty, made common-sense seem out of place. The whole black fog, the sea, the earth itself, seemed to be pressing down his will! The longer he delayed, the weaker he grew.

A slight shifting of his position caused him all at once to encounter the eyes of the unseen presence with his own! The stout-nerved young fellow was startled to the very heart. Was the unseen presence startled also? At all events, the shock found Balder Helwyse his tongue, seldom before tied up without his consent.

"I hope I'm not disturbing your solitude. You are not a noisy neighbor, sir."

So flat fell the words on the blank darkness, it seemed as if there could never be a reply. Nevertheless, a reply came.

"You must come much nearer me than you are, to disturb my solitude. It does not consist in being without a companion."

The quality of this voice of darkness was peculiar. It sounded old, yet of an age that had not outlived the devil of youth. Probably the invisibility of the speaker enhanced its effect. With most of the elements of pleasing, it was nevertheless repulsive. It was soft, fluent, polished, but savage license was not far off, hard held by a slender leash; an underlying suggestion of harsh discordance. The utterance, though somewhat rapid, was carefully distinct.

Helwyse had the gift of familiarity,—of that rare kind of familiarity which does not degenerate into contempt. But there was an incongruity about this person, hard to assimilate. In a couple of not very original sentences, he had wrought upon his listener an effect of depraved intellectual power, strangely combined with artless simplicity,—an unspeakably distasteful conjunction! Imagination, freed from the check of the senses, easily becomes grotesque; and Helwyse, unable to see his companion, had no difficulty in picturing him as a grisly monster, having a satanic head set upon the ingenuous shoulders of a child. And what was Helwyse himself? No longer, surely, the gravely humorous moralizer? The laws of harmony forbid! He is a monster likewise; say—since grotesqueness is in vogue—the heart of Lucifer burning beneath the cool brain of a Grecian sage. The symbolism is not inapt, since Helwyse, while afflicted with pride and ambition as abstract as boundless, had, at the same time, a logical, fearless brain, and keen delight in beauty.

"I was just thinking," remarked the latter monster, "that this was a good place for confidential conversation."

"You believe, then, that talking relieves the mind?" rejoined the former, softly.

"I believe a thief or a murderer would be glad of an hour—such as now passes—to impart the story of what is dragging him to Hell. And even the best houses are better for an airing!"

"A pregnant idea! There are certainly some topics one would like to discuss, free from the restraint that responsibility imposes. Have you ever reflected on the subject of omnipotence?"

Somewhat confounded at this bold question, Helwyse hesitated a moment.

"I can't see you, remember, any more than you can see me," insinuated the voice, demurely.

"I believe I have sometimes asked myself whether it were obtainable,—how it might best be approximated," admitted Helwyse, cautiously; for he began to feel that even darkness might be too transparent for the utterance of some thoughts.

"But you never got a satisfactory answer, and are not therefore omnipotent? Well, the reason probably is, that you started wrongly. Did it ever occur to you to try the method of sin?"

"To obtain omnipotence? No!"

"It wouldn't be right,—eh?" chuckled the voice. "But then one must lay aside prejudice if one wants to be all-powerful! Now, sin denotes separation; the very etymology of the word should have attracted the attention of an ambitious man, such as you seem to be. It is a path separate from all other paths, and therefore worth exploring."

"It leads to weakness, not to power!"

"If followed in the wrong spirit, very true. But the wise man sins and is strong! See how frank I am!—But don't let me monopolize the conversation."

"I should like to hear your argument, if you have one. You are a prophet of new things."

"Sin is an old force, though it may be applied in new ways. Well, you will admit that the true sinner is the only true reformer and philosopher among men? No? I will explain, then. The world is full of discordances, for which man is not to blame. His endeavor to meet and harmonize this discordance is called sin. His indignation at disorder, rebellion against it, attempts to right it, are crimes! That is the vulgar argument which wise men smile at."

"I may be very dull; but I think your explanations need explaining."

"We'll take some examples. What is the liar, but one who sees the false relations of things, and seeks to put them in the true? The mission of the thief, again, is to equalize the notoriously unjust distribution of wealth. A fundamental defect in the principles of human association gave birth to the murderer; and as for the adulterer, he is an immortal protest against the absurd laws which interfere between the sexes. Are not these men, and others of similar stamp, the bulwarks of true society,—our leaders towards justice and freedom?"

Whether this were satire, madness, or earnest, Helwyse could not determine. The night-fog had got into his brain. He made shift, however, to say that the criminal class were not, as a mere matter of fact, the most powerful.

"Again you misapprehend me," rejoined the voice, with perfect suavity. "No doubt there are many weak and foolish persons who commit crimes,—nay, I will admit that the vast majority of criminals are weak and foolish; but that does not affect the dignity of the true sinner,—he who sins from exalted motives. Ignorance is the only real crime, polluting deeds that, wisely done, are sublime. Sin is culture!"

"Were I, then, from motives of self-culture, to kill you, I should be taking a long step towards rising in your estimation?" put in Helwyse.

"Admirable!" softly exclaimed the voice, in a tone as of an approving pat on the back. "Certainly, I should be the last to deny it! But would it not be more for the general good, were I, who have long been a student of these things, to kill a seeming novice like you? It would assure me of having had one sincere disciple."

"I wonder whether he's really mad?" mused Balder Helwyse, shuddering a little in the dampness.

"But, badinage aside," resumed this loquacious voice, "although there is so much talk and dispute about evil, very few people know what evil essentially is. Now, there are some things, the mere doing of which by the most involuntary agent would at once stamp his soul with the conviction of ineffable sin. He would have touched the essence of evil. And if a wise man has done that, he has had in his hand the key to omnipotence!"

"It is easily had, then. A man need but take his Leviticus and Deuteronomy, and run through the catalogue of crimes. He would be sure of finding the key hidden beneath some of them."

"No; you do Moses scant justice. He—shrewd soul!—was too cunning to fall into such an error as that. He forbade a few insignificant and harmless acts, which every one is liable to commit. His policy was no less simple than sagacious. By amusing mankind with such trumpery, he lured them off the scent of true sin. Believe me, the artifice was no idle one. Should mankind learn the secret, a generation would not pass before the world would be turned upside down, and its present Ruler buried in the ruins!"

At this point, surely, Helwyse got up and went to his stateroom without listening to another word?—Not so. The Lucifer in him was getting the better of the sage. He wanted to hear all that the voice of darkness had to say. There might be something new, something instructive in it. He might hear a word that would unbar the door he had striven so long to open. He aimed at knowledge and power beyond recognized human reach. He had taken thought with himself keenly and deeply, but was still uncertain and unsatisfied. Here opened a new avenue, so untried as to transcend common criticism. The temptation to omnipotence is a grand thing, and may have shaken greater men than Helwyse; and he had trained himself to regard it—not exactly as a temptation. As for good or bad methods,—at a certain intellectual height such distinctions vanish. Vulgar immorality he would turn from as from anything vulgar; but refined, philosophic immorality, as a weapon of power,—there was fascination in it.

—Folly and delusion!—

But Helwyse was only Helwyse, careering through pitchy darkness, on a viewless sea, with a plausible voice at his ear insinuating villanous thoughts with an air of devilish good-fellowship!

The "Empire State" was at this moment four and a half miles northeast of the schooner whose bowsprit she was destined to carry away. The steamer was making about ten knots an hour: the schooner was slowly drifting with the tide into the line of the steamer's course. The catastrophe was therefore about twenty-seven minutes distant.

IX.

The Voice of Darkness.

The fog-whistle screeched dismally. Helwyse took his feet off the camp-stool in front of him, and sat upright.

"Do you know this secret of sin?" he asked.

"It must, of course, be an object of speculation to a thoughtful man," answered the voice, modestly parrying the question. "But I assure you that only a man of intellect—of genius—has in him the intelligence, the sublime reach of soul, which could attain the full solution of the problem; they who merely blunder into it would fail to grasp the grand significance of the idea."

"But you affirm that whoever fairly masters the problem of absolute sin would have God and His kingdom at his mercy?"

"I am loath to appear boastful; but I apprehend the fact to be not unlike what you suggest," the voice replied, with a subdued gusto. "It would depend upon our hypothetical person's discretion, and his views as to the claims of the august Being who has so long controlled the destinies of the human race, how much the existing order of things might have to fear from him. I should imagine that the august Being, if He be as wise as they say He is, would be careful how He treated this hypothetical person!"

"You are a liar," said Helwyse, unceremoniously. "Why is not Satan, who must possess this all-powerful knowledge, supreme over the universe?"

Instead of taking offence (as Helwyse, to do him justice, hoped it would; for his Berserker blood, which boiled only at heaven-and-hell temperature, was beginning to stir in him),—so far from being offended, the voice only uttered its peculiar quiet chuckle.

"Your frankness charms me! it proves you worthy to learn. Satan—supposing there be such a personage—divides, with the other august Being, the sovereignty of the spiritual world. Were I a cynic, I should say he owned at least half of the physical world into the bargain! But Satan is only a spirit, and his power over men is but as the power of a dream. Were a Satan to arise in the flesh, so that men could see and touch him, and hear his voice with their fleshy ears,—there were a Satan! Already has the Incarnation of goodness appeared to mankind, and, though the world be moved to virtue only slowly and with reluctance, mark how mighty has been his influence! What think you, then, would be the power of a Christ of evil, showing to men the path they already grope for? I tell you, the human race would be his only; Hell, full to bursting with their hurrying souls, would outweigh Heaven in the balance; the teller of the secret would be king above all,—forever!"

The sinuous voice twined round the listener's mind, swaddling the vigorous limbs into imbecile inertia. But when before now did a sane human brain let itself be duped by sophistry? This case were worth marking, if only because it is unparalleled.

"And the only punishable sin is ignorance!" muttered Helwyse.

"Well, I have thought so, too. And I have questioned whether a man might have power over himself, to put his hand to evil or to good alike, and to remain impartial and impassive; and so make evil and good alike minister to his culture and raise him upwards!"

"The question does credit to your wit," chimed in the voice of darkness. "Whoever has in him the making of a deity must learn the nature of opposites. The soldier will not join battle without studying the tactics of the enemy. Without experimental knowledge of both evil and good, none but a fool would believe that man can become all-powerful."

"From the care with which you avoid speaking the name of God, if from no other cause, I should suppose you to be the Devil himself!" observed Helwyse, bluntly.

"Well, profanity is vulgar! As to my being the Devil, it is too dark here for either denial or acknowledgment to be of practical use. But (to be serious)—about this secret—"

The voice paused interrogatively. Lucifer, speaking through Helwyse's lips, demanded sullenly:

"Well, what is the secret?"

What, indeed! Why, there is no such secret;—it is a bugbear! But the moral perversion of the person who could soberly ask the question that Helwyse asked is not so easily disposed of. It met, indeed, with full recognition. As for the subtile voice, having accomplished its main purpose, it began now to evade the point and to run into digressions; until the collision came, and ended the conversation forever.

"Unfortunately," said the voice, "the secret is not such as may be told in a word. Like all profound knowledge, it can only be communicated by leading the learner, step by step, over the ground traversed by the original discoverer. Let me, as a sort of preliminary, suppose a case."

Hereupon ensued a considerable silence, and Helwyse seemed once more a detached atom, flying through infinite darkness without guide or control. Where was he?—what was he? Did the world exist,—the broad earth, the sunny sky, the beauty, the sound, the order and sweet succession of nature? Was he a shadow that had dreamed for a moment a strange dream, and would anon be quenched, and know what had seemed Self no more? Strangely, through the doubt and uncertainty, Helwyse felt the pressure of his shoulders against the cabin wall, and the touch of the dead cigar between his fingers.

The voice, resuming, restored him to a reality that seemed less trustworthy than the doubt. The tone was not quite the same as heretofore. The smooth mocking had given place to a hurried excitement, alien to the philosophic temperament.

"A man kidnaps the child of his enemy, through the child to revenge himself. Kill it?—no! he is no short-sighted bungler; he has refinement, foresight, understanding. She is but an infant,—open and impressible, warm and sanguine! He isolates her from sight and reach. He pries into her nature with keenest delicacy,—no leaf is unread. Being learnt, he works upon it; touches each budding trait with gentlest impulse. No violence! he seems to leave her to her own development; yet nothing goes against his will. More than half is left to nature, but his scarce perceptible touches bias nature. Ah! the idealization of education!"

"This sounds more real than hypothetical!" thought Helwyse.

"So cunning was he, he reversed in her mind the universal law. Evil was good; good, evil. She grew fast and strong, for evil is the sweeter food; it is rich earth to the plant. She never knew that evil existed, yet evil was all she knew! For whatever is forced reacts; he never taught her positive sin, lest she perversely turn to good."

"Did he mean insensibly to initiate her into the knowledge of absolute sin?"

"Such would be his purpose,—such would be his purpose. To make her a devil, without the chance of knowing it possible to be anything else!"

"He was a fool," growled Helwyse. "The plan is folly,—impracticable in twenty ways. A soul cannot be so influenced. Devils are not made by education. The only devil would be the educator!"

But the voice had forgotten his presence. It ceased not to mutter to itself while he was speaking, and now it broke forth again.

"Years have passed,—she is a woman now. She knows not that the world exists. All is yet latent within her. But the time is at hand when the hidden forces shall flower! Plunged into life, with nothing to hold by, no truth, no divine help; her marvellous powers and passions in full strength,—all trained to drag her down,—not one aspiring, maddened by new thoughts, limitless opportunities opening before her,—she will plunge into such an abyss of sin as has been undreamt of since the Deluge!"

"Well,—what of it? what is the upshot?" questioned Helwyse with sullen impatience. The emotion now apparent in the voice, uncanny though it was, counteracted the spell wrought by its purely intellectual depravity. Helwyse was perhaps beginning to understand that he had ventured his stock of virgin gold for a handful of unclean wastepaper!

"He will come back,—her father,—my enemy! I have waited for him from youth to age. I have seen him in my dreams, and in visions. I am with him continually,—we talk together. At first, cringingly and softly, I lead him to recall the past, to speak of the dead wife,—the lost child,—her baby ways and words. I lure him on till imagination has fired his love and given life and vividness to his memory. Then I whisper,—She lives! she is near! in a moment he shall behold her! And while his heart beats and he trembles, I bring her forth in her beauty. Take her! your daughter! the one devil on earth; but devils shall spring like grass in the track of her footsteps!"

The voice had worked itself into a frenzy, and, forgetting caution, had crazily exposed itself. Its owner was probably some poor lunatic, subject to fits of madness. But Helwyse was full of scorn and anger, born of that bitterest disappointment which admits not even the poor consolation of having worthily aspired. He had been duped,—and by the cobwebs of a madman's brain! He broke into a short laugh, harsh to the ear, and answering to no mirthful impulse.

"So! you are the hero of your story? You have brooded all your life over a crazy scheme of stabbing a father through his child, until you have become as blind as you are vicious! As for the girl, you may have made her ignorant and stupid, or even idiotic; but that she should become queen of Hell or anything of that kind—"

He stopped, for his unseen companion was evidently beyond hearing him. The man seemed to be actually struggling in a fit,— gasping and choking. It was a piteous business,—not less piteous than revolting. But Helwyse felt no pity,—only ugly, hateful, unrelenting anger, needing not much stirring to blaze forth in fearful passion. Where now were his wise saws,—his philosophic indifference? Self-respect is the pith of such supports; which being gone, the supports fail.

"My music,—my music!" gasped the voice; "my music, or I shall die!"

"Die? Yes, it were well you should die. You cumber the earth! Shall I do it?" Helwyse muttered to his heart,—"merely as a means of culture!"

Perhaps it was said only in a mood of sardonic jesting. The next moment, no doubt, Balder Helwyse would have retired to his cabin, leaving the voice of darkness forever. But at that moment the hurried flash of a lantern on the captain's bridge fell full on the young man's face and shoulders, gleaming in his eyes, and lighting up the masses of yellow hair and mighty beard. He was standing with one hand resting on the taffrail. The dim halo of the fog, folding him about, made him look like a spirit.

X.

Helwyse Resists the Devil.

As the light so fell, hoarse voices shouted, and then a concussion shivered through the steamer, and her headway was slackened. But of this Helwyse knew nothing; for the voice had burst forth in a cry of fear, amazement, and hate; and in another breath he found himself clutched tightly in long, wiry arms, and felt panting breath hot against his face.

He struggled at first to free himself,—but he was held in the grip of a madman! Then did the turbid current of his blood begin to leap and tingle, and strange half thoughts darted through his mind like deformed spectres, capering as they flew! The bulwark of his will was overthrown; he could not poise himself long enough to recover his self-sway. He was sliding headlong down a steep, the velocity momently increasing.

Was it Balder Helwyse that was struggling thus furiously, his body full of fire, his brain of madness, his heart quick-beating with savage, wicked, thirsty joy? His soul—his own no longer—was bestridden by a frantic demon, who, brimming over with hot glee, drove him whirling blindly on, with an ever-growing purpose that surcharged each smallest artery, and furnished a condensed dart of malice wherewith to stab and stab again the opposing soul. He waxed every instant madder, wickeder, more devilishly exultant; and now, although panting, breathless, pricking at every pore from the agony of the strain, he could scarce forbear screaming with delight! for he felt he was gaining, and—O ecstasy!—knew that his adversary felt it also, and that his heart was as full of black despair and terror as was his conqueror's of intolerable triumph! Gaining still!

Strange, that all through this wild frenzy in which body and soul were rapt, the essential part of Balder Helwyse seemed to be looking on, with a curious, repellent twist of feature, commenting on what was going forward, and noting, with quiet interest and precision, each varying phase of the struggle,—noting, as of significance, that the sway of the demon of murder made the idea of other crimes seem beyond words congenial, enticing, delicious!

Steadily through this storm of lawless fury has the predestined victory been drawing near! The throbbing of his enemy's heart,—Helwyse feels it; did ever lover so rejoice in the palpitations of his mistress? O the wine of life! drunk from the cup of murder! Hear how the wretch's voice breaks choking from his throat!—he would beg for mercy, but cannot, shall not! Keep your fingers in his throat; the other hand creeps warily downwards. Now hurl him up,—over!—

But with what an ugly gulp the black water swallowed his body!

XI.

A Dead Weight.

Was it not well done? Tempted to covet imaginary wickedness, Helwyse was ripe for real crime,—and who so worthy to suffer as the tempter?

He leaned panting against taffrail. His predominant feeling was that he had been ensnared. His judgment had been drugged, and he had been lured on to evil. An infamous conspiracy!

His breath regained, he stood upright and in a mechanical manner arranged his disordered dress. His haversack was gone,—had been torn from his shoulders and carried overboard. An awkward loss! for it contained, among other things, valuable letters and papers given him by his father; not to mention a notebook of his own, and Uncle Glyphic's miniature. His dead enemy had carried off the proofs of his murderer's identity!

Not till now did Helwyse become aware of an unusual tumult on the steamer. Had they seen the deed?—He stood with set teeth, one hand on the taffrail. Rather than be taken alive, he would leap over!

But it soon became evident that the nucleus of excitement was elsewhere. The "Empire State" was at a standstill. Captain and mates were shouting to one another and at the sailors. By the flying light of the lanterns Helwyse caught glimpses of the sails and tall masts of a schooner. He began to comprehend what had happened.

"Thank God! that saves me," he said with a sense of relaxation. Then he turned and peered fearfully into the black abyss beyond the stern. Nothing there! nothing save the heavy breathing of remorseless waves.

The statistics of things God has been thanked for,—what piquant instances would such a collection afford! Any unusual stir of emotion seems to impel a reference to something higher than the world. Only a bloodless calm appears to be secure from God's interference. It is worthy of remark that this was the first time in Helwyse's career—at least since his arrival at years of discretion—that he had thanked God for anything. This was not owing to his being of a specially ungrateful disposition, but to peculiar ideas upon the subject of a Supreme Being. God, he believed, was no more than the highest phase of man; and in any man of sufficient natural endowment, he saw a possible God; just as every American citizen is a possible President! What is of moment at present, however, is the fact that the young man's first inconsistency of word with creed dates at the time his self-control forsook him on board the midnight steamer.

In that thanksgiving prayer his passion passed away. After unnaturally distending every sense and faculty, it suddenly ebbed, leaving the consciousness of an irritating vacuum. Something must be done to fill it. One drawback to crime seems to be its insufficiency to itself. It creates a craving which needs must be fed. The demon returns, demanding a fresh task; and he returns again forever!

Helwyse, therefore, plunged into the midst of the uproar consequent on the collision, and tried to absorb the common excitement,—to identify himself with other men; no longer to be apart from them and above them. But he did not succeed. It seemed as though he would never feel excitement or warmth in the blood again! His deed was a dead weight that steadied him spite of his best efforts. His aim has hitherto been, not to forget himself;—let him forget himself now if he can!

The uproar was over all too soon, and the steamer once more under way.

"No serious harm done, sir!—no harm done!" observed a spruce steward.

"No; no harm."

"By the way, sir,—thought I heard some one sing out aft just afore we struck. You heard it, sir? Thought some fellow'd gone overboard, may be!"

"I saw no one," answered Helwyse; nor had he. But he turned away, fearing that the brisk steward might read prevarication in his face. No, he had seen no one; but he had heard a plunge! He revolted from the memory of it, but it would not be banished. Had there been a soul in the body before it made that dive? even for a few minutes afterwards? He would have given much to know! In theorizing about crime, he had always maintained the motive to be all in all. But now, though unable to controvert the logic of his assertion, he felt it told less than the whole truth. He recognised a divine conservative virtue in straws, and grasped at the smallest! Through the long torture of self-questioning and indecision, let us not follow him. Uncertainty is a ghastly element in such a matter.

He groped his way back to the taffrail. Why, he knew not; but there he was at last. He might safely soliloquize now; there was no listener. He might light a cigar and smoke; no one would see him. Yet, no; for, on second thoughts, his cigars had gone with the haversack!

He bent over the slender iron railing. Where was—it now? Miles away by this time, swinging, swaying down—down—down to the bottom of the Sound! Slowly turning over as it sinks, its arms now thrown out, now doubled underneath; the legs sprawling helplessly; the head wagging loosely on the dead neck. Down—down, pitching slowly head forwards; righting, and going down standing, the hair floating straight on end. Down! O, would it never be done sinking—sinking—sinking? Was the sea deep as Hell?

But when it reached the bottom, would it rest there? No, not even there. It would drift uneasily about for a while on the dark sand, the green gloom of the water above it. Every hour it would grow less and less heavy; by and by it would begin slowly to rise—rise! Horrible it looked now; not like itself, that had been horrible enough before. Rising,—rising. O fearful thing! why come to tell dead men's tales here? You are done with the world. What wants mankind with you? Begone! sink, and rise no more! It will not sink; still it rises, and the green gloom lightens as it slowly buoys upwards. The light rests shrinkingly on it, revealing the dreadful features. The limbs are no longer pliant, but stiff,—terribly stiff and unyielding. Still it rises, nearer and nearer to the surface. See where the throat was gripped! Up it comes at last in the morning sun, among the sparkling, laughing, pure blue waves,—the swollen, dead thing!—dead in the midst of the world's life, hideous amidst the world's beauty. It bobs and floats, and will sink no more; would rise to heaven if it could! No need for that. The tide takes it and creeps stealthily with it towards the shore, and casts it, with shudder and recoil, upon the beach. There it lies.

Such visions haunted Helwyse as he leaned over the taffrail. He had not suspected, at starting, upon how long a voyage he was bound. How many hours might it be since he and the cook had so merrily dined together? Was such a contrast possible? Surely no more monstrous delusion than this of Time ever imposed upon mankind! For months and years he jogs on with us, a dull and sober-paced pedestrian. Then comes a sudden eternity! But Time thrusts a clock in our faces, and shows us that the hands have marked a minute only. Shall we put faith in him?

Helwyse suffered from a vivid imagination. He went not to his room that night. He kept the deck, and tried to talk with the men, following them about and asking aimless questions, until they began to give him short answers. Where were his pride and his serene superiority to the friendship or enmity of his race? where his philosophic self-criticism and fanciful badinage? his resolute, conquering eyes? his bearing of graceful, careless authority? Had all these attributes been packed in his haversack, and cast with that upon the waters? and would they, no more than he to whose care they had been intrusted, ever return?

With each new hour, morning seemed farther off. In his objectless wanderings, Helwyse came to the well of the engine-room and hung over it, gazing at the bright, swift-sliding machinery, studying the parts, tracing the subtle transmission of force from piece to piece. Here at last was companionship for him! The engine was a beautiful combination,—so polished, effective, and logical; like the minds of some philosophers, moving with superhuman regularity and power, but lifeless!

Helwyse watched it long, till finally its monotony wearied him. It was doing admirable work, but it never swerved from its course at the call of sentiment or emotion. Its travesty of life was repulsive. Machinery is the most admirable invention of man, but is modelled after no heavenly prototype, and will have no part in the millennium. It seems to annul space and time, yet gives us no taste of eternity. Man lives quicker by it, but not more. With another kind of weapon must the true victory over matter be achieved!

XII.

More Vagaries.

Most benign and beautiful was the morning. The "Empire State" emerged from the fog and left it, a rosy cloud, astern. The chasing waves sparkled and danced for joy. The sun was up, fresh and unstained as yesterday. Night, that had changed so much, had left the sun un-dimmed. With the same power and brightness as for innumerable past centuries, his glorious glance colored the gray sky blue. Helwyse—he was at the stern taffrail again—looked at the marvellous sphere with unwinking eyes, until it blurred and swam before him, and danced in colored rings. It warmed his face, but penetrated no deeper. Looking away, black suns moved everywhere before his eyes, and the earth looked dim and shabby, as though blighted by a curse.

Helwyse had not slept, partly from disinclination to the solitude of his berth, partly because the thought of awakening dismayed him. Nevertheless, he could scarcely believe in what had happened, now. He stood upon the very spot; here was the semicircle of railing, the camp-stools, the white cabin-wall against which he had leaned. But the black-ness of night had so utterly past away that it seemed as though the deed done in it must in some manner have vanished likewise. What is fact at one time looks unreal at another. It must be associated with all times and moods before it can be fully comprehended and accepted.

Glancing down at the deck, Helwyse saw there the cigar he had been smoking the night before, flattened out by the tread of a foot, and lying close beside it a sparkling ring. He picked it up; it was a diamond of purest water, curiously caught between the mouths of two little ser-pents, whose golden and black bodies, twisted round each other, formed the hoop. Realizing, after a moment, from whose finger it must have fallen, he had an impulse to fling it far into the sea; but his second thought was not to part from it. The idea of its former owner must indeed always be hateful to his murderer; but the bond between their souls was closer and more indissoluble than that between man and wife; and of so unnatural a union this ring was a fair emblem. Unnat-ural though the union were, to Helwyse it seemed at the time better than total solitude.

He felt heavy and inelastic,—averse to himself, but still more to society. He wished to see men and women, yet not to be seen of them.

He had used to be ready in speech, and willing to listen; now, no subject interested him save one,—on which his lips must be forever closed. When the sun had made himself thoroughly at home on earth and in heaven, Helwyse went to his stateroom, feeling unclean from the soul outwards. While making his toilet, he took care to leave the window-blind up, that he might at any time see the blue sky and water, and the bright shore, with its foliage and occasional houses. He shrank from severing, even for an instant, his communication with the beneficent spirit of nature. And yet Nature could not comfort him,—in his extremest need he found her most barren. He had been wont to rejoice in her as the creature of his own senses; but when he asked her to sympathize with his pain, she laughed at him,—the magnificent coquette!—and bade him, since she was only the reflection of himself, be content with his own sympathy. Truly, if man and Nature be thus allied, and God be but man developed, then is self-sufficiency the only virtue worth cultivating, and idolatry must begin at home!

His efforts to improve his appearance were not satisfactory; the loss of his toilet articles embarrassed him not a little; and he, moreover, lacked zest to enter into the business with his customary care. And what he did was done not merely for his own satisfaction, as heretofore, but with an eye to the criticisms of other people. His naively unconscious independence had got a blow. After doing his best he went out, pale and heavy-eyed, the diamond ring on his finger.

The passengers had begun to assemble in the cabin. It seemed to Helwyse, as he entered, that one and all turned and stared at him with suspicious curiosity. He half expected to see an accuser rise up and point a dreadful finger at him. But in truth the sensation he created was no more than common; it was his morbid sensitiveness, which for the first time took note of it. He had been accustomed to look at himself as at a third person, in whose faults or successes he was alike interested; but although his present mental attitude might have moved him to smile, he, in fact, felt no such impulse. The hue of his deed had permeated all possible forms of himself, thus barring him from any standpoint whence to see its humorous aspect. The sun would not shine on it!

As time passed on, however, and no one offered to denounce him, Helwyse began to be more at ease. Seeing the steward with whom he had spoken the night before, he asked him whereabouts he supposed the schooner was.

"O, she'll be in by night, sir, safe enough. Wind's freshened up a good bit since; wouldn't take her long to rig a new bowsprit. Beg pardon, sir, did you happen to know the party next door to you?"

"I know no one. What about him?"

"Can't find him nowhere, sir. Door locked this morning; hadn't used his bed; must have come aboard, for there was a violin lying on the bed in a black box, for all the world like a coffin, sir. Queer, ain't it?"

The steward was called away, but Helwyse's uneasiness had returned. Did this fellow suspect nothing? The student of men could not read his face; the power of insight seemed to have left him. Reason could tell him that it was impossible he should be suspected, but reason no longer satisfied him.

He left the cabin and once more sought the deck, harried and anxious. Why could not he be stolid and indifferent, as were many worse criminals than he? Or was his disquiet a gauge of his moral accountability? By as much as he was more finely gifted than other men, was the stain of sin upon his soul more ineffaceable? Last night, ignorance was the only evil; but had he been satisfied with less wisdom, might he not have sinned with more impunity? Nevertheless, Balder Helwyse would hardly have been willing to purchase greater ease at the price of being less a man.

The steamer descended the narrow and swift current of East River, rounded Castle Garden, and reached her pier before eight o'clock. Shoulder to shoulder with the other passengers, Helwyse descended the gangplank. The official who took his ticket eyed him so closely that there was the beginning of an impulse in his weary brain to knock the fellow down. Finding himself not interfered with, however, he passed on to the rattling street, beginning to understand that the attention he excited was not owing to a visible brand of Cain, but to his beard and hair which were at variance with the fashion of that day. He was neither more nor less a cynosure than at other times. But he was more sensitive to notice, and it now occurred to him that his unique appearance was unsafe as well as irksome. Were a certain body found, in connection with evidence more or less circumstantial, how readily might he be pointed out! He fancied himself reading the description in a newspaper, and realized how many and how easily noted were his peculiarities. His carelessness of public remark had been folly. The sooner his peculiarities were amended, the better!

At the corner of the street stood a couple of policemen,—ponderous, powerful men, able between them to carry to jail the most refractory criminal. One path was open to Helwyse, whereby to recover his self-respect, and regain his true footing with the world; and that led into the hands of those policemen! With a revulsion of feeling perhaps less strange than it seems, he walked up to them, resolved to surrender himself on a charge of murder. It was the simplest issue to his embarrassments.

"Policemen!" he began, with a return of his assured voice and bearing. They stared at him, and one said, "How?"

"Direct me to the best hotel near here!" said Helwyse.

They stared, and told him the way to the Astor House.

There had been but the briefest hesitation in Helwyse's mind, but during that pause he had reconsidered his resolve and said No to it. Remembering some episodes of his past history, he cannot hastily be accused of vulgar fear of death. In his case, indeed, it may have required more courage to close his mouth than to open it. Be that as it might, the question as to the degree and nature of his guilt was still unsettled in his mind. Moreover, had he been clear on this point, he yet distrusted the competence of human laws to do him justice. He shrank from surrender, less as affecting his person than as superseding his judgment. But, failing himself and mankind, to what other court can he appeal? Should the fitting tribunal appear, will he have the nerve to face it?

He did not go to the Astor House, notwithstanding the trouble he had taken to ask his way thither. He coasted along the more obscure thoroughfares, seeming to find something congenial in them. Here were people, many of whom had also committed crimes, whose eyes he need not shun to meet, who were his brethren. To be sure, they gave him no friendly glances, taking him for some dainty aristocrat, whom idle curiosity had led to their domains. But Helwyse knew the secret of his kinship; and he perhaps indulged a wild momentary dream of proclaiming himself to them, entering into their life, and vanishing from that world that had known him heretofore. It is a shorter step than is generally supposed, from human height to human degradation.

A pale girl with handsome features, careless expression, and somewhat disordered hair, leant out of a low window, her loose dress falling partly open from her bosom as she did so.

"Where are you going, my love?" inquired she, with a professionally attractive smile. "Aren't you going to give me a lock of that sweet yellow hair?—there's a duck!"

It so happened that Helwyse had never before been openly accosted by a member of this class of the community. Was this infringement of the rule the result of his own fall, or of the girl's exceptional effrontery? He had an indignant glance ready poised, but forbore to hurl it! The worst crime of the young woman was that she disposed of herself at a rate of remuneration exactly corresponding to the value of the commodity; whereas he, less economical and orderly, had mortgaged his own soul by disposing of some one else's body, and was, if anything, out of pocket by the transaction! Undoubtedly the young woman had the best of it; very likely, had she been aware of the circumstances, she would not have deigned him so much as a smile. He therefore neither yielded to her solicitations nor rebuked them, but passed on. The adventure rectified his fraternizing impulse. Albeit standing accountant for so great a sin, the mire was as yet alien to him.

But there was pertinence in the young woman's question; where was he going, indeed? Since the catastrophe on board the steamer, he had forgotten Doctor Glyphic. He felt small inclination to meet his relative now; but certain considerations of personal interest no longer wore the same color as yesterday. Robbed of his self-respect, he could ill afford to surrender worldly wealth into the bargain. On the other hand, to palm himself off on his uncle for a true man was adding hypocrisy to his other crime.

Such an objection, however, could hardly have turned the scale. Great crimes are magnets of smaller ones. It was necessary for Helwyse to alter the whole scheme of his life-voyage; and since he had failed in beating up against the wind, why not make all sail before it? Meanwhile, it was easier to call on Doctor Glyphic than to devise a new course of action; and thus, had matters been allowed to take their natural turn, mere inertia might have brought about their meeting.

But the irony of events turns our sternest resolves to ridicule. On the next street-corner was a hair-dresser's shop, its genial little proprietor, plump and smug, rubbing his hands and smiling in the doorway. Beholding the commanding figure of the yellow-bearded young aristocrat, afar off, his professional mouth watered over him. What a harvest for shears and razor was here! Dare he hope that to him would be intrusted the glorious task of reaping it?

As Helwyse gained the corner, his weary eyes took in the smiling hair-dresser, the little room beyond cheerful with sunshine and colored paper-hangings, and the padded chair for customers to recline in. Here might he rest awhile, and rise up a new man,—a stranger to himself and to all who had known him. It was fitting that the inward change should take effect without; not to mention that the wearing of so conspicuous a mane was as unsafe as it was unsuitable.

He entered the shop, therefore,—the proprietor backing and bowing before him,—and sat down with a sigh in the padded chair. Immediately he was enveloped in a light linen robe, a towel was tucked in round his neck by deft caressing fingers, the soothing murmur of a voice was in his ear, and presently sounded the *click-click* of shears. The descendant of the Vikings closed his eyes and felt comfortable.

The peculiar color and luxuriance of Balder's hair and beard were marked attributes of the Helwyse line. In these days of ponderous genealogies, who would be surprised to learn that the family sprang from that Balder, surnamed the Beautiful, who was the sun-god of Scandinavian mythology? Certain of his distinctive characteristics, both physical and mental, would appear to have been perpetuated with marvellous distinctness throughout the descent; above all, the golden locks, the blue eyes, and the sunny disposition.

For the rest, so far as sober history can trace them back, they seem to have been a noble and adventurous race of men, loving the sea, but often taking a high part in the political affairs of the nation. The sons were uniformly fair, but the daughters dark,—owing, it was said, to the first mother of the line having been a dark-eyed woman. But the advent of a dark-eyed heir had been foretold from the earliest times, not without ominous (albeit obscure) hints as to the part he would play in the family history. The precise wording of none of these old prophecies has come down to us; but they seem in general to have intimated that the dark-eyed Helwyse would bring the race to a ruinous and disgraceful end, saving on the accomplishment of conditions too improbable to deserve recording. The dead must return to life, the living forsake their identity, love unite the blood of the victim to that of the destroyer,—and other yet stranger things must happen before the danger could be averted.

The superstitious reverence paid to enigmatical utterances of this kind has long ago passed away; and, if any meaning ever attaches to them, it is apt to be sadly commonplace. Nevertheless, when Balder was born, and the hereditary blue eyes were found wanting, the circumstance was doubtless the occasion of much half serious banter among those to whom the ominous prophecies were familiar. Certainly the young man had already made one grave mistake; and he could hardly have followed it up by a more disgraceful retreat than this to the hairdresser's saloon. The ghosts of his heroic forefathers in Valhalla would disown his shorn head with indignant scorn; for their golden locks had ever been sacred to them as their honor. When the Roman Empire was invaded by the Goths and Vandals, a Helwyse—so runs the tale—was taken prisoner and brought before the Roman General. The latter summoned a barber and a headsman, and informed the captive that he might choose between forfeiting his head, and that which grew upon it. As to the precise words in which the Northern warrior couched his reply, historians vary; but they are agreed on the important point that his head was chopped off without delay!

Did the memory of these things bring no blush to Balder's

cheeks? There he sat, as indifferent, to all outward seeming, as though he were asleep. But this may have been the apathy consequent on the abandonment of lofty pretensions and sublime ambitions; betraying proud sensitiveness rather than base lack of feeling. Balder Helwyse was not the first man of parts to appear in an undignified and unheroic light. The foremost man of all this world once whined like a sick girl for his physic, and preposterously overestimated his swimming powers; yet his greatness found him out!

In sober earnest, however, what real importance attaches to Helwyse's doings at this juncture? Physically and mentally weary, he may have acted from the most ordinary motives. As to his entertaining any superstitious crotchets about having his hair cut,—the spirit of the age forbid it!

XIII.

Through A Glass.

The hair-dresser had the quality—now rare among his class—of unlimited and self-enjoying loquacity; soothing, because its little waves lapsed in objectless prattle on the beach of the apprehension, to be attended to or not at pleasure. The sentences were without regular head or tail, and were connected by a friendly arrangement between themselves, rather than by any logical sequence; while the recurring pauses at interesting epochs of work wrought a recognition of how caressing had been the easy voice, and accumulated a lazy disposition to hear it continue.

After decking Helwyse for the sacrifice, he had murmured confidentially in his ear, "Hair, sir?—or beard, sir?—or both?—little of both, sir? Just so. Hair first, please, sir. Love-ly morning!"

And thereupon began to clip and coo and whisk softly about, in the highest state of barberic joy. As he worked, inspired by the curly, flowing glossy locks which, to his eye, called inarticulately for the tools of his trade, his undulating monologue welled forth until Coleridge might have envied him. Helwyse heard the sound, but let the words go by to that unknown limbo whither all sounds, good or bad, have been flying since time began.

By and by the hair was done; there ensued a plying of brushes, a blowing down the neck, and a shaking out of the linen apron.

"Will you cast your eyes on the mirror now, sir, please?"

"No,—go on and finish, first," replied Helwyse; and forthwith a cushion was insinuated beneath his head, and his feet were elevated upon a rest. He heard the preparation of the warm lather, and anon the knowing strapping of a razor. He put up his hand and stroked his beard for the last time, wondering how he would look without it.

"Never saw the like before, sir; must have annoyed you dreadful!" remarked the commiserating barber, as he passed the preparatory scissors round his customer's jaw, mowing the great golden sheaf at one sweep. He spoke of it as though it were a cancer or other painful excrescence, the removal of which would be to the sufferer a boon unspeakable.

Helwyse's face expressed neither anguish nor relief; he presently lost himself in thoughts of his own, only returning to the perception of outside things when the barber asked him whether he, also, had ever attended camp-meeting; the subject being evidently one which had been held forth upon for some time past.

"No?" continued the little man who by long practice had acquired a wonderful power of interpreting silence. "Well, it's a great thing, sir; and a right curious thing is experiencing religion, too! A great blessing I've found it, sir; there's a peace dwells with me, as the minister says, right along all the time now. Does the razor please you, sir? Ah! I was a wild and godless being once, although always reckoned a smart hand with the razor;—Satan never took my cunning hand, as the poet says, away from me. Yes, there was a time when I was how-d'y'-do with all the bloods around the place, and a good business I used to do out of them, too, sir; but religion is a peace there's no understanding, as the Good Book says; and if I don't make all I used to, I save twice as much,—and that's the good of it, sir. Beau-ti-ful chin is yours, sir, I declare!"

"Do you believe in the orthodox faith?" demanded Helwyse; "in miracles, and the Trinity, and so forth?"

"Everything we're told to believe in I believe, I hope, sir; and as quick as I hear anything more, why, I'm ready to believe that also, provided only it comes through orthodox channels, as the saying is. Ah, sir, it's the unquestioning belief that brings the happiness. I wouldn't have anything explained to me, not if I could! and my faith is such, that what goes against it I never would believe, not if you proved it to me black and white, sir! Love-ly skin you've got, sir,—it's just like a woman's. The intellect is a snare, that's what it is,—ah, yes! You think with me, sir, don't you?"

But Helwyse had relapsed into silence. The little hair-dresser was happy, was he?—happy, and hopeful, and conscious of spiritual progress?—had no misgivings and feared no danger,—because he had eliminated reason from his scheme of religion! Divine reason,—could man live without it? A snare?—Well, had not Balder found it so?

True, that was not reason's fault, but his who misused reason. True, also, that he who believed on others' authority believed not ideas but men, and was destitute of self-reliance or dignity. Yet the hair-dresser seemed to find in that very dependence his best happiness, and to have built up a factitious self-respect from the very ruin of true dignity. His position was the antipodes of Balder's, yet, if results were evidence, it was tenable and more successful.

This plump, superficial, smiling little hair-dresser was a person of no importance, yet it happened to him to modify not only Helwyse's external aspect, but the aspect of his mind as well,—by the presentation of a new idea; for strange to say, Helwyse had never chanced to doubt that seraphim were higher than cherubim, or that independence was the only ladder to heaven. To be taught by one avowedly without intellect is humiliating; but the experience of many will furnish examples of a singular disregard of this kind of proprieties.

When the shaving was done to the artist's satisfaction, he held the mirror before his customer's face. Helwyse looked narrowly at his reflection, as was natural in making the acquaintance of one who was to be his near and intimate companion. He beheld a set of features strongly yet gracefully built, but shorn of a certain warm, manly attractiveness. The immediate visibility of mouth and chin—index of so large a part of man's nature—startled him. He was dismayed at the ease wherewith the working of emotion might now be traced. Man wholly unveiled to himself is indeed an awful spectacle, be the dissection-room that of the surgeon or of the psychologist. Hardly might angels themselves endure it. A measure of ignorance of ourselves is wise, because consciousness of a weakness may lead us to give it rein. Perfect strength can coexist only with perfect knowledge, but neither is attainable by man. Man should pay to be screened from himself, lest his sword fail,—lest the Gorgon's head on his breast change him to stone.

The gracious, outflowering veil of Balder Helwyse's life had vanished, leaving nakedness. Henceforth he must depend on fence, feint and guard, not on the downright sword-stroke. With Adam, the fig-leaf succeeded innocence as a garment; for Helwyse, artificial address must do duty as a fig-leaf. The day of guiltless sincerity was past; gone likewise the day of open acknowledgment of guilt. Now dawned the day of counterfeiting,—not always the shortest of our mortal year.

On the whole, Helwyse's new face pleased him not. He felt self-estranged and self-distrustful. Standing on the borders of a darker land, the thoughts and deeds of his past life swarmed in review before his eyes. Many a seeming trifling event now showed as the forewarning of harm to come. The day's journey once over, we see its issue prophesied in each trumpery raven and cloud that we have met since morning. However, the omens would have read as well another way; for nature, like man, is twofold, and can be as glibly quoted to Satan's advantage as to God's.

"Very well done!" said Helwyse to the barber, passing a hand over the close-cropped head and polished chin. "The only trouble is, it cannot be done once for all."

As the little man smilingly remarked, however, the charge was but ten cents. His customer paid it and went out, and was seen by the hairdresser to walk listlessly up the street. The improvement in his personal appearance had not mended his spirits. Indeed, it cannot be disguised that his trouble was more serious than lay within a barber's skill altogether to set right.

Were man potentially omniscient, then might Balder's late deed be no crime, but a simple exercise of prerogative. But is knowledge of evil real knowledge? God is goodness and man is evil. God knows both good and evil. Man knows evil—knows himself—only; knows God only in so far as he ceases to be man and admits God. But this simple truth becomes confused if we fancy a possible God in man.

This was Balder's difficulty. Possessed of a strong, comprehensive mind, he had made a providence of himself; confounded intelligence with integrity; used the moral principle not as a law of action but as a means of insight. The temptation so to do is strong in proportion as the mind is greatly gifted. But experience shows no good results from yielding to it. Blind moral instinct, if not safer, is more comfortable!

Not the deed alone, but the revelation it brought, preyed on the young man's peace. If he were a criminal today, then was the whole argument of his past life criminal likewise. Yesterday's deed was the logical outcome of a course of thought extending over many yesterdays. Why, then, had not his present gloom impended also, and warned him beforehand? Because, while parleying with the Devil, he looks angelic; but having given our soft-spoken interlocutor house-room, he makes up for lost time by becoming direfully sincere!

On first facing the world in his new guise, Helwyse felt an embarrassment which he fancied everybody must remark. But, in fact (as he was not long discovering), he was no longer remarkable; the barber had wiped out his individuality. It was what he had wished, and yet his insignificance annoyed him. The stare of the world had put him out of countenance; yet when it stopped staring he was still unsatisfied. What can be the solution of this paradox?

It perhaps was the occasion of his seeking the upper part of the city, where houses were more scarce and there were fewer people to be unconcerned! In country solitudes he could still be the chief figure. He entered Broadway at the point where Grace Church stands, and passed on through the sparsely inhabited region now known as Union Square. The streets hereabouts were but roughly marked out, and were left in many places to the imagination. On the corner of Twenty-third Street was a low whitewashed inn, whose spreading roof overshadowed the girdling balcony. Farmers' wagons were housed beneath the adjoining shed, and one was drawn up before the door, its driver conversing with a personage in shirtsleeves and straw hat, answering to the name of Corporal Thompson.

Helwyse perhaps stopped at the Corporal's hospitable little establishment to rest himself and get some breakfast; but whether or not, his walk did not end here, but continued up Broadway, and after passing a large kitchen-garden (whose owner, a stout Dutchman, was pacing its central path, smoking a long clay pipe which he took from his lips only to growl guttural orders to the gardeners who were stooping here and there over the beds), emerged into open country, where only an occasional Irish shanty broke the solitude.

How long the young man walked he never knew; but at length, from the summit of a low hill, he looked northwest and saw the gleam of Hudson River. Leaving the road he struck across rocky fields which finally brought him to the riverbank. A stony promontory jutted into the water, and on this (having clambered to its outer extremity) Helwyse sat down, his feet overhanging the swirling current. The tide was just past the flood.

About two hundred yards up stream, to the northward, stood a small wooden house, on the beach in front of which a shabby old mariner was bailing out his boat. Southwards, some miles away, curved the shadowed edge of the city, a spire mounting here and there, a pencilled mist of smoke from chimneys, a fringe of thready masts around the farthest point. In front slid ceaselessly away the vast sweep of levelled water, and still it came undiminished on. The opposing shore was a mile distant, its rocky front gradually gaining abruptness and height until lost round the northern curve. But directly opposite Helwyse's promontory, the stony wall was for some way especially precipitous and high, its lofty brink serried with a thick phalanx of trees.

This spot finally monopolized the adventurer's attention; had he been in Germany, he would have looked for gray castle-towers rising behind the foliage. The place looked inaccessible and romantic, and was undeniably picturesque. New York was far enough away to be mistaken for—say—Alexandria; while the broad river certainly took its rise in as prehistoric an age as the Nile itself. Perhaps in the early morning of the world some chieftain built his stronghold there, and fought notable battles and gave mighty feasts; and later married, and begat stalwart sons, or a daughter beautiful as earth and sky! Where today were her youth and beauty, her loving noble heart, her warm melodious voice, her eyes full of dark light? Why were there no such women now?—not warped, imperfect, only half alive in body and spirit; but charged from the heart outwards with pure divine vitality,—natures vivid as fire, yet by strength serene!

"Why did not I live when she lived, to marry her?" muttered Helwyse in a dream. "A woman whose infinite variety age could not alter nor custom stale! A true wife would have kept me from error.

What man can comprehend the world, if he puts half the world away? Now it is too late; she might have helped me rise to greatness, but not to bear disgrace. Ah, Balder Helwyse, poor fool! you babble as if she stood before you to take or leave. *You* rise to greatness? You never had the germs of greatness in you! You are so little that not the goddess Freya herself could have made you tall! Through what delusion did you fancy yourself better than any other worm?"

There was an interval, not more than a rod or two in width, in the tree-hedge which lined the opposite cliff. Through this one might get a narrow glimpse of what lay beyond. A strip of grassy lawn extended in front of what seemed to be the stone corner of a house. The distance obscured detail, but it looked massively built, though not after the modern style. As Helwise gazed, sharpening his eyes to discern more clearly, he saw a figure moving across the lawn directly towards him. Advancing to the brink of the cliff, it there paused and seemed to return his glance. Helwyse could not tell whether it were man or woman. Had the river only been narrower!

The next moment he remembered his telescope, and, taking it from its case, he was at a bound within one hundred yards of the western shore. Man or woman? he steadied the glass on his knee and looked again. A woman, surely,—but how strangely dressed! Such a costume had not been in vogue since Damascus was a new name in men's mouths. Balder gazed and gazed. Accurately to distinguish the features was impossible,—tantalizingly so; for the gazer was convinced that she was both young and beautiful. Her motions, her bearing, the graceful peculiarity of her garb,—a hundred nameless evidences made it sure. How delightful to watch her in her unconsciousness! yet Helwyse felt a delicacy in thus stealing on her without her knowledge or consent. But the misgiving was not strong enough to shut up his telescope; perhaps it added a zest to the enjoyment.

"The very princess you were just now dreaming of! the most beautiful and complete woman! Would I were the prince to win thee!"

This aspiration was whispered, as though its object were within conversable distance. Balder could be imaginative enough when the humor took him.

Hardly had the whisper passed his lips when he saw the princess majestically turn her lovely head, slowly and heedfully, until her glance seemed directly to meet his own. His cheeks burned; it was as if she had actually overheard him. Was she gracious or offended? He saw her stretch towards him her arms, and then, with a gesture of beautiful power, clasp her hands and draw them in to her bosom.

Prince Balder's hand trembled, the telescope slipped; the quick effort to regain it lent it an impetus that shot it far into the water. It had done its work and was gone forever. The beautiful princess was once more a vague speck across a mile of rapid river; now, even the speck had moved beyond the trees and was out of sight!

The episode had come so unexpected, and so quickly passed, that now it seemed never to have been at all! But Helwyse had yielded himself unreservedly to the influence of the moment. Following so aptly the fanciful creation of his thought, the apparition had acquired peculiar significance. The abrupt disappearance afflicted him like a positive loss.

Did he, then, soberly believe himself and the princess to have exchanged glances (not to speak of thoughts) across a river a mile wide? Perhaps he merely courted a fancy from which the test of reason was deliberately withheld. Spirits not being amenable to material laws, what was the odds (so far as exchange of spiritual sentiment was concerned) whether the prince and princess were separated by miles or inches?

But however plausible the fancy, it was over. Helwyse leaned back on the rock, drew his hat over his eyes, folded his hands beneath his head, and appeared to sleep.

XIV.

The Tower of Babel.

In a perfect state of society, where people will think and act in harmony with only the purest æsthetic laws, a knowledge of stenography and photography will suffice for the creation of perfect works of art. But until that epoch comes, the artist must be content to do the grouping, toning, and proportioning of his picture for himself, under penalty of redundancy and confusion. People nowadays seldom do or think the right thing at the fitting moment; insomuch that the biographer, if he would be intelligible, must use his own discretion in arranging his materials.

Now, in view of the rough shaking which late events had given Balder and his opinions, it is doing no violence to probability to fancy him taking an early opportunity to pass these opinions in review. It would be easy, by a glance at the magic ring, to reproduce his meditations just as they passed through his brain. Brevity and pertinence, however, counsel us to recall a dialogue which had taken place about three years before.

Balder and his father were then in the North of England; and the latter (who never concerned himself with any save the plainest and most practical philosophy) was not a little startled at an analogy drawn by his son between the cloud-cap on Helvellyn's head and the Almighty! Premising that the cloud-cap, though apparently stable, was really created by the continuous passage of warmer air through a cold region around the summit of the mountain, whereby it was for a moment condensed into visibility and then swept on,—having postulated this fact, and disregarding the elder's remark that he believed not a word of it,—Balder went on to say that God was only a set of attributes,—in a word, the perfection of all human attributes,—and not at all an individual!

"And what has that to do with your cloud-making theory?" demanded Thor, with scorn.

"The perfect human attributes," replied Balder, unruffled, "correspond to the region of condensation,—the cold place, you understand."

"Do they? Well?"

"The constant condensation of the warm current from below corresponds to the taking on of these attributes by a ceaseless succession of human souls. Filling out the Divine character, they lose identity, and so make room for others."

"What are these attributes?"

"They are ineffable,—they are omniscience,—the comprehension of the whole creative idea."

"You expect me to believe that,—eh?" growled Thor.

"If I could believe you understood it, dear old sceptic!" returned Balder, with affectionate irreverence, throwing his arm across his father's broad shoulders. "I say that every soul of right capacity, living for culture, and not afraid of itself, will at last reach that highest point. It is the sublime goal of man, and no human life is complete unless in gaining it. Many fail, but not all. I will not! No, I am not blasphemous; I think life without definite aim not worth having; and that aim, the highest conceivable."

Thor, having stared in silence at his descendant, came out with a stentorian Viking laugh, which Balder sustained with perfect good humor.

"Ho, ho!—the devil is in you, son!—in those black eyes of yours,—ho, ho! No other Helwyse ever had such eyes,—or such ideas either! Well, but supposing you passed the condensation point, what then?"

Balder, who was entirely in earnest about the matter, answered gravely,—

"I cease to be; but what was I becomes the pure, life-giving, spiritual substance, and enters into fresh personalities, and so passes up again in endless circulation."

"Hum! and how with the evil ones, boy?"

"As with all waste matter; they are cast aside, and, as distinct souls, are gradually annihilated. But they may still manure the soil, and involuntarily help the growth of others. Sooner or later, in one or another form, all come into use."

"For all I see, then," quoth Thor, "your devils come to the same end as your gods!"

"There is the same kind of difference," returned the philosopher, "as between light and earth,—both of which help the growth of flowers; but light gives color and beauty, earth only the insipid matter. I would rather be the light."

"Another thing," proceeded Thor, ignoring this distinction; "admitting all else, how do you account for your region of condensation?"

"By the necessity of perfection," answered Balder, after some consideration. "There would be no meaning in existence unless it tended towards perfection. But you have hit on the unanswerable question."

Thor shook his head and huge grizzled beard. "German University humbug!" growled he. "Get you into a scrape some day. The cloud's not made in that way, I tell you! Come, let's go back to the inn."

"Take my arm," said Balder; and as together they descended the spur of the mountain, he added lovingly, "I'll bring no clouds across your sky, my dear old man!" So the hospitable inn received them.

The discussion between the two was never renewed; but Balder held to his creed. He elaborated and fortified what had been mere outline before. No dogma can be conceived which many circumstances will not seem to confirm and justify. But we cannot attempt to keep abreast of Balder's deductions. There are as many theological systems as individual souls; and no system can be wholly apprehended by any one save its author.

Mastery of men and things,—supreme knowledge to the end of supreme power,—such seems to have been his ambition,—an ambition too abstract and lofty for much rivalry. Nature and human nature were at once his laboratory and his instruments. His senses were to him outlets of divinity. The good and evil of such a scheme scarce need pointing out. It was the apotheosis of self-respect; but self-respect raised to such a height becomes self-worship; human vision dazzles at the sublimity of the prospect; at the moment of greatest weakness the soul arrogates invincible power, and falls! For, the mightier man is, the more absolutely does he need the support of a mightier Man than he can ever be.

No doubt Balder had often been assailed by doubts and weariness; the path had seemed too long and arduous, and he had secretly pined for some swift issue from perplexity and delay. In such a moment was it that the voice of darkness gained his ear, and, like a will-o'-the-wisp, lured him to calamity. Verily, it is not easy to be God. Only builders of the Tower of Babel know the awfulness of its overthrow.

Balder's spirit lay prostrate among the ruins, too stunned and bewildered to see the reason or justice of his fall. Such a state is dangerous, for, the better part of the mind being either occupied with its disaster or stupefied by it, the superficial part is readily moved to folly or extravagance,—to deeds and thoughts which a saner moment would scout and ridicule. Well is it, then, if the blind steps are guided to better foothold than they know how to choose. Angels are said to be particularly watchful over those who sleep; perhaps, also, during the darkness which follows on moral perversion.

XV.

Charon's Ferry.

After lying motionless for half an hour, Balder suddenly sat upright and settled his hat on his head. A new purpose had come to him which, arriving later than it might have done, made him wish to act upon it without delay.

The old mariner had by this time bailed out his boat, and, having shipped a mast in the forward thwart, was dropping down stream. As he neared the promontory Balder hailed him:—

"Hullo! skipper, take me across?"

The skipper, without replying, steered shorewards, the other clambering down the rock to meet him. After a brief parley, during which the old fellow closely scrutinized his intending passenger from head to foot, a bargain was struck, and they put forth, tacking diagonally across stream. For Balder, having charged his imagination with castles, warlike chieftains, and beautiful princesses, had finally arrived at the conclusion that the stone house was an enchanter's castle; the figure he had seen, an imprisoned lady; himself, a knight-errant bound to rescue her and give the wicked enchanter his deserts. This idea possessed his brain for the moment more vividly than do realities most men. The plumed helmet was on his head, he glittered with shining arms and sword, his heart warmed and throbbed with visions of conflict and bold emprise. The commonplace assumed an aspect of grandeur and magnificence in harmony with his chivalric mania. The leaky craft in which he sat became a majestic barge; the skipper, some wrinkled Charon who doubtless had ferried many a brave knight to his death beneath yonder castle's walls. That seeming birch-stump on the farther shore was the castle champion, armed cap-a-pie in silver harness and ready with drawn sword to do battle against all comers. Trim the sail, ferryman, and steer thy skilfullest!

The kind of insanity which sees in outward manifestation the fantasies of the mind is an affection incident at times to every one. An artist sees beauties in a landscape, an artisan in pulleys and levers, and either may be so far insane in the eyes of the other. Nature discovers grandeur, beauty, or truth according as the quality abides in the seer. In this view Balder or Don Quixote was no more insane than other people. Their eyes bore true witness to what was in their minds, and the sanest eyes can do no more. Their minds were, perhaps, out of focus; but who can cast the first stone?

The skipper, when not masquerading as Charon, was a lean, brown, and wrinkled old salt, neither complete nor clean of garb, and bulging as to one lank cheek with a quid of tobacco. At first he sat silent, dividing his attention between the conduct of his boat and his passenger.

"Whereabouts will yer land, Captain?" he asked when they were fairly under way.

"Wherever there is a path upwards. Who is the owner of the castle?"

"The castle? Well, there ain't many rightly knows just what his name is," answered Charon, cocking his gray eye rather quizzically. "Some says one thing, some another. I have heard tell he was Davy Jones himself!"

"Have you ever seen him?"

"Well, I don't know; I've seen something that might have been him; but there's no telling! he can fix himself up to look like pretty much anything, they say. There ain't many calls up to the castle, anyway."

"Why not?"

"Well, there's a big wall all around the place, for one thing, and never a gate in it; so without yer dives under ground and up again, there don't seem no easy way of getting in."

"Does the owner never come out, then?"

"Well, he can get out, I expect, when he wants to," replied the wrinkled humorist, with a weather-beaten grin. "They do say he whips off on a broomstick about once a month and steers for Boston!" His fashion of utterance was a leisurely sing-song, like the roll of a vessel anchored in a ground-swell.

"Why does he go there?" demanded Prince Balder, with the air of finding nothing extravagant or improbable in the sailor's yarn. The latter (a little doubting whether his interlocutor were a simpleton or a "deep one") answered, after a moment's pause,—to replenish his imagination perhaps,—

"Well, in course, I knows nothing what he does; but they do say he coasts around to all the hotels and overhauls the log. He's been laying for some one this twenty year. My idea, it's about time he hailed him!"

"What does he want with him?"

"Well, yer see, what folks say is, this chap had played some game or other off on Davy; so Davy he puts a rod in pickle and vows he'd be even with the chap, yet.

"Yer see,—I'll tell yer," continued Charon, leaning forward on his knee and speaking confidentially; "just as this chap was putting off,—with some of Davy's belongings, likely,—Davy up and cuts a slice of flesh and blood off him. Well, he takes this slice and fixes it up one way or another, and makes a witch out of it,—handsome as she can be,—enough to draw a chap's heart right out through his jacket. Now, being as she's his own flesh and blood, d' yer see, this chap I'm telling yer on 's bound to come back after her afore he dies. Well, soon as Davy gets hold on him, he ups with him to the place yonder and outs with the witch. 'Here yer are, my dear friend!' says he (as civil as may be), 'here's yer own flesh and blood a-waiting for yer!' Well, the chap grabs for her, and once he touches her there ain't no letting go no more. Off she starts on her broomstick, he along behind, till they gets over Hell gate—" Charon checked himself, made an ominous downward gesture with his right forefinger, and emphasized it by spitting solemnly to leeward.

"Did you ever meet him,—this man?" asked Helwyse, rousing himself from a brown study and looking Charon in the eyes.

"Well, now, I couldn't tell for certain as I ever met him," replied the other, returning the look with an odd wrinkling of the features. "But it's nigh on twenty year that I fetched a man across this very spot, and back again in the evening, that might have been him. Leastways, he was the last caller ever I took over to that house."

"I am the first since he—eh?"

"Well, yer are; and, Captain,—no offence to you,—but allowing for a lot of hair he had, he was like enough to you to be yer twin brother!"

"Or even myself! So Davy Jones goes by the name of Doctor Glyphic in these parts, does he?" said Balder, with a sudden, incisive smile, which almost cut through the old ferryman's self-possession. The boat at the same moment glided into a little cove, and the passenger jumped ashore. Charon stood deferentially touching his weatherstained hat, too much mystified to speak. But the fare which Helwyse handed him restored his voice.

"Thank yer, Captain,—thank yer kindly!—hope no offence, Captain,—a chap picks up a deal of gossip in twenty year, and—"

"No offence in the world!" cried Helwyse; "I take you for a powerful enchanter, who seems to steer one way, when he is in fact taking his passenger in another. Where are you bound?"

"Well, I was dropping down a bit to see if the schooner ain't around yet. She'd ought to be in by now, if nothing ain't runned into her in the fog."

Helwyse paused a moment, eying Charon sharply. "The schooner

'Resurrection,'" he began, and, seeing he had hit the mark, continued, "was run into last night on Long Island Sound, and had her bowsprit carried away. But no serious damage was done, and she'll be in by night, if the wind holds."

With this he bade the awe-stricken old yarn-spinner farewell, and, with secret laughter at his bewilderment, turned to the narrow zigzag path that climbed the bank, passing the birch-stump champion without a glance of recognition. A few vigorous minutes brought him to the summit, whence, facing round, he saw the broad river crawl beneath him; the little boat, with Charon in the stern, drift downwards; and beyond, the whole rough length of Manhattan Island.

A few days before Thor Helwyse's departure for Europe (some four years after his wife's death) he had left a certain little boy and girl in charge of the nurse,—a woman in whose faithfulness he placed the utmost confidence,—and had crossed from Brooklyn to New Jersey, to say good by to Brother Hiero. Returning at night he found one of the children—his son Balder—locked up in the nursery; the nurse and the little girl had disappeared, nor did Thor again set eyes on either of them.

Balder, as he grew up, often questioned his father concerning various events which had happened beyond the reach of his childish memory; and among other stories, no doubt this of the farewell visit to Uncle Glyphic had been often told with all the details. By no miracle, therefore, but simply by an acute mental process, associating together time, place, and description, was Balder enabled so to dumfounder old Charon.

Embarking on a phantom quest, his brain full of whimsical visions, Balder had thus unexpectedly stepped into the path of his legitimate affair. The accident (for no better reason than that it was such) inspired him with a superficial cheerfulness. He had landed some distance below his uncle Glyphic's house,—for such indeed it was,—and he now took his way towards it through trees and underbrush. It was so situated, and so thickly surrounded with foliage, as to be visible from no point in the vicinity. Had the site been chosen with a view to concealment, the builder could not have succeeded better. Remembering the eccentricity of his uncle's character, as portrayed in many an anecdote, Balder would not have been surprised to find him living under ground, or in a pyramid.

On arriving at the wall whereof the ferryman had told him, he found it a truly formidable affair, some twelve feet high and built of brick. To scale it without a ladder was impossible; but Balder, never doubting that there was a gate somewhere, set out in search of it.

It was tiresome walking over the uneven ground and through obstructing bushes, branches, and stumps. The tall brick barrier seemed as interminable as unbroken. How many houses, thought Balder, might have been built from the material thus wasted! If ever he came into possession of the place, he resolved to present the brick to his friend Charon, that he might replace his wooden shanty with something more durable and convenient, and perhaps build a dock for the schooner "Resurrection" to lie in. It must have taken a fortune to put up such a wall; were the enclosure proportionally valuable, it was worth while crossing the ocean to see it. Still more wall! fully a mile of it already, and yet further it rambled on through leafy thickets. But no signs of a gate!

"I believe the Devil really does live here!" exclaimed Balder, in impatient heat; "and the only way in or out is on a broomstick,—or by diving under ground, as Charon said!"

Stumbling onwards awhile farther, he suddenly came again upon the riverbank, having skirted the whole length of the wall. There was actually no getting in! The castle was impregnable.

Helwyse sat down at the foot of a birch-tree which grew a few yards from the wall.

"How does my uncle manage about his butcher and baker, I wonder! He might at least have provided a derrick for victualling his stronghold. Perhaps he hauls up provisions by ropes over the face of the cliff. No doubt, Charon knew about it. Shall I go down and look?"

It was provoking—having come so far to call on a relative—to be put off with a mile or two of brick wall. The gate must have been walled up since his father's time, for Thor had never mentioned any deficiency in that respect. But Balder's determination was piqued,—not to mention his curiosity. Had the path from Mr. MacGentle's office to Doctor Glyphic's door been straight and unobstructed, the young man might have wandered aside and never reached the end. As it was, he was goaded into the resolution to see his uncle at all hazards. An additional spur was the thought of the gracious apparition which he had seen—or dreamt he saw—from the farther bank. Was she indeed but an apparition?—or the single reality amidst the throng of fantasies evoked by his overwrought mind?—beaconing him through misty errors to a fate better than he knew! In all seriousness, who could she be? Had Doctor Glyphic crowned his eccentricities by marrying, and begetting a daughter?

These speculations were interrupted by the clear, joyous note of a bird, just above Balder's head. It was such a note as might have been uttered by a paradisical cuckoo with the breath of a brighter world in his throat. Looking up, he saw a beautiful little fowl perched on the topmost twig of the birch-tree. It had a slender bill, and on its head a crest of splendid feathers, which it set up at Balder in a most coquettish manner. The next moment it flew over the wall, and from the farther side warbled an invitation to follow.

Although he could not fly, Balder reflected that he could climb, and that the top of the tree would show him more than he could see now. The birch looked tolerably climbable and was amply high; as to toughness, he thought not about it. Beneath what frivolous disguises does destiny mask her approach! Discretion is a virtue; yet, had Balder been discreet enough to examine the tree before getting into it, the ultimate consequences are incalculable!

As it was (and marvelling why he had not thought of doing it before) he set stoutly to work, and, despite his jackboots, was soon among the upper branches. The birch trembled and groaned unheeded. The bird (an Egyptian bird,–a hoopoe,–descendant of a pair brought by Doctor Glyphic from the Nile a quarter of a century ago),–the hoopoe was fluttering and warbling and setting its brilliant cap at the young man more captivatingly than ever. A glance over the enclosure showed a beautifully fertile and luxurious expanse, damasked with soft green grass and studded with flowers and trees. A few hundred yards away billowed the white tops of an apple-orchard in full bloom. Southward, half seen through boughs and leaves, rose an anomalous structure of brick, glass, and stone, which could only be the famous house on whose design and decoration old Hiero Glyphic had spent years and fortunes.

The tract was like an oasis in a forbidding land. The soil had none of the sandy and clayey consistency peculiar to New Jersey, but was deep and rich as an English valley. The sunshine rested more warmly and mellowly here than elsewhere. The southern breeze acquired a tropical flavor in loitering across it. The hoopoe had seemed out of place on the hither side the wall, but now looked as much at home as though the Hudson had been the Nile indeed.

"My uncle," said Balder to himself, as he swayed among the branches of his birch-tree, "has really succeeded very well in transporting a piece of Egypt to America. Were I on the other side of the wall, no doubt I might appreciate it also!"

The hoopoe responded encouragingly, the tree cracked, and Balder felt with dismay that it was tottering beneath him. There was no time to climb down again. With a dismal croak, the faithless birch leaned slowly through the air. There was nothing to be done but to go with it; and Balder, even as he descended, was able to imagine how absurd he must appear. The tree fell, but was intercepted at half its height by the top of the wall. The upper half of the stem, with its human fruit still attached to it, bent bowlike towards the earth, the trunk not being quite separated from the root.

Helwyse had thus far managed to keep his presence of mind, and now, glancing downwards, he saw the ground not eight feet below. He loosed his hold, and the next instant stood in the soft grass. The birch had been his broomstick. Meanwhile the hoopoe, with a triumphant note, flew off towards the house to tell the news.

XVI.

Legend and Chronicle.

Hiero Glyphic's house came not into the world complete at a birth, but was the result of an irregular growth, progressing through many years. Originally a single-gabled edifice, its only peculiarity had been that it was brick instead of wooden. Here, red and unornamented as the house itself, the future Egyptologist was born. The parallel between him and his dwelling was maintained more or less closely to the end.

He was the first pledge of affection between his mother and father, and the last also; for shortly after his advent the latter parent, a retired undertaker by profession, failed from this world. The widow was much younger than her husband, and handsome to boot. Nevertheless, several years passed before she married again. Her second lord was likewise elderly, but differed from the first in being enormously wealthy. The issue of this union was a daughter, the Helen of our story, a pretty, dark-eyed little thing, petted and indulged by all the family, and reigning undisputed over all.

Meanwhile the old brick house had been deserted, Mrs. Glyphic having accompanied her second husband to his sumptuous residence in Brooklyn. But in process of time Hiero (or, as he was then called, Henry) took it into his head to return to the original family mansion and live there. No objection was made; in truth, Henry's oddities, awkwardnesses, and propensity to dabble in queer branches of research and experiment may have allayed the parting pangs. Back he blundered, therefore, to the banks of the Hudson, and established himself in his birthplace. What he did there during the next few years will never be known. Grisly stories about the man in the brick house were current among the country people. A devil was said to be his familiar friend; nay, it was whispered that he himself was the arch-fiend! But nothing positively supernatural, or even unholy, was ever proved to have taken place. The recluse had the command of as much money as he could spend, and no doubt he wrought with it miracles beyond the vulgar comprehension. His mind had no more real depth than a looking-glass with a crack in it, and its images were disjointed and confused. There are many such men, but few possess unlimited means of carrying their crack-brained fancies into fact.

During this—which may be called the second—period of Glyphic's career, he made several anomalous additions to the brick house, all after designs of his own. He moreover furnished it anew throughout, in a manner that made the upholsterers stare. Each room—so reads the legend—was fitted up in the style of a different country, according to Glyphic's notion of it! He was said to live in one apartment or another according as it was his whim to be Spaniard, Turk, Russian, Hindoo, or Chinaman. He also applied himself to gardening, and enclosed seven hundred acres of ground adjoining the house with a picket fence, forerunner of the famous brick wall. The whole tract was dug out and manured to the depth of many feet, till it was by far the most fertile spot in the State. The larger trees were not disturbed, but the lesser were forced to give place to new and rare importations from foreign countries. Gorgeous were the hosts of flowers, like banks of sunset clouds; the lawns showed the finest turf out of England; there was a kitchen-garden rich and big enough to feed an army of epicures all their lives. In short, the place was a concentrated extract of the world at large, where one might at the same moment be a recluse and a cosmopolitan. Here might one live independent of the world, yet sipping the cream thereof; and might persuade himself that all beyond these seven hundred enchanted acres was but a diffused reflection of the concrete existence between the cliff and the fence.

But to this second period succeeded finally the third,—that which witnessed the birth and growth of the Egyptian mania. Its natal moment has not been precisely determined; perhaps it was a gradual accretion. Mr. Glyphic's relatives in Brooklyn were one day electrified by the news that the quondam Henry—now Hiero—purposed instant departure for Europe and Egypt. Before starting, however, he built the brick wall round his estate, shutting it out forever from human eyes. Then he vanished, and for nine years was seen no more.

His return was heralded by the arrival at the port of New York of a mountain of freight, described in the invoice as the property of Doctor Hiero Glyphic of New Jersey. The boxes, as they stood piled together on the wharf, might have furnished timber sufficient to build a town. They contained the fruits of Doctor Glyphic's antiquarian researches.

The Doctor himself—where he picked up his learned title is unknown—was accompanied by a slender, swarthy young factotum who answered to the name of Manetho. He was introduced to the Brooklyn relatives as the pupil, assistant, and adopted son of Hiero Glyphic. The latter, physically broadened, browned, and thickened by his travels, was intellectually the same good-natured, fussy, flighty original as ever; shallow, enthusiastic, incoherent, energetic.

He and his adopted son shut themselves up behind the brick wall; but it soon transpired that extensive additions were making to the old house. Beyond this elementary fact conjecture had the field to itself. Both architects and builders were imported from another State and sworn to secrecy, while the high wall and the hedge of trees baffled prying eyes. Quantities of red granite and many blocks of precious marbles were understood to be using in the work. The opinion gained that such an Oriental palace was building as never had been seen outside an Arabian fairy-tale.

By and by the work was done, the workmen disappeared. But whoever hoped that now the mystery would be revealed, and the Oriental palace be made the scene of a gorgeous house-warming, was disappointed. The dwellers behind the wall emerged not from their seclusion, nor were others invited to relieve it. In due course of time Doctor Glyphic's worthy stepfather died. The widow and her daughter continued to live in Brooklyn until the former's death, which took place a few years afterwards. Then Helen came to her brother, and the Brooklyn house was put under lock and key, and so remained till Helen's marriage, when it was set in order for the bridal pair. But Thor's wife died as they were on the point of moving thither, and he sold it four years later and left America forever.

After his departure less was known, than before of how things went on behind the brick wall. The gateway was filled in with masonry. No one was ever seen entering the enclosure or leaving it; though it was supposed that, somehow or other, communication was occasionally had with the outside world. As knowledge dwindled, legend grew, and wild were the tales told of the invisible Doctor and his foster-son. In his youth, the former had been suspected of simple witchcraft, but he was not let off so easily now. Manetho was first dubbed a genie whom the Doctor had brought out of Egypt. Afterwards it was hinted that these two worthies were in fact one and the same demon, who by some infernal jugglery was able to appear twain during the daytime, but resumed his proper shape at night, and cut up all manner of unholy capers.

By another version, Doctor Glyphic died in Egypt, not before bargaining with the Prince of Darkness that his body should return home in charge of a condemned soul under the guise of Manetho. During the day, affirmed these theorists, the body was inspired by the soul with phantom life; but became a mummy at night, when the condemned soul suffered torments till morning. With sunrise the ghastly drama began anew. This state of things must continue until the sun shone all night long within the brick wall enclosure.

A third, more moderate account is that to which we have already listened from Charon's lips. And he perhaps built on a broader basis of truth than did the other yarn-spinners. But under whatever form the legend appeared, there was always mingled with it a vaguely mysterious whisper relating to the alleged presence in the Doctor's Den (so the enclosure was nicknamed) of an apparition in female form. What or whence she was no one pretended soberly to conjecture. Even her personal aspect was the subject of vehement dispute; some maintaining her to be of more than human beauty, while others swore by their heads that she was so hideous fire would not burn her! These damned her for a malignant witch; those upheld her as a heavenly angel, urged by love divine to expiate, through voluntary suffering, the nameless crimes of the demoniac Doctor. But unless the redemption were effected within a certain time, she must be swallowed up with him in common destruction. Were the how and wherefore of these alternatives called in question, the answer was a wise shake of the head!

The gentle reader will believe no one of the fantastic legends here recorded; possibly they were not believed by their very fabricators. They are useful only as tending to show the moral atmosphere of the house and its occupants. There is sometimes a subtile symbolic element inwoven with such tales, which—though not the truth—helps us to apprehend the truth when we come to know it. Moreover, the fanciful parts of history are to the facts as clouds to a landscape; a picture is incomplete without them; they aid in bringing out the distances, and cast lights and shadows over tracts else harsh and bare.

Beyond what he had gathered from the ancient mariner, Balder Helwyse knew nothing of these fearful fables. This perhaps accounted for the boldness wherewith he pursued his way towards the mysterious house, following in the airy wake of the clear-throated little hoopoe.

XVII.

Face To Face.

The ground-plan of the house was like a capital H placed endwise towards the river. The northern side consisted of the original brick building and the additions of the second period; the southern was that stone edifice which so few persons had been lucky enough to see. The centre or crosspiece comprised the grand entrance-hall and staircase, heavily panelled with dark oak, and the floor flagged with squares of black and white marbles.

This entrance-hall opened eastward into a generous conservatory, filling the whole square court between the wings at that end. The corresponding western court was devoted to the roomy portico. Two or three broad steps mounted to a balcony twenty feet deep and nearly twice as wide, protected by a lofty roof supported on slender Moorish columns. Crossing this, one came to the hall-door, likewise Moorish in arch and ornamentation. Considered room by room and part by part, the house was good and often beautiful; taken as a whole, it was the craziest amalgamation of incongruities ever conceived by human brain.

Balder, approaching from the north, trod enjoyingly the silken grass. No misgiving had he; his uncle would hardly be from home, nor would he be apt to discredit his nephew's identity. His face had already been evidence to more than one former knower of his father, and why not also to his uncle?

The house was more than half a mile in a direct line from the birch-tree, and presented an imposing appearance; but on drawing near, the odd architectural discrepancies became noticeable. Side by side with the prosy Americanism of the northern wing, sprang gracefully the Moorish columns of the portico; beyond, uprose in massive granite, quaintly inscribed and carved, and strengthened by heavy pilasters, the ponderous Egyptian features of the southern portion. The latter was neither storied nor windowed, and, as Balder conjectured, probably contained but a single vast room, lighted from within.

Meanwhile there were no signs of an inhabitant, either in the house or out of it. It wore in parts an air of emptiness and neglect, not exactly as though gone to seed, but as if little human love and care had been expended there. The deepset windows of the brick wing, like the sunken eyes of an old woman, peered at the visitor with dusky forlornness. Lonely and stern on the other side stood the Egyptian pilasters, as though unused to the eye of man; the hieroglyphics along the cornice intensified the impression of desertion. As the young man set foot beneath the portico, he laid a hand on one of the slender pillars, to assure himself that it was real, and not a vision. Cool, solid marble met his grasp; the building did not vanish in a peal of thunder, with an echo of demoniac laughter. Yes, all was real!

But the stillness was impressive, and Balder struck the pillar sharply with his palm, merely for the sake of hearing a noise. There was no answering sound, so, after a moment's hesitation, he walked to the door,—which stood ajar,—purposing to call in the aid of bell and knocker. Neither of these civilized appliances was to be found. While debating whether to use his voice or to enter and use his eyes, the note of the hoopoe fell on his ear. An instant after came an answering note, deeper, sweeter, and stronger,—it thrilled to Balder's heart, bringing to his mind, by some subtle process, the goddess of the cliff.

He crossed the oak-panelled hall (where the essence of mediæval England lingered) and came to the threshold of the conservatory. It was a scene confusedly beautiful. The air, as it touched his face, was tropically warm and indolent with voluptuous fragrance of flowers and plants. Luxuriant shrubs, with broad-drooping leaves, stood motionless in the heat. Two palm-trees uplifted their heavy plumes forty feet aloft, on slender stalks, brushing the high glass roof. In the midst of the conservatory a pool slumbered between rocky margins, overgrown with a profusion of reeds, grasses, and water-plants. There floated the giant leaves and blossoms of the tropic waterlily; and on a fragment of rock rising above the surface dozed a small crocodile, not more than four feet long, but looking as old, dried up, and coldly cruel as sin itself!

The place looked like an Indian jungle, and Balder half expected to see the glancing spits of a tiger crouching beneath the overarching leaves; or a naked savage with bow and arrows. But amid all this vegetable luxuriance appeared no human being,—no animal save the evil crocodile. Whence, then, that melodious voice,—clear essence of nature's sweetest utterances?

At the left of the conservatory was a door, the entrance to the Egyptian temple. It was square and heavy-browed, flanked by short thick columns rising from a base of sculptured papyrus-leaves, and flowering in lotus capitals. Three marble steps led to the threshold, while on either side reclined a sphinx in polished granite, softened, however, by a delicate flowering vine, which had been trained to cling round their necks. On the deep panels of the door were mystic emblems carved in relief. A line of hieroglyphics inscribed the lintel in deep blue, red, and black,—to what purport Balder could not divine.

At the opposite side of the conservatory was a corresponding door, veiled by an ample fold of silken tapestry, cunningly handworked in representation of a moon half veiled in clouds, shining athwart a stormy sea. By her light a laboring ship was warned off the rocks to leeward. The room (one of the later additions) by its external promise might have been the bower of some fashionable beauty thousands of years ago.

Balder looked from one of these doors to the other, doubting at which to apply. The tapestry curtain was swept aside at the base, leaving a small passage clear to the room beyond. In this opening now appeared the bright-crested head and eyes of the hoopoe, peeping mischievously at the intruder, who forthwith stepped down into the conservatory, holding forth to the little bird a friendly finger. The bird eyed him critically, then launched itself on the air, and, alighting on a spray above his head, warbled out a brilliant call.

Hereupon was heard within a quick rustling movement; the curtain was thrust aside, and a youthful woman issued forth amongst the warm plants. She was within a few feet of Balder Helwyse before seeming to realize his presence. She caught herself motionless in an instant. The sparkle of laughter in her eyes sank in a black depth of wonder. Her eyes filled themselves with Balder as a lake is filled with sunshine; and he, the man of the Wilie and philosopher, could only return her gaze in voiceless admiration.

Were a face and form of primal perfection to appear among men, might not its divine originality repel an ordinary observer, used to consider beautiful such abortions of the Creator's design as sin and degeneration have produced? Not easily can one imagine what a real man or woman would look like. Painting nor sculpture can teach us; we must learn, if at all, from living, electric flesh and blood.

This young woman was tall and erect with youthful majesty. She stood like the rejoicing upgush of a living fountain. Her contour was subtile with womanly power,—suggesting the spring of the panther, the glide of the serpent. Warm she seemed from the bosom of nature. One felt from her the influence of trees, the calm of meadows, the high freedom of the blue air, the happiness of hills. She might have been the sister of the sun.

The moulding finger of God seemed freshly to have touched her face. It was simple and harmonious as a chord of music, yet inexhaustible in its variety. It recalled no other face, yet might be seen in it the germs of a mighty nation, that should begin from her and among a myriad resemblances evolve no perfect duplicate. No angel's countenance, but warmest human clay, which must undergo some change before reaching heaven. The sphinx, before the gloom of her riddle had dimmed her primal joy,—before men vexed themselves to unravel God's webs from without instead of from within,—might have looked thus; or such perhaps was Isis in the first flush of her divinity,—fresh from Him who made her immortally young and fair.

Her black hair was crowned with a low, compact turban,—a purple and white twist of some fine cottony substance, striped with gold. Round her wide, low brow fitted a band of jewelled gold, three fingers' breadth, from which at each temple depended a broad, flat chain of woven coral, following the margin of the cheeks and falling loose on the shoulders. A golden serpent coiled round her smooth throat and drooped its head low down in her bosom. Her elastic feet, arched like a dolphin's back, were sandalled; the bright-colored straps, crossing one another halfway to the knee, set dazzlingly off the clear, dusky whiteness of the skin.

From her shoulders fell a long full robe of purple byssus, over an underdress of white which readied the knee. This tunic was confined at the waist by a hundred-fold girdle, embroidered with rainbow flowers and fastened in a broad knot below the bosom, the low-hanging ends heavy with fringe. The outer robe, with its long drooping sleeves falling open at the elbow, was ample enough wholly to envelop the figure, but was now girded up and one fold brought round and thrust beneath the girdle in front, to give freedom of motion. A rare perfume emanated from her like the evening breath of orange-blossoms.

Balder was no unworthy balance to this picture, though his else stately features showed too much the stimulus of modern thought. He was eminent by culture; she by nature only. But Balder's culture had not greatened him. Greatness is not of the brain, save as allied to the deep, pure chords which thrill at the base of the human symphony. He might have stood for our age; she, for that more primitive but profounder era which is at once man's beginning and his goal.

Balder's eyes could not frankly hold their own against her gaze of awful simplicity. All he had ever done amiss arose and put him to the blush. Nevertheless, he would not admit his inferiority; instead of dropping his eyes he closed the soul behind them, and sharpened them with a shallow, out-striking light. Without understanding the change, she felt it and was troubled. Loftily majestic as were her form and features, she was feminine to the core,—tender and finely perceptive. The incisive masculine gaze abashed her. She raised one hand deprecatingly, and her lips moved, though without sound.

He relented at this, and straightway her expression again shifted, and she smiled so radiantly that Balder almost looked to see whence came the light! The wondrous lines of her face curved and softened; all that was grave vanished. A tree standing in the sober beauty of shadow, when suddenly lit by the sun, changes as she changed; for sunshine is the laughter of the world.

The smile refreshed her courage, for she came nearer and made a sideways movement with her arm, apparently with the expectation that it would pass through the stalwart young man as readily as through the air. On encountering solid substance, she drew startled back, half in alarm and wholly in surprise. Balder had felt her touch, first as a benediction; then it chilled him, through remembrance of a deed forever debarring him from aught so pure and innocent as she. The subtleties of his philosophy might have cajoled him anywhere save in her presence. There, he felt unmistakably guilty; yet from irrational dread that she, whose intuitions seemed so swift and deep, might grasp the cause of his discomposure, he strove to hide it. Last of all the world should she know his crime!

Scarce two minutes since their meeting, yet perhaps a large proportion of their lives had meanwhile been charmed away. No word had been spoken,—eyes had superseded tongues. Nay, was ordinary conversation possible with a young goddess such as this? So perfect seemed her mastery over those profounder elements of intercourse underlying speech, which are higher and more direct than the mechanism of articulate words, that perhaps the latter method was unknown to her.

Nevertheless, one must say something. But what?—with what sentence of supreme significance should he begin? Moreover, what language should he use? for she, whose look and bearing were so alien to the land and age, might likewise be a stranger to modern dialects. But Aryan or Semitic was not precisely at the tip of Balder's tongue!

In the midst of his embarrassment, the startling note of the hoopoe pierced his ear, and precipitated him into asking that great elemental question which all created things are forever putting to one another,—

"What is your name?"

XVIII.

The Hoopoe and the Crocodile.

"Gnulemah!" she answered, laying a finger on the head of her golden serpent, and uttering the name as though it were of the only woman in the world.

But the next moment she found time to realize that something unprecedented had occurred, and her wonder trembled on the brink of dismay.

"Speaks in my language!" she exclaimed below her breath; "but is not Hiero."

Until Balder's arrival, then, Hiero would seem to have been the only talking animal she had known. The singularity of this did not at first strike the young man. Gnulemah was the arch-wonder; yet she so fully justified herself as to seem very nature; and by dint of her magic reality, what else had been wonderful seemed natural. Balder was in fairy-land.

He fell easily into the fairy-land humor.

"I am a being like yourself," said he, with a smile; "and not dumb like your plants and animals."

"Understood!—answered!" exclaimed Gnulemah again, in a tremor. As morning spreads up the sky, did the sweet blood flow outward to warm her face and neck. As the blush deepened, her eyelids fell, and she shielded her beautiful embarrassment with her raised hands. A pathos in the simple grace of this action drew tears unawares to Balder's eyes.

What was in her mind? what might she be? Had she lived always in this enchanted spot, companionless (for poor old Hiero could scarcely serve her turn) and ignorant perhaps that the world held other beings endowed like herself with human gifts? Had she vainly sought throughout nature for some kinship more intimate than nature could yield her, and thus at length fancied herself a unique, independently created soul, imperial over all things? Since her whole world was comprised between the wall and the river, no doubt she believed the reality of things extended no further.

In Balder she had found a creature like, yet pleasingly unlike herself, palpable to feeling as to sight, and gifted with that articulate utterance which till now she had accounted her almost peculiar faculty.

Delightful might be the discovery, but awesome too, frightening her back by its very tendency to draw her forward.

Whether or not this were the solution of Gnulemah's mystery, Balder recognized quiet to be his cue towards her. Probably he could not do better than to get the ear of Doctor Hiero, and establish himself upon a footing more conventional than the present one. His next step accordingly was to ask after him by name.

She peeped at the questioner between her fingers, but ventured not quite to emerge from behind them, as she answered,–her primary attempt at description,–

"Hiero is–Hiero!"

"And how long have you been here?" inquired Balder with a smile.

Gnulemah forgot her embarrassment in wondering how so remarkable a creature happened to ask questions whose answers her whole world knew!

"We are always here!" she exclaimed; and added, after a moment's doubtful scrutiny, "Are you a spirit?"

"An embodied spirit,–yes!" answered he, smiling again.

"One of those I see beyond,"–she pointed towards the cliff,–"that move and seem to live, but are only shadows in the great picture? No! for I cannot touch them nor speak with them; they never answer me; they are shadows." She paused and seemed to struggle with her bewilderment.

"They are shadows!" repeated Helwyse to himself.

Though no Hermetic philosopher, he was aware of a symbolic truth in the fanciful dogma. Outside his immediate circle, the world is a shadow to every man; his fellow-beings are no more than apparitions, till he grasps them by the hand. So to Gnulemah the cliff and the garden wall were her limits of real existence. The great picture outside could be true for her only after she had gone forth and felt as well as seen it.

Fancy aside, however, was not hers a condition morally and mentally deplorable? Exquisitely developed in body, must not her mind have grown rank with weeds,–beautiful perhaps, but poisonous? Herein Balder fancied he could trace the one-sided influence of his crackbrained uncle.–Whether his daughter or not, Gnulemah was evidently a victim of his experimental mania. What particular crotchet could he have been humoring in this case? Was it an attempt to get back to the early sense of the human race?

The materials for such an evolution were certainly of tempting excellence. In point of beauty and apparent natural capacity,

Gnulemah might claim equality with the noblest daughter of the Pharaohs. The grand primary problem of how to isolate her from all contact with the outside world was, under the existing circumstances, easy of solution. Beyond this there needed little positive treatment. Her creed must arise from her own instinctive and intuitive impressions. Of all beyond the reach of her hands, she trust to her eyes alone for information; no marvel, therefore, if her conclusions concerning the great intangible phenomena of the universe were fantastic as the veriest heathen myths. The self-evolved feelings and impulses of a black-eyed nymph like Gnulemah were not likely to be orthodox. She was probably no better than a worshipper of vain delusions and idols of the imagination.

Her attire—a style of costume such as might have been the fashion in the days of Cheops or Tuthmosis—showed a carrying out of the Doctor's whim,—a matching of the external to the internal conditions of the age he aimed to reproduce. The project seemed, on the whole, to have been well conceived and consistently prosecuted. It was seldom that Uncle Hiero achieved so harmonious a piece of work; but the idea showed greater moral obliquity than Balder would have looked for in the old gentleman.

But there was no deep sincerity in the young man's strictures. There before him stood the woman Gnulemah,—purple, white, and gold; a vivid, breathing, warm-hued life; a soul and body rich with Oriental splendor. There she stood, her hair flowing dark and silky from beneath her twisted turban, her eyes,—black melted loadstones; the broad Egyptian pendants gleaming and glowing from temple to shoulder. The golden serpent seemed to writhe on her bosom, informed from its wearer with a subtle vitality. Through all dominated a grand repose, like the calm of nature, which storms may prove but not disthrone!

There she stood,—enchanted princess, witch, goddess,—woman at all events, palpable and undeniable. She must be accepted for what she was, civilized or uncivilized, heathen or Christian. She was a perfected achievement,—vain to argue how she might have been made better. Who says that an evening cloud, gorgeous in purple and heavenly gold, were more usefully employed fertilizing a garden-patch?

Balder Helwyse, moreover, was not a simple utilitarian; he was almost ready to make a religion of beauty. If he blamed his uncle for shutting up this superb creature within herself, he failed not to admire the result of the imprisonment. He knew he was beholding as rare a spectacle as ever man's eyes were blessed withal; nor was he slow to perceive the psychological interest of the situation. To a student of mankind, if to no one else, Gnulemah was beyond estimation precious. But had Balder forgotten what fruit his tree of philosophy had already yielded him?

At all events, he forbore to press his question as to the whereabouts of Uncle Hiero, who would turn up sooner or later. It was enough for the present to know that he still existed. Meanwhile he would sound the depths of this fresh nature, undisturbed.

The hoopoe (who had played an important part in promoting the acquaintance thus far) forsook his perch above Balder's head, and after hovering for a moment in mid-air, as if to select the best spot, he alighted on the mossy cushion at the foot of the twin palm-trees. Such a couch might Adam and Eve have rejoiced to find in Paradise. Balder took the hint, and without more ado threw himself down there, while Gnulemah half knelt, half sat beside him, propped on her arm, her warm fingers buried in the cool moss. The little master-of-ceremonies remained, with a fine sense of propriety, between the two, preening and fluttering his brilliant feathers and casting diamond glances sidelong.

"You remember nothing before coming to this place, Gnulemah?"

"Only dream-memories, that grow dimmer. Before this, I was a spirit in the great picture, and when my lamp goes out I shall return thither."

"Your lamp, Gnulemah?—what lamp?"

"How can you understand me and yet not know what I know? My lamp is the light of my life; it burns always in the temple yonder; when it goes out my life will become a darkness, for I am Gnulemah, the daughter of fire!"

"I knew not that my uncle was a poet," muttered Balder to himself. "A daughter of fire,—yes, there is lightning in her eyes!" Aloud he said, secretly alluding to the manner of his descent into the garden,—

"I dropped from the sky into your world, Gnulemah. Though we can talk together, whatever we tell each other will be new."

She caught the idea of a lifetime spent instructing this delightful being, and receiving in return instruction from him. She entered at once the charming vista.

"Tell me," she began, bending towards him in her earnestness, "are there others like you?—are they bright and beautiful as you are?—or do they look like Hiero?"

Balder laughed, and flushed, and his heart warmed pleasurably. Here was a compliment from the very soul of nature. And albeit the lovely flatterer's experience of men was avowedly most limited, yet her taste was unvitiated as her sincerity, and her judgment may therefore have been more valuable than that of the most practised belle of fashion. But he answered modestly,—

"Hiero and I are both men, and there are as many men as stars in heaven, and as many women as men, myriads of men and women, Gnulemah!"

She lifted her face and hand in eloquent astonishment.

"O, what a world!" she exclaimed in her low-toned way. "But are the women all like me?"

"There is not one like you," answered Balder, with the quiet emphasis of conviction. How refreshing was it thus to set aside conventionalism! Her ingenuousness brought forth the like from him.

"Have you never wished to go beyond the wall?" he asked her.

"Yes, often!" she said, fingering the golden serpent thoughtfully. "But that could not be unless I put out the lamp. Sometimes I get tired of this world,—it has changed since I first came to it."

"Is it less beautiful?"

"It is smaller than it used to be," said Gnulemah, pensively. "Once the house was so high, it seemed to touch heaven;—see how it has dwindled since then! And so with other things that are on earth. The stars and the sun and clouds, they have not changed!"

"That is a consolation, is it not?" observed Balder, between a smile and a sigh. Gnulemah was not the first to charge upon the world the alterations in the individual; nor the first, either, to find comfort in the constancy of Heaven.

She went on, won to further confidence by her listener's sympathy,—

"I used to hope the wall would one day become so low that I might pass over it. But it has ceased to change, and is still too high. Shall I ever see the other side?"

"It can be broken down if need be. But you might go far before finding a world so fair as this. Perhaps it would be better to stand on the cliff, and only look forth across the river."

"I cannot stay always here," returned Gnulemah, shaking her turbaned head, with its gleaming bandeau and rattling pendants. "But no wall is between me and the sky; the flame of my lamp goes upward, and why should not Gnulemah?"

"A friend is the only world one does not tire of," he replied after a pause. "You have lacked companions."

Gnulemah glanced down at the hoopoe, who forthwith warbled aloud and fluttered up to her shoulder. The bird was her companion, and so, likewise, were the plants and flowers. Gnulemah could converse with them in their own language. Nature was her friend and confidant, and intimately communed with her.

All this was conveyed to Balder's apprehension, not by words, but by some subtle expressiveness of eye and gesture. Gnulemah could give voiceless utterances in a manner pregnant and felicitous almost beyond belief.

"I meet also a beautiful maiden in the looking-glass," she added; "her face and motion are always the same as my own. But though she seems to speak, her voice never reaches me; and she smiles, but only when I smile; and mourns only when I mourn. We can never reach each other; but there is more in her than in my birds and flowers."

"She is the shadow of yourself; no reality, Gnulemah."

"Are we shadows of each other, then? is she weary of her world, as I of mine? shall we both escape to some other,—or only pass each into the other's, and be separated as before?"

Balder, like wise men before him, was at some loss how to bring his wisdom to bear here. He could not in one sentence explain the complicated phenomena in question. Fortunately, however, Gnulemah (who had apparently not yet learned to appeal from her own to another's judgment) seemed hardly to expect a solution to problems upon which she had expended much private thought.

"I have come to look on her as though she were myself, and she tells me secrets which no one else can know. Some things she tells me that I do not care to hear, but they are always true. I can see changes in; her face that I feel in my own heart."

"Does she teach you that you grow every day more beautiful?" He was willing to prove whether Gnulemah could thus be disconcerted. Many a woman had he known, surprisingly innocent until a chance word or glance betrayed profoundest depths.

"Our beauty is like the garden, which is beautiful every day, though no day is just like another. But the changes I mean are in the spirit that looks back at me from her eyes, when I enter deeply into them."

What connection could, after all, subsist between beauty and vanity in one who neither had rivals nor aught to rival for? Doubtless she enjoyed her beauty,—the more, as her taste was pure of conventional falsities. How much of worldly experience would it take to vitiate that integrity in her? Would it not be better to leave her to end her life, restricted to the same innocent and lovely companionship which had been hers thus far? Here the hoopoe, startled at some movement that Balder made, abandoned his perch on his mistress's shoulder, and flew to the top of the palm-tree. Had the day when such friends would suffice her needs gone by?

Yes, it was now too late. No one who has beheld the sun can

thenceforth dispense with it. Balder had shone across the beautiful recluse's path, and linked her to outside realities by a chain which, whether he went or stayed, would never break. Flowers, birds, shadows in the mirror,—less than nothing would these things be to her from this hour on.

Heretofore the intercourse between the two had been tentative and incoherent,—a doubtful, aimless grappling with strange conditions which seemed delightful, but might mask unknown dangers. No solid basis of mutual acquaintanceship had been even approached. Balder, accustomed though he was to woman's society, knew not how to apply his experience here; while Gnulemah had not yet perhaps decided whether her visitor were natural or supernatural. The man was probably the less at ease of the two, finding himself in a pass through which tradition nor culture could pilot him. Gnulemah, being used to daily communion with things mysterious to her understanding, would scarcely have altered her demeanor had Balder turned out to be a genie!

But the first step towards fixing the relations between them was already taken. The young man's abrupt movement of his hand to his face (probably with purpose to stroke the beard no longer growing there) had not only scared away the hoopoe, but had flashed on Gnulemah a ray from the diamond ring.

She rose to her feet suddenly, yet easily as a startled serpent rears erect its body. Vivid emotion lightened in her face. Balder knew not what to make of the look she gleamed at him.

"What are you?" she asked, her voice sunk to almost a whisper. "Hiero?—are you Hiero?"

Balder stared confounded,—partly inclined to smile!

"Come back,—transfigured!" she went on, her eyes deepening with awe. What did it mean? Somewhat disturbed, Balder got also on his feet. As he did so, Gnulemah crouched before him, holding out her hands like a suppliant. An onlooker might have fancied that the would-be God had found his worshipper at last!

"My name is Balder," his Deityship managed to say. As he spoke, the sun rounded the corner of the house, and the light fell brightly on him, Gnulemah kneeling in shadow. The glory of his splendid youth seemed to have shone out from within him in sudden effulgence.

"Balder!" she slowly repeated, still gazing up at him.

"There is a relationship between us," said he, a vague uneasiness urging him to take refuge behind the quaint fantasy, "You are the daughter of fire, and I the descendant of the sun!"

He spoke the unpremeditated notion which the sunburst had created in his brain,—spoke not seriously nor yet lightly. He had as much right to his genealogy as she to hers.

But what a strange effect his words wrought on her! She clasped her hands together quickly in a kind pf ecstasy.

"The sun,–Balder! I have prayed to him,–he as come to me,– Balder, my God!" With how divine an accent did her full low voice give him the name to which he had dared aspire! He was God–and her God!

He perhaps divined one part of the process through which her mind must have gone; but he could not find a word to answer, whether of acceptance or disclaimer. He turned pale,–his heart sick. Had the recognition of his Godhood been too tardy? Gnulemah fancied he repulsed her, and her passion kindled,–only religious passion, but it seared him!

"Do not be cold to me, Balder!"–his name as she uttered it moved him as a blasphemy. "In my lonely kneelings I have felt you! my eyes close, my hands grow together, my breath flutters, every breath is joy and fear! I think 'He is with me,–the Being I adore!' but when I opened my eyes, He was gone,–Balder!"

Still motionless and seeming-deaf stood the Divinity, bathed in mocking sunlight. He was powerless to stop her from unveiling to him, as to a visible God the sacred places of her maiden heart. That sublime office whose reversion he had boldly courted, in the possession shrivelled his soul to nothing and left him dead. It was not easy to be God,–even over one human being!

But Gnulemah, in her mighty earnestness, knelt nearer, so that the edge of Balder's sunlight smote the golden ornaments that clung round her outstretched arms. She almost touched him, but though his spirit recoiled, the doltish flesh would not be moved.

"It was not to be always so," she continued, an appealing vehemence quivering through her tones. "Some day I was to see Him and know Him more clearly. Shine on me, Balder! am not I your priestess? in the morning do not I worship you, and at noon, and in the evening? At night do not I kneel at your altar and pray you to care for me while I sleep? Hear me, Balder! I see you in all things,–they are your thoughts and meet again in you! The sun himself is but your shadow! Do not I know you, my Balder? Be not clouded from your servant! Leave me not,–take me with you where you go!"

It was at this moment that the young man's mind, stumbling stupidly hither and thither, chanced to encounter that picture of the courtesan, leaning from the open window in the city street, beckoning him to come. She took Gnulemah's place, beckoning, making a hateful parody of Gnulemah's expression and gestures. Could a devil take the consecrated place of angels? or was the angel a worse devil in disguise?

In the same day, to him the same man, could two such voices speak,—such faces look? And could the germ of Godhead abide in a soul liable to the irony of such vicarious solicitation?

Speech or motion was still denied him. His priestess, strengthened by religious passion, was bold to touch with hers his divine hand, on the finger of which demoniacally glittered the murder-token. The hand was so cold and lax that even the smooth warmth of her soft fingers failed to put life in it.

"You have taken Hiero to yourself,—take me also! be my God as well as his, for I shall be alone now he is gone. This ring which he always wore—"

Balder roughly snatched back his hand.

"Hiero's ring?"

"Why do you look so?—is it not a sign to me from him?"

"Hiero's ring?—tell me, Gnulemah, is this Hiero's ring?—Stop—stand up! No—call me Satan!—Hiero's ring!"

"Where is Hiero, then?" demanded Gnulemah, rising and dilating. "You wear his ring,—what have you done with him?—Is there no God?"

The words came riding on the waves of deep-drawn breaths, for her soul was in a tumult. Her life had thus far been like a quiet sequestered pool, reflecting only the sky, and the ferns and flowers that bent above its margin; ignorant, moreover, of its own depth and nature. Now, invaded by storm, God and nature seemed swept away and lost, and a terror of loneliness darkened over it.

"Is there no Balder?" reiterated Gnulemah. But all at once the fierceness in her eyes melted, as lightning is followed by summer rain. She came so near,—he standing dulled with horror of his discovery,—came so near that her breath touched him, and he could hear the faint rustling of the white byssus on her bosom, and the soft tinkle of the broad pendants that glowed against her black hair; and could see how profoundly real her beauty was. Mighty and beneficent must be the force or the law which could combine the rude elements into such a form of life as this!

"Let me live for you and serve you! Though the world has no Balder, may not I have mine? You shall be everything to me! Without you I cannot be; but I want no other God if I have my Balder!"

This was another matter! Nevertheless,—so subtle is the boundary between love human and divine,—Gnulemah in these first passionate moments may easily have deemed the one no less sublime than the other.

But there was no danger of Balder's falling into such an error. The distinction was clear to him. Yet with remorse and abasement strove the defiant impulse to pluck and eat—forgetful of this world and the next the royal fruit so fairly held to his lips! For herein fails the divinity of nature,—she can minister as well to man's depravity as to his exaltation; which could not happen were she one with God. Nay, man had need be strong with Divine inspiration, before communing unharmed with nature's dangerous loveliness.

His hand in Gnulemah's was now neither cold nor lax. She raised it in impetuous homage to her forehead. The diamond left a mark there; first white, then red. For a breath or two, their eyes saw depths in each other beyond words' fathoming....

A door was closed above; and the echo stole down stairs and crept with a hollow whisper into the conservatory. The little lord chamberlain fluttered down from his lofty perch and hovered between the two faces, his penetrating note sounding like a warning, Gnulemah drew back, and a swift blush let fall its rosy veil from the golden gleam of her jewelled forehead-band to below the head of the serpent which twisted round her neck.

One parting look she gave Balder, pregnant of new wonder, fear, and joy. Then she turned and glided with quick ophidian grace to the doorway from which she had first appeared, and was eclipsed by the curtain. The inner door shut; she was gone. Dull, dull and colorless was the conservatory. The hoopoe had flown out through the hall to the open air. Only the crocodile continued to keep Balder company.

After standing a few moments, he once more threw himself down on the moss couch beneath the palm-trees. There he reclined as before, supported on his elbow, and turned the diamond ring this way and that on his finger in moody preoccupation.

Was the crocodile asleep, or stealthily watching him?

XIX.

Before Sundown.

If Balder Helwyse had been in a vein for self-criticism at this juncture, the review might probably have dissatisfied him. He possessed qualities which make men great. He could have discharged august offices, for he saw things in large relations and yet minutely. His mind and courage could rise to any enterprise, and carry it with ease and cheerfully. His nature was even more receptive than active. He had force of thought to electrify nations.

But his was the old story of the stargazer walking into the well, who might have studied the stars in the well, but could not be warned of the well by the stars. He had whistled grand chances down the wind, reaching after what was superhuman. His hunger had been vast, but the food wherewith he had filled himself nourished him not, and suddenly he had collapsed. His first actual step towards realizing his lofty aspirations had landed him low amongst earth's common criminals,—nor had the harm stopped there. That defiant impulse to which he had just now been on the point of yielding had not dared so much as to have shown its face before his unvitiated will. He was disorganized and at the mercy of events, because without law sufficient to keep and guide himself.

Though fallen, there was in him somewhat giantlike, perhaps easier to see now than before,—as the ruin seems vaster than the perfect building. The travail of a soul like Balder's must issue greatly, whether for good or ill. He could not remain long inchoate, but the elements would combine to make something either darker or fairer than had been before. Meanwhile, in the uncrystallized solution the curious analyst might detect traits bright or sinister, ordinarily invisible. Here were softness, impetuosity, romantic imagination, and tender fire, enough to set up half a dozen poets. Again, there was a fund of malignity, coldness, and subtlety adequate to the making an Iago. Here, too, were the clear sceptical intellect, the fertility and versatile power of brain, which only the loftier minds of the world have shown.

Such seemingly incongruous qualities are, in the human crucible, so mingled, proportioned, and refined, as to form a seeming simple and transparent whole. We may feel the presence of a spirit weighty, strong, deep, without understanding the how and why of impression.

Only at critical moments, such as this in Balder's life, can we point out the joining lines.

Balder's present attitude, viewed from whatever side, was no less irksome than ignoble. One misfortune was with diabolic ingenuity dovetailed into another. It was bad enough to have killed a man; but the victim was his own uncle, and the father—at least the foster-father—of Gnulemah. And she, forsooth, must idolize the murderer; and, finally, his heart must leap forth in passionate response to hers at the moment—partly perhaps for the reason—that every honest motive forbade it. That look and touch, at the molten point of various emotions, had welded their spirits together at once and lastingly.

What next? For Gnulemah and for himself what course was least disastrous?—the heroic line,—to leave her without a word?—or, concealing what he was, should he stay and be happy in her arms? Was there a third alternative?

"To part would be yet worse for her than for me. She would think I had deceived her. And, love apart, how can I leave her whose only protector I have killed? That deed puts me in his place; so love and duty are at one for once. Her Balder,—her God,—she calls me. She is my universe; the depth and limit of my knowledge and power are gauged by her. Such is the issue of my aspirations!"

He breathed out a half laugh, ending in a sigh. "But loving her is sweeter than to inform creation!" he added, aloud.

The crocodile made no reply. Balder went on, fingering the telltale ring and talking with himself; the earth, meanwhile, slowly turning her warm shoulder to the western sun. A still half light filled the conservatory as with a clear mellow liquor, and the rich leaves, and blossoms stood breathless with delight. The painfully rigid contraction of Balder's features was softening away; he was coming into harmony with the sensuous beauty of the scene, or its refined voluptuousness—serene, unambitious, content with time and careless of eternity—interpreted his altered temper.

Be happy in the sunlight, O men and women! Love and kiss,—bow down and worship each the other! Who can tell of another joy like this? Everlasting knows it not, for only the flavor of death can give it perfection! Save for the foreshadow of midnight, noonday were not beautiful. But when night comes, sink ye in one another's arms, and sleep! Heaven on earth is a richer, stronger draught than Heaven; but pray that in vouchsafing death, it cheat ye not of annihilation!

He had forgotten that there was anything ugly in the world, or that the blindest cannot always escape the Gorgon. He recked not the risk of bringing a being such as Gnulemah face to face with modern life, nor bethought him that the secret in his heart would still be nearer it than love could come. Neither, during this fortunate moment, did fear of discovery harass him.

Oddly, too, it was not to domestic comforts,—the love of wife, children, and friends,—nor yet to the absorbing duties of a profession, that Balder looked for a shield against inward trouble. Hope held him no more than fear; his happiness must consist in freedom from both. He thought only of the Gnulemah of today,—unique, beautiful, untamed, divinely ignorant; but whose heart walked before, leading the giddy mind by paths the wisest dared not tempt. The sounds of her voice, the shiftings of her expression, her look, her touch,—he recalled them all. He centred time and space in her. Change, new conditions, succession of events,—these came not near her. Their life should know neither past nor future, but abide a constant Now,—until the end!

His lips followed his thought with soundless movement. Handsome lips they were,—the under, full, but sharply defined from the bulwark-chin; the upper, slender, boldly curved, firm, yet sensitive;—the mouth was a compendium of the man's physical nature. His eyes, large and almost as dark as Gnulemah's, albeit far different in effect,—were now in-looking; the pupils, always extraordinarily large and brilliant, almost filled the space between the eyelids. His hair clung round his head in yellow curls; the dark dense eyebrows arched at ease. With velvet doublet and well-moulded limbs, in the enchanted evening-glow, he looked the ideal fairy prince,—noble, wise, and valiant; conquering fate for love's sake. They were brave princes,—they of old time. But one wonders whether the giants and enchanters, nowadays, are not stronger and subtler than they used to be!

XX.

Between Waking and Sleeping.

There was an old woman in the house who went by the name of Nurse; her duties being to cook the meals and preserve a sort of order in such of the rooms as were occupied by the family. Since the greater part of the house was uninhabited, and there were only two mouths to feed beside her own, Nurse was not without leisure moments. How were they employed?

Not in gossiping, for she had no cronies. Not in millinery and dressmaking, for there were no admiring eyes to reward such labors. Not in gadding, for she might not pass the imprisoning wall. Not even in reading, perhaps because she was not much of a proficient in that art.

The truth is that—to the outward eye at least—she was uniformly idle. For years past she had spent many hours of each night in the corner of the kitchen fireplace, which was as large, roomy, and smoke-seasoned as any in storybooks or mediæval halls. Here sat she, winter and summer, her body bent forward over her knees, her disfigured face supported on one hand, while the other lay across her breast. This was her common position, and she seldom moved to change it. She hummed tunes to herself sometimes,—not hymn tunes,—but never was heard to utter an articulate word. Often you might have thought her asleep,—but no! when you least expected it a shining black eye was fixed oh you; an eye which, two hundred years ago, would have convicted its owner of witchcraft. It was the only bright thing about the poor woman.

Whenever the master of the house came to the kitchen, Nurse's witch-eye followed him animallike; no movement of his, no expression, seemed to escape it. A curious observer might sometimes have re-marked in her, during the few moments after the man's entrance, a muffled agitation, an irregularity of the breath, an obscure anxiety and suspense. This, however, would soon subside, and rarely recur during his stay. The phenomenon had been observable daily for nearly a score of years, yet nothing had meantime happened to explain or justify it. Had an original dread—groundless or not—prolonged its phantom exis-tence precisely because it had never met with justification?

Often for weeks at a time, complete silence would obtain between master and Nurse. He would enter and ramble hither and thither the ample kitchen; eat what had been prepared for him, and be off again without a word or glance of acknowledgment. Or, again, pacing irregularly to and fro before the fireplace, he would pour forth long disjointed rhapsodies, wild speculations, hopes, and misgivings; his mood changing from solemn to gay, and round through gusty passion to morbid gloom. But never did he address his words to Nurse so much as to himself or to some imaginary interlocutor; and she for her part never answered him a syllable, but sat in silence through it all. Yet was she ever alert to listen, and sometimes the subdued trembling would come on and the obstruction of breath. But when the talker, in midexcitement of speech, snatched his violin and drew from it melodies weirdly exquisite, soothing his diseased thoughts and harmonizing them, Nurse would become once more composed; the phantom danger was again put off, and the violinist would presently fall into silence,—sometimes into sleep. But still, while he slept, the witch-eye watched him; though with an expression of yearning, uncouth intensity which seldom ventured forth while he was awake.

With Gnulemah, Nurse's intercourse became yearly more and more infrequent. As the child arose to womanhood, she grew apart from the voiceless creature who had cared for her infancy. It was not Gnulemah's fault, whose heart was never barren of loving impulses. But mother, father, were words whose meaning she had never been taught; and had Nurse comprehended the unconscious thirst and hunger of the girl's soul,—unconscious, but not therefore harmless,—she might have tried, by dint of affectionate observances and companionship, to represent the motherly office which she had filled in the beginning. But this was not to be. Some hidden agency had forced the two ever farther asunder. Moreover, Gnulemah developed rapidly, while Nurse underwent a process of gradual congealment,—her wits and emotions became torpid. Besides this, she was the victim of disfigurement, physical as well as spiritual; while Gnulemah, both naturally and by training, was sensitive to beauty and ugliness. Other surface causes no doubt there were, in addition to the hidden one, which was perhaps the most potent of all.

A considerable time had passed since Gnulemah's departure, when Balder became aware that he was not alone in the conservatory. His thoughts were all of Gnulemah, and he looked quickly round in expectation of seeing her. The apparition of a widely different object startled him to his feet.

A female figure stood before him, wrapped in sad-colored garments of anomalous description, her head tied up in dark turbanlike folds of cloth. A lock of rusty black hair escaped from beneath this headdress and hung down beside her face. She might once have been tall and erect, but her form now sagged to the left, losing both height and dignity. Her visage, seamed and furrowed by the scar of some terrible calamity, had lost its natural contour. The left eye was extinguished, but the right remained,–the only feature in its original state. It was dark and bright, and possessed, by very virtue of its disfigured environment, a repulsive kind of beauty. Its influence was peculiar. In itself, it postulated an owner in the prime of life, handsome and graceful. But, one's attention wandering, the woman's actual ugliness impressed itself with an intensity enhanced by the imaginary contrast.

A grotesque analogy was thus brought to light. The woman was dual. Her right side lived; the left–blind, inert, and soulless–was dragged about a dead weight. It was an unnatural emphasizing of the spiritual-material composition of mankind. Observable, moreover, was her strange method of disguising emotion. There was no muscular constraint; she simply turned her blank left side to the spectator, with an effect like the interposition of a dead wall!

Such, on Balder's perhaps abnormally excited apprehension, was the impression the nurse produced. She, on her part, was perhaps more disconcerted than he. Her single eye settled upon him in a panic of surprise. The dressing of the scene gave Balder a grisly reminder of the first moments of Gnulemah's eloquent astonishment. There was as great an apparent difference between the superb Egyptian and this poor creature, as between good and evil; but there was also the disagreeable suggestion of a similar kind of relationship. Gnulemah, withered, stifled, and degraded by some unmentionable curse, might have become a thing not unlike this woman.

"Have we met before, madam?" asked Helwyse, impelled to the question by what he took for a bewildered recognition in her eye.

She moved her lips, but made no audible answer.

"I am Balder Helwyse," he added; for he had made up his mind that all concealments (save one) were unnecessary.

A grotesque quake of emotion travelled through the woman's body, and she gave utterance to a harsh inarticulate sound. She came confusedly forwards, groping with hands outstretched. Balder, though not wont to fail in courtesy to the sorriest hag, could scarce forbear recoiling; especially because he fancied that an expression of affectionate interest was struggling to get through the scarred incrustation of the woman's nature.

Perhaps she marked his inward shrinking, for she checked herself, and, slowly turning her lifeless screen, hid behind it. It was impotent deprecation translated into flesh,–at once ludicrous and painful. The young man found so much difficulty in restraining the manifestation of his distaste, that he blushed in the twilight at his own rudeness. He would do his best to redeem himself.

"Doctor Hiero Glyphic is my uncle," said he, moving to get on Nurse's right side, and speaking in his pleasantest tone. "Is he at home? I have come a long way to see him."

Preoccupied by his amiable purpose to reassure the woman, Helwyse had got to the end of this speech before realizing the ghastly mockery involved in it. Nevertheless, it was well. Even thus falsely and boldly must he henceforth speak and act. By a happy accident he had opened the path, and must see to it that his further steps did not retrograde.

Still Nurse answered not a word, which was the less surprising, inasmuch as she had been dumb for a quarter of a century past. But Balder, supposing her silence to proceed from stupidity or deafness, repeated more loudly and peremptorily,—

"Doctor Glyphic,—is he here? is he alive?"

He felt a morbid curiosity to hear what reply would be made to the question whose answer only he could know. But he was puzzled to observe that it appeared to throw Nurse into a state of agitation as great as though she had herself been the perpetrator of Balder's crime! She stood quaking and irresolute, now peeping for a moment from behind her screen, then dodging back with an increase of panic.

This display—rendered more uncouth by its voicelessness—revolted the æsthetic sensibilities of Helwyse. Besides, what was the meaning of it? Had it actually been Davy Jones with whom he had striven on the midnight sea? and had his adversary, instead of drowning, spread his bat-wings for home, and left his supposititious murderer to disquiet himself in vain? Verily, a practical joke worthy its author!

This conceit revealed others, as a lightning-flash the midnight landscape. Balder was encircled by witchcraft,—had been ferried by a real Charon to no imaginary Hades. The quaint secluded beauty of circumstance was an illusion, soon to be dispelled. Gnulemah herself—miserable thought!—was perhaps a thing of evil; what if this very hag were she in another form? Glancing round in the deepening twilight, Balder fancied the dark, still plants and tropic shrubs assumed demoniac forms, bending and crowding about him. The old witch yonder was muttering some infernal spell; already he felt numbness in his limbs, dizziness in his brain.

The devils are gathering nearer. A heavy, heated atmosphere quivers before his eyes, or else the witch and her unholy crew are uniting in a reeling dance. In vain does Balder try to shut his eyes and escape the giddy spectacle; they stare widely open and see things super-natural. Nor can he ward off these with his hands, which are rigid before him, and defy his will. The devilish jig becomes wilder, and careers through the air, Balder sweeping with it. In mid-whirl, he sees the crocodile,—cold, motionless, waiting with long, dry jaws—for what?

A cry breaks from him. With a wrench that strains his heart he bursts loose from the devil's bonds that confine his limbs. The witch has vanished, and Helwyse seems to himself to fall headlong from a vast height, striking the earth at last helpless and broken.

"Gnulemah!"

Gasping out that name, he becomes insensible.

Beneath an outside of respectable composure have turmoiled the tides of such remorse and pain as only a man at once largely and finely made can feel. Added to the mental excitement carried through many phases to the point of distraction, have been bodily exertion and want of food and sleep. The apparition of unnatural ugliness, of behavior strange as her looks, coming upon him in this untoward condition, needed not the heat of the conservatory and stupefying perfume of the flowers to bring on the brief delirium and final unconsciousness. As he lies there let us remember that his last word threw back the unworthy, dark misgiving, that beauty and deformity, good and bad, could by any jugglery become convertible.

As a mere matter of fact, Nurse was no witch, nor had she, of her own will and knowledge, done Balder any harm. On the contrary, she was already at work, with trembling hands and painfully thumping heart, to relieve his sad case. She was touched and agitated to a singular degree. It was not the first time in the patient's life that she had tended him. The reader has guessed her secret,—that she had known Balder before he knew himself, and cared for him when his only cares had been to eat and sleep. She knew her baby through his manly stature and mature features, less from his likeness to his father than from certain uneffaced traces of infantine form and expression. She was of gypsy blood, and had looked on few human faces since last seeing his. He did not recognize her until some time afterwards. All things considered, it was hardly possible he should do so.

It was curious to observe how awkwardly she now managed emotions that had once flowed but too readily. She was moved by impulses which she had long forgotten how to interpret. Her only outlet for tenderness was her solitary eye, which might well have given way under the strain thus put upon it.

But by and by the inward heat began to thaw the stiff outward crust, which had been hardening for so many years. Glimpses there were of the handy, affectionate, sympathizing woman, emerging from fossilization. Her withered heart once more hungered and thirsted, and the strange duality tended to melt back again into unity.

Balder's attack at length yielded, and a drowsy consciousness returned, memory and reason being still partly in abeyance. His heavy, half closed eyes rested on darkness. A crooning sound was in his ear,—a nursery lullaby, wordless but soothing. Where was he? Had he been ill? Was he in his cradle at home? Was Salome sitting by to watch him and give him his medicine? Yes, very ill he was, but would be better in the morning; and meanwhile he would be a good boy, and not cry and make a fuss and trouble Salome.

"Nurse,—Sal!—I say, Sal!"

Salome bent over him as of old.

"Had such a funny dream, Sal! dreamt I was grown up, and—killed a man! What makes you shake so, Sal? it wasn't true, you know! And I'm going to be a good boy and go to sleep. Good night! give a kiss from me—to—my—little—"

So sinks he into slumber, profound as ever wooed his childhood; his head pillowed in Salome's lap, his funny dream forgotten.

XXI.

We Pick Up Another Thread.

Darkness and silence reigned in the conservatory; the group of the sleeping man and attendant woman was lost in the warm gloom, and scarcely a motion—the low drawing of a breath—told of their presence.

A great gray owl, which had passed the daylight in some obscure corner, launched darkling forth on the air and winged hither and thither,—once or twice fanning the sleeper's face with silent pinions. The crocodile lazily edged off the stone, plumped quietly into the water, and clambered up the hither margin of the pool, there coming to another long pause. A snail, making a night-journey across the floor, found in its path a diamond, sparkling with a light of its own. The snail extended a cool cautious tentacle,—recoiled it fastidiously and shaped a new course. A broad petal from a tall flowering-shrub dropped wavering down, and seemed about to light on Balder's forehead; but, swerving at the last moment, came to rest on the scaly head of the crocodile. The night waited and listened, as though for something to happen,—for some one to appear! Salome, too, was waiting for some one;—was it for the dead?

Meantime, pictures from the past glimmered through her memory. When, in our magic mirror, we saw her struck down by the hand of her lover, she was far from being the repulsive object she is now. Indeed, but for that chance word let fall yesterday, about her having been badly burnt, we might be at a loss to justify our recognition of her.

After Manetho's rude dismissal of her, she fled—not knowing whither better—to Thor Helwyse, who was living widowed in his Brooklyn house, with his infant son and daughter. Because she had been Helen's attendant, she besought Helen's husband to give her a home. She was in sore trouble, but said no more than this; and Thor, suspecting nothing of her connection with Manetho, gladly received her as nurse to his children.

But past sins and imprudences would find out Salome no less than others. At the critical moment for herself and her fortunes, the house took fire. She risked her life to save Thor's daughter, was herself burned past recognition, and (one misfortune treading on another's heels) balanced on death's verge for a month or two. She got well, in part; but the faculty of speech had left her, and beauty of face and figure was forever gone.

In her manifold wretchedness, and after such devotion shown, it was not in Thor's warm heart to part with her; so, losing much, she gained something. She remained with her benefactor, whose manly courtesy ever forbore to probe the secret of her woman's heart, over which as over her face she always wore a veil. The world saw Salome no more. She sat in the nursery, watching year by year the dark-eyed little maiden playing with the fair-haired boy. Broad-shouldered Thor would come in, with his grand, kindly face and royal beard; would kiss the little girl and tussle with the boy, mightily laughing the while at the former's solicitude for her playmate; would throw himself on the groaning sofa, and exclaim in his deep voice,—

"God bless their dear little souls! Why, Nurse! when did a brother and sister ever love each other like that,—eh?"

Salome probably was not unhappy then; indeed,—whether she knew it or not,—she was at her happiest. But new events were at hand; Thor, growing yearly more restless, at length resolved to sell his house and go to Europe, taking with him Salome and both the children. Everything was ready, down to the packing of Salome's box. A day or two before the sailing, Thor went to New Jersey, to bid farewell to his eccentric brother-in-law. It was a warm summer day, and the children played from morning till night in the front yard, while Nurse sat in the window and kept her eye on them. Her thoughts, perhaps, travelled elsewhere.

Since her misfortune she had, no doubt, had more opportunity than most women for reflection: silence breeds thought. What she thought about, no one knew; but she could hardly have forgotten Manetho. On this last evening, when at the point of leaving America forever, it would have been strange had no memory of him passed through her mind.

She had not heard his name in the last four years, and she knew that he suspected nothing of her whereabouts. Had he ever wished to see her? she wondered and thought, "He would not know me if he did see me!" With that came a tumultuous longing once more to look upon him. Too late! Why had she not thought of this before? Now must her last memory of him be still as when, disfigured by sudden rage, he turned upon her and struck her on the bosom. There was the scar yet; the fire had spared it! It was a keepsake which, as time passed, Salome strangely learned to love!

It was growing dusk,—time for the children to come in. They were sitting deep in the abundant grass, weaving necklaces out of dandelion-stems. Nurse leaned out of window and beckoned to attract their attention. But either they were too much absorbed to notice her, or they were wilfully blind; so Nurse rose to go out and fetch them.

Before reaching the open front door, she stopped short and her heart seemed to turn over. A tall dark man was leaning over the fence, talking with the little girl. Nurse shrank within the shadow of the door, and thence peeped and listened,—as well as her beating pulses would let her.

"I know where fairyland is," says the man, in the soft, engaging tone that the listener so well remembers. "Come! shall we go together and visit it?"

"He come too?" asks the little maiden, nodding towards the boy, who is portentously busy over his dandelions.

"He may if he likes," the man answers with a smile. "But we must make haste, or fairyland will be shut up!"

It flashes into Salome's head what this portends. She had heard this man vow revenge on Thor long ago, and she now sees how he means to keep his oath. He has shrewdly improved the opportunity of Thor's absence, and has come intending to carry off either his son or his daughter. Fortune, it seems, had chosen for him the dark-eyed little girl. See! he stoops and lifts her gently over the wall, and they are off for fairyland!

Rush out, Salome! alarm the neighborhood and force the kidnapper to give up his booty! After Thor's kindness to you, will you be false to him? Besides, what motive have you for unfaithfulness? Grant that you love Manetho,—what harm, save to his revengeful passion, could result from thwarting him?

Salome acted oddly on this occasion,—it would seem, irrationally. But that which appears to the spectator but a trivial modification may have vital weight with the actor. Had Manetho taken Balder, for example, Salome might have pursued another and more intelligible course than the one she actually took. She hurried out of the door and caught Manetho by the arm before he was twenty paces on his way. He turned, savage but frightened, setting down the little girl but not letting go her hand. She was in her happiest humor, and informed Nurse that she was to be queen of fairyland!

Nurse lifted the veil from her face and looked steadfastly at Manetho with her one eye. It was enough,—he saw in her but a hideous object,—would never know her for the bright girl he had once professed to love. Salome gave one sob, containing more of womanly emotion than could be written down in many words, and then was quiet and self-possessed. Manetho did not offer to escape, but stood on his guard; half prepared, however,—from something in the woman's manner,—to find her a confederate.

"S'e come too?" chirped the unconscious little maiden.

But Manetho's attention was turned to some words that Salome was writing in a little blank-book which she always carried in her pocket She offered to help him carry off the child, on condition of being herself one of the party!

He looked narrowly at the woman, but could make nothing by his scrutiny. Was it love for the child that prompted her behavior? No; for she could easily have raised the neighborhood against him. She completely puzzled him, and she would give no explanations. What if he should accept her offer? She would be an advantage as well as an inconvenience. The child would have the care to which it had been accustomed, and Manetho would thus be spared much embarrassment. When the woman's help became superfluous, it would not be difficult to give her the slip.

There was small leisure for reflection. An agreement was made,—on Salome's part, with a secret sense of intense triumph, not unmixed with fear and pain. She caught up Master Balder and his dandelions, kissed and hugged him violently, and locked him into the nursery; where he was found some hours afterwards by his father, in a state of great hunger and indignation. But the little dark-haired maiden was no more. She was gone to her kingdom of fairyland, and Nurse with her. Long mourned Balder for his vanished playmate!

Salome has kept her secret well. And now, there she sits, her long-lost baby's head in her lap, thinking of old times; and the longer she thinks, the more she softens and expands. Has she done a great wrong in her life? Surely she has suffered greatly, and in a manner that might well wither her to the core. But there must still have been a germ of life in the shrivelled seed, which this night—memorable in her existence—has begun to quicken.

By and by come a few tears, with a struggle at first, then more easily. Kind darkness lets us think of Salome bright and comely as in the old days, with the added grace of inward beauty wrought by sad experience. But, in truth, she is marred past earthly recovery. Nothing removes a soul so far from human sympathy as self-repression,—especially for any merely human end!

The night creeps reluctantly westward; the gray owl wings back to his shady corner; the adventurous snail, halfway up the palm-tree, glues himself to the bark and turns in for a nap. The crocodile has resumed his old position on the rock in the pool, and the flower petal floats on the water. Here comes the brilliant hoopoe with his smart crest and clear chirrup, impatient to bid Gnulemah good morning! All is as before, save that the group beneath the palm-trees has disappeared!

Balder slept late, yet, on awakening, he thought he must be dreaming still. He could not distinguish imagination from reality. His mind had temporarily lost its grasp, his will its authority. Where was he? Was it years or hours since he had entered Boston harbor?

Suddenly rose before him the vision of the deadly struggle on the midnight sea. Round this central point the rest crystallized in order. His heart sank, and he sighed most heavily. But presently he rose to his elbow and stared about in bewilderment. Had he ever seen this room before? How came he here?

He was lying on a carved bedstead, furnished with sheets of fine linen and a counterpane of blue embroidered satin; but all bearing an appearance of great age. The room was oval, like a bird's-egg halved lengthwise; the smoothly vaulted ceiling being frescoed with a crowd of figures. The rich and costly furniture harmonized with the bedstead, and bore the same marks of age. The chairs and lounge were satin-covered; the sumptuous toilet-table was fitted with a mirror of true crystal; the arched window was curtained with azure satin and lace. It was a chamber fit for a princess of the old *régime*, unaltered since its fair occupant last abode in it.

Balder now examined the frescos which covered wall and ceiling. The subject seemed at the first glance to be a Last Judgment, or something of that nature. A mingled rush of forms mounted on one side to the bright zenith, and thence lapsed confusedly down the opposite descent. The dark end of the room presented a cloud of gloomily fantastic shapes, swerved from the main stream, and becoming darker and more formless the farther they receded, till at the last they were lost in a murky shadow. Not entirely lost, however; for as Balder gazed awfully thitherward, the shadow seemed to resolve itself into a mass of intertwined and struggling beings, neither animal nor human, but combining the more unholy traits of both.

But from the centre of the upward stream shone forms and faces of angelic beauty; yet, on looking more narrowly, Balder discerned in each one some ghastly peculiarity, revealing itself just when enjoyment of the beauty was on the point of becoming complete. Such was the effect that the most angelic forms were translated into mocking demons, and where the light seemed brightest there was the spiritual darkness most profound.

In the zenith was a white lustre which obliterated distinction of form as much as did the cloudy obscurity at the end of the room. Now the design seemed about to unfold itself; then again it eluded the gazer's grasp. Suddenly at length it stood revealed. A gigantic face, with wide-floating hair and beard, looked down into Balder's own. Its expression was of infinite malignity and despair. The impersonation of all that is wicked and miserable, its place was at the top of Heaven; it was moulded of those aspiring forms of light, and was the goal which the brightest attained. Moreover, either by some ugly coincidence or how otherwise he could not conceive, this countenance of supreme evil was the very reflex of Balder's,—a portrait minutely true, and, despite its satanic expression, growing every moment more unmistakable.

Was this accident, or the contrivance of an unknown and unfathomable malice? Balder, Lord of Heaven, instinct with the essence of Hell! A grim satire on his religious speculations! But what satirist had been bitter enough so to forestall the years?—for the painting must have been designed while Balder was still an infant.

He threw himself off the bed and stepped to the window, and saw the blue sky and the river rhyming it. The breath of the orchard visited him, and he was greeted by the green grass and trees, He sighed with relief. There had been three mornings since his return to America. For the first he had blessed his own senses; the second had looked him out of countenance but the third came with a benediction, serene and mighty, such as Balder's soul had not hitherto been open to.

"This is more than a plaster heaven," said he, looking up; "but I fear, Balder Helwyse, your only heaven, thus far, has been of plaster. You have seen this morning how the God of such a heaven looks. How about the God of this larger Heaven, think you?"

Presently he turned away from the window; but he had quaffed so deeply of the morning glory, that the sinister frescos no longer depressed him. They were ridiculously unimportant,—nothing more than stains on the wall, in fact. Balder could not tell why he felt light-hearted. It was solemn light-heartedness,—not the gayety of sensuous spirits, such as he had experienced heretofore. It had little to do with physical well-being, for the young man was still faint and dizzy, and weak from hunger. Behold, then, at the foot of the bed, a carved table covered with a damask cloth and crowned with an abundant breakfast; not an ordinary breakfast of coffee, rolls, omelette, and beefsteak, but a pastoral breakfast,—fresh milk, bread and honey and fruit and mellow cheese,—such food as Adam might have begun the day with.

In face of the yet unsolved mystery of his own presence in the room, this new surprise caused Balder no special wonder. Beyond the apparition of the ugly dumb woman, he recollected nothing of the previous evening's experience. Could she have transported him hither? Well, he would not let himself be disturbed by apparent miracles. "No doubt the explanation is simple," thought he; and with that he began his toilet. The dressing-table displayed a variety of dainty articles such as a lady might be supposed to use,—pearl-handled brushes, enamelled powder-boxes, slender vases of Meissen porcelain, a fanciful ring-stand; from the half open drawer a rich glimpse of an Indian fan; a pair of delicate kid gloves, which only a woman's hands could have worn, were thrown carelessly on the table. There were still the little wrinkles in the fingers, but time had changed the pristine white to dingy yellow.

"Whose hands could have worn them? whose chamber was this?" mused Balder. "Not Gnulemah's; she knows nothing of kid gloves and powder! and these things were in use before she was born. Whose face was reflected in this glass, when those gloves were thrown down here? Was that her marriage-bed? Were children born in it?"

His seizure of the night before must have dulled the edge of his wit, else he had scarce asked questions which chance now answered for him. A scratch on one corner of the polished mirror-surface showed, on closer inspection, a name and a date written with a diamond. Shading off the light with his hand, Balder read, "Helen, 1831."

"My mother's name; the year I was born. My mother!" he repeated softly, taking up the old yellow gloves. "And this room was my birthplace,—and my little sister's! My mother's things, as she left them; for father once told me that he never entered her room after she was buried. She died here; and here my little sister and I began to live. And here I am, again,—really the same little helpless innocent baby who cried on that bed so long ago. Only not innocent now! Perhaps, not helpless, either!

"How happy that barber was yesterday! prattled about being born again. Cannot I be born again,—today,—in this room? Here I first began, and have come round the world to my starting-point. I will begin afresh this morning."

And heavily as he was weighted in the new race, he would not be disheartened. Unuttered resolves brightened his eyes and made his courage high.

Before beginning breakfast, he returned to the window and drank again of the divine blue and green. From the branch of a near tree the hoopoe startled him and made him color. Was the bird an emissary from Gnulemah? Balder's mouth drew back, and his chin and eyes strengthened, as though some part of his unuttered resolves were recalled by the thought of her.

When he was ready to go, he turned at the door, and threw a parting glance round the dainty old-fashioned chamber, trying to gather into one all the thoughts, memories, and resolves connected with it. He had nearly forgotten the frescos; the victorious sunshine had reduced the figures, satanic or beautiful, to a meaningless agglomeration of wandering lines and faded colors. As for his own portrait, it was no longer distinguishable.

XXII.

Heart and Head.

Balder easily found his way to the conservatory, but it was empty,—Gnulemah, at least, was not there! The tapestry curtain in her doorway was pushed aside, the door itself open. Where should he seek her?

As he stood in doubt, he saw lying at his feet a violet. Picking it up, he saw another some distance beyond it, and still another on the threshold which he had just crossed. They were Gnulemah's footsteps,—the scent of this sweet quarry, teaching him how to follow her. So he followed, nor let one fragrant trace escape him; and presently he had a nosegay of them.

She was out of doors, then. Truly, on such a day as this, where else should she be? What walls could presume to hold her? Her loveliness was at one with nature's, and they attracted each other. To the solitary nymph, her mighty playmate had been all-sufficient; for she saw not the earth and sky as they appear nowadays to mankind, but the divine meaning which they clothe. Thus she could converse with animals, and could read plants and stones more profoundly than botanist or geologist. She followed inward to her own fresh and beautiful soul the sympathies which allied her to outward things, and found there their true prototypes.

But when the strong magnetism of a new human spirit began to act upon her, these fine communings with nature suffered disturbance. In such thunderstorms as the meeting of the electric forces must engender, there was need of a trustworthier safeguard than simple perception of a divine purpose underlying creation. Only the personal God is strong enough to govern the relations of soul with soul. Barren of Eve, Adam would not have fallen; but with her he will one day not only retrieve his fall, but climb to a sublimer height than any to which he could have aspired alone.

Balder strolled out on the wide lawn. Southwestward wound an avenue of great trees, overshadowing the narrow footpath that stole beneath them. To the right, round the northern corner of the house, he could see far off the white tops of the blossoming apple-trees; and beyond, the river. The orchard perfume came riding on the untamed breeze, and whispered a fragrant secret in the young man's ear. Orchardward he pursued his search.

As he went on, Gnulemah grew every moment nearer. At length he caught the flutter of her mantle amidst the foliage, and presently saw her on the brink of the precipice, looking out across the broad blue river. Thus had he, through his glass, darkly, seen her stand the day before. Were the crossing a river and the flight of a day all that divided his past life from what he thought awaited him now!

While yet at a distance, he called to her,—not from impatience, but because he stood in awe of the meeting, and wanted the first moments over. His voice touched Gnulemah like a beloved hand, and turned her towards him. Her face, which had not learned to be the mask of emotion, but was instead the full and immediate index thereof, brightened with joy; and as he came near, the joy increased. Yet a seriousness deep down in her eyes, marked the shadow of a night and the dawn of another day. A spiritual chemistry had been working in her.

She did not move forward to meet him but stood delighting in the sense of his ever-growing nearness. When at length he stood close before her, she drew a long, pleasant breath and said,—

"A beautiful morning!"

This was no commonplace greeting, for it was not made in a commonplace manner. It said that his coming had consummated the else imperfect beauty of nature, and won its expression from Gnulemah's lips. The commonplace wondered to find itself transmuted into a compliment of fine gold!

Gnulemah's attire today was more Dianalike than yesterday's, and looked as appropriate to her as leaves to trees or clouds to the sky. Her dress, indeed, was not so much a conventional appendage as a living, sensitive part of her, which might be supposed to change its color and style in sympathy with her shifting moods and surroundings, yet never losing certain distinctive traits which had their foundation in her individual nature.

"A beautiful morning!" returned Balder, taking her hand. "Were you expecting me?"

"I feared you might not show yourself to me again," she answered, with sudden tears twinkling on her eyelashes. She seemed more tenderly human and approachable today than heretofore. Had she found her mountain-height of unmated solitude untenable?—found in herself a yielding woman, and in Balder the strength that is a man? This descent, which was a sweet ascent, made her endlessly more lovable.

"I come here always when I feel lonely," continued she. "If it had not been for this place, with its great outlook, I should often have been too lonely to stay in the world."

"We all need an outlook to a larger, world, Gnulemah."

"Besides, you came to me from the other side!" said she glancing in his face.

"Did you see me there?" Balder was on the point of asking; but he was wise enough to refrain. If he could believe it true, let him not tempt his happiness; if faith were weak, why build a barrier against it? So he kept silence.

"You found my violets!" whispered Gnulemah, with a shy smile. "You understand all I do and am; it is happiness to be with you."

They sat down by mutual consent beneath a crooked old apple-tree, which yet blossomed as pure and fresh as did the youngest in the orchard. From beneath this white and perfumed tent was a view of the distant city.

Gnulemah could not be called talkative, yet in giving her thoughts expression she outdid vocabularies. Many fine muscles there were around her eyes, at the corners of her mouth, and especially in the upper lip,—whose subtile curvings and contractions spoke volumes of question, appeal, observation. Her form by its endless shiftings uttered delicate phrases of pleasure, surprise, or love; her hands and fingers were orators, and eloquent were the curlings and tappings of her Arab feet.

This kind of language would be blank to one used rather to hear words than to feel them; but Balder, in, his present exalted mood, delighted in it. Was there any enjoyment more refined than to see his thought, before he had given it breath, lighten in the eyes of this daughter of fire? and with his own eyes to catch the first pure glimmer of her yet unborn fancies? A language genial of intimacy, for the talkers must feel in order to utterance,—must meet each other, from the heart outward, at every point. The human form is made of meanings. It is the full thought of its Creator, comprising all other thoughts. Is it blind chance or lifeless expediency that moulds the curves of woman's bosom, builds up man's forehead like a citadel, and sets his head on his shoulders? Is beauty beautiful, or are we cozened by congenial ugliness? But Balder's philosophic scepticism should never have braved a test like Gnulemah!

Except music, painting, sculpture,—all the arts and inspiration of them,—waited on the nib of the pen, such talk as passed between these two could not be written. Some things—and those not the least profound and admirable of life—transcend the cunning of man to interpret them, unless to an apprehension as fine as they! We are fain to content ourselves with the husks.

"It must be happy there!" said Gnulemah, looking cityward. "So many Balders and Gnulemahs!"

"Why happy?" asked the man of the world, with a faint smile.

"We are only two, and have known each other today and yesterday. But they, you said, are as many as the stars, and have been together many yesterdays."

Such was the woman's unclinched argument, leaving her listener to draw the inference. He would not forestall her enlightenment from the grim page of his own experience. But do not many pure and loving souls pass through the world without once noticing how bad most of the roads are, and how vexed the climates? So might not the earthly heaven of Gnulemah's imagination tenderly blind her to the unheavenly earth of Balder's knowledge?

Through his abstraction Balder felt on his hand a touch soft as the flowing of a breath, yet pregnant of indefinite apprehension. When two clouds meet, there is a hush and calm; but the first seeming-trifling lightning-flash brings on the storm whereby earth's face is altered. So Balder, full-charged as the thundercloud, awaited fearfully the first vivid word which should light the way for those he had resolved to speak.

"I see you with my open eyes, Balder, and touch you and hear you. Is this the end I thought would come? Balder, are you greatest?" With full trust she appealed to him to testify concerning himself. This was the seriousness he had marked beneath the smile.

"Are you content it should be so?"

She plucked a blade of grass and tied it in a knot, and began, drawing a trembling breath between each few words,—

"O Balder,—if I must kneel to you as to the last and greatest of all,—if there is nothing too holy to be seen and touched,—if there is no Presence too sublime for me to comprehend—"

"What then?" asked he, meeting her troubled look with a strong, cheerful glance.

"Then the world is less beautiful than I thought it; the sun is less bright, and I am no more pleasing to myself." Tears began to flow down her noble cheeks; but Balder's eyes grew brighter, seeing which, Gnulemah was encouraged to continue.

"How could I be happy? for either must I draw myself apart from you—O Balder!—or else live as your equal, and so degrade you; for I am not a goddess!"

"Then there are no goddesses on earth, nor gods! Gnulemah, you need not shrink from me for that."

The beautiful woman smiled through her sparkling eyelashes. She could love and reverence the man who, as a deity, bewildered and disappointed her. But was the intuition therefore false which had revealed to her the grand conception of a supreme, eternal God?

They sat silent for a while, and neither looked in the other's face. They had struck a sacred chord, and the sweet, powerful sound thrilled Balder no less than Gnulemah. But presently he looked up; his cheeks warmed, and his heart swelled out. He was about to put in jeopardy his most immediate jewel, and the very greatness of the risk gave him courage. Not to the world, that could not judge him righteously, would he confess his crime,—but to the woman he loved and who loved him. Her verdict could not fail to be just and true.

Could a woman's judgment of her lover be impartial? Yes, if her instincts be pure and harmonious, and her worldly knowledge that of a child. Her discrimination between right and wrong would be at once accurate and involuntary, like the test of poison. Love for the criminal would but sharpen her intuition. The sentence would not be spoken, but would be readable in eyes untainted alike by prejudice or sophistry.

Gnulemah was thus made the touchstone of Balder's morality. He stood ready to abide by her decision. Her understanding of the case should first be made full; then, if condemned by her look, he would publish his crime to the world, and suffer its penalty. But should her eyes absolve him, then was crime an illusion, evil but undeveloped good, the stain of blood a prejudice, and Cain no outcast, but the venerable forefather of true freedom.

Unsearchable is the heart of man. Balder had looked forward to condemnation with a wholesome solemnity which cheered while it chastened him. But the thought of acquittal, and at Gnulemah's hands, appalled him. The implicit consequences to humanity seemed more formidable than the worst which condemnation could bring upon himself. So much had he lately changed his point of view, that only the fear of seeing his former creed confirmed could have now availed to stifle his confession.

But that fear did not much disquiet him; he trusted too deeply in his judge to believe that she would justify it. In short, Gnulemah was in his opinion right-minded, exactly in proportion as she should convict him of being in the wrong. Balder resigned the helm of his vessel, laden as she was with the fruits of years of thought and speculation, at the critical moment of her voyage,—resigned her to the guidance of a woman's unreasoning intuition. He might almost as well have averred that the highest reach of intellect is to a perception of the better worth and wisdom of an unlearned heart.

XXIII.

Balder Tells an Untruth.

By way of enheartening himself for what he was to do, Balder kissed the posy of Gnulemah's fragrant footsteps. He kept his eyes down, lest she should see something in them to distract her attention from his story. He must go artfully to work,—gain her assent to the abstract principles before marshalling them against himself.

Meanwhile Gnulemah had picked up a gold beetle, and was examining it with a certain grave interest.

"I never told you how I came by this ring of Hiero's. It was the night before I first saw you, Gnulemah."

"The ring guided you to me!" said she, glancing at his downcast visage.

"Perhaps it did!" he muttered, struck by the ingenious superstition; and he eyed the keen diamond half suspiciously. How fiercely the little serpents were struggling for it! "But Hiero—he has lost it, and you will see him no more!"

"You are with me!" returns she, shining out at him from beneath her level brows. What should she know of death and parting?

Balder still forbore to raise his face. Gnulemah was in a frolicsome humor, the reaction of her foregoing solemnity. But Balder, who deemed this hour the gravest of his life, was taken aback by her unseasonable gayety. Casting about for means to sober her,—an ungracious thing for a lover to do!—he hit upon the gold beetle.

"Dead; the poor little beetle! Do you know what death is, Gnulemah?"

"It is what makes life. The sun dies every night, to get life for the morning. And trees die when cold comes, so as to smile out in green leaves again,—greener than if there had been no death. So it is with all things."

"Not with everything," said Balder, taking her light-heartedness very gravely. "That gold beetle in your hand is dead, and will never live or move again."

But at that Gnulemah smiled; and bringing her hand, with the beetle in it, near her perfect lips, she lent it a full warm breath,—enough to have enlivened an Egyptian scarabæus,—and behold! the beetle spread its wings and whizzed away. Before Balder could recover from this unexpected refutation, the lovely witch followed up her advantage.

"You thought, perhaps, that Hiero was as dead as the little beetle; but he lives more beautifully in you!"

He looked startled up, his large eyes glittering blackly in the paleness of his face. Gnulemah, with the serenity of a victorious disputant willing to make allowances, continued,—

"It may be different in the outside world from which you come; but here death ends nothing, but makes life new and strong."

After a silence of some duration, poor Balder renewed his attack from another quarter.

"What would you think of one who put to death a creature you loved?"

She smiled, and shook her glowing pendants.

"Only God puts to death; and no one would hurt a thing I love!"

"What should you think of one who put to death a man?"

Gnulemah looked for a moment perplexed and indignant. Then, to Balder's great discomfiture, she laughed like a bird-chorus.

"Why do you imagine what cannot be? Would you and Hiero kill each other? The gray owl kills little mice, but that is to eat them. Would you eat Hiero—"

"Don't laugh, Gnulemah!" besought he. "I should kill him, not as animals kill one another, but from rage and hatred."

"Hatred!" repeated Gnulemah, dislikingly; "hatred,—what is it?"

"A passion of men's hearts,—the wish that evil may befall others. When the hatred is bitter enough, and the opportunity fair, they kill!"

Gnulemah shuddered slightly and looked sad. Then she leaned towards Balder and touched his shoulder persuasively.

"Never think of such things, or talk of them! Could you hate anyone, Balder? or kill him if you did?"

With that glorious presence so near him,—her voice so close to his ear,—how could he answer her? His heart awoke, and beat and drove the tingling blood tumultuously forth to the remotest veins. She saw the flush, and caught the passionate brilliancy of his eyes. Happy and afraid, she drew back, saying in haste,—

"You have not told me yet about the ring!"

That was not wisely said! Balder checked himself with a sudden, strong hand, and held still,—his brows lowered down and his lips settled together,—until his pulses were quiet and his cheeks once more pale.

"I will tell you," he said; "but to understand, you must first hear some other things." He hesitated, face to face with an analysis of murder. The position was at once stimulating and appalling. To dissect and reduce to its elements that grisly murder-devil which had once possessed his own soul, and whose writhings beneath the scalpel he would therefore feel as his own—here loomed a prospect large and terrible! Nevertheless, Balder took up the knife.

The white petal of an apple-blossom, part from its calyx, came floating earthwards; but a breeze caught it and wafted it aloft. It sank again, and was again arrested and borne skywards. Finally is disappeared over the cliff-edge.

"The weight that made it fall is of the earth," said Balder (both he and Gnulemah had been watching the petal's course). "The breeze that buoyed it up was from heaven, and so it is with man. Were there no heavenly support, he would fall at once, but whether or not, he always tends to fall."

Gnulemah objected, "It loves the air better than the earth!"

"When man begins to fall, he becomes mad, and thinks he is not falling, but that earth is heaven, to which he is rising. But since earth is not like heaven, infinite, he does not wish others to enjoy it, lest his own pleasure be marred."

"How can that be?" said the unwilling Gnulemah. "What can make men so happy on earth as other men?"

"Each wants all power for himself," rejoined Balder, his voice growing stern as he pursued his theme. "They want to hurl their fellows out of the world, even to annihilation. Every moment this hatred is let grow in the heart's garden, it spreads and strengthens, till it gains dominion and makes men slaves, and madder than before. Each will be above his rival,—his enemy! he will be absolute master over him. And from that resolve is born murder!"

"Why do you tell Gnulemah this?" she asked, lifting her head like a majestic serpent. But she could not stop him now. His voice, measured at first, was now driven by emotion.

"Murder comes next; and many a man, had fear or impotence not withheld him, would have done murder a thousand times. But sometimes the demon leaps up and masters impotence and fear. The man is drunk with immeasurable selfishness,—greater than the universe can satisfy; which would fain make one victim after another, till all the human race should be destroyed; and then would it turn against Heaven and God. Save for man's mortal frailty, the population of the world would ever and anon be swept away by some giant murderer.

"Wickedness grows faster, the wickeder it is; he who has been wicked once will easily be so again,—the more easily as his crime was great. Even though through all his mortal life he sin no more, yet his drift is thitherward! Only the air of Heaven breathing through his soul after death can make him pure."

Balder was speaking out all the gloom and terror which had been silently gathering within him since his fatal night. As he spoke, his mind expanded, and perceived things before unknown. As the reasons for condemnation multiplied, he did but push on the harder, striking at each tender spot in his own armor. And as the day turned fatally against him, his face looked great and heroic, and his voice sounded almost triumphant.

Thus far, he had only generalized; now, he was come to his own plight. On several points he had been painfully in doubt: whether he had done the deed in self-defence; whether he had meant to do it; whether it had not been a blind, mad accident, since swollen by fevered imagination into the likeness of wilful crime. But against such doubts arrayed itself the ineffaceable memory of that wild joy which had filled his soul, when he had felt his enemy in his power! Had the man survived, Balder might still have doubted; being dead, doubts were but cowardly sophistry.

But during the brief pause he made, came a backward recoil of that impulse which had swept him on. All at once he was cold, and wavered. Gnulemah was sitting with her elbow on her knee, her strange eyes fixed upon him. Had he duly considered what effect all this might have on her? In aiming at his own life, might not the sword pass also through hers? Abruptly to behold sin,—to find in the first man she had learnt to know, the sinner,—to be left this burden on her untried soul,—might this not ruin more than her earthly happiness? Did she still love him, such love could end only in misery; should she hate him who of all men was bound to protect her defencelessness,—that were misery indeed!

This misgiving, arresting his hand at the instant of delivering the final blow, almost discouraged the much-tried man. He glanced sullenly toward the edge of the cliff, only a few yards off. A new thought jarred through his nerves! He got up and walked to the brink. Full sixty feet to the bottom.

Gnulemah also rose slowly, and stretched herself like a tired child, sending a lazy tension through every noble limb and polished muscle. She sighed with a deep breathing in and out, and pressed her hands against her temples.

"I was not made to understand such things. Tell me of what you have done or seen—I shall understand that. The things my love does not enter only trouble me and make me sad."

As she spoke, she turned away towards the house. She saw, or thought she saw, a man's figure stealing cautiously behind a clump of bushes near the north-eastern corner. Her listlessness fell from, her like a mantle, and she watched, motionless!

Her last words had goaded Balder past bearing. As she turned away, his face looked grim and forlorn. He balanced with half raised arms on the cliff's brink. The river slumbered bluely on below, peace was aloft in the sky, and joy in the trees and grass. But in the man were darkness and despair and loathing of his God-given life!

The thing he meditated was not to be, however. Close in shore a little boat glided into view, beating up against stream. In the stern, the sheet in one hand and the tiller in the other, sat Balder's old friend Charon. He nodded up at the young man with a recognizing grin. Then he laid his tiller-hand aside his brown cheek and sang out,—

"Look out there, Capt'n! Davy Jones's got back,—run foul of you!"

The next moment he put down the helm and ran out.

Meantime Balder, coloring from shame, had stepped back from his dangerous position; and the peril was past. But the paltering irresolution which he had at all points displayed urged him to redeem himself,—else was he lower than a criminal. He went towards Gnulemah,—knelt down,—caught her dress,—he knew not what he did! In a blind dance of sentences he told her that he was a murderer, that all he had said pointed at himself, that with his own hands he had killed Hiero, whose body now lay at the bottom of the sea; many frantic words he spoke. Thus, without art or rhetoric, roughly dragged forth by head and ears, came his momentous confession into the world. Gnulemah had more than once striven to check it, but in vain. When he had come to an end, and stood tense and quivering as a bowstring whose arrow has just flown, these words reached him:—

"Hiero is not dead; he is there behind the trees."

Stiffly he turned and stared bewildered. Landscape, sky, Gnulemah, swam before his eyes in fragments, like images in troubled water. She put out her arm and tenderly supported him.

"Where?" said he at length.

"Near the house,—there!" she pointed.

Balder began to walk forward doubtfully. But, suddenly realizing what lay before him, clearness and vigor ebbed back. He saw a figure turn the corner of the house. Then he leapt out and ran like a staghound!

XXIV.

Uncle Hiero At Last.

In a couple of minutes Balder was at the house, breathless: the figure was nowhere to be seen. He sprang across the broad portico, and hurried with sounding feet through the oaken hall. Should he go up stairs, or on to the conservatory? The sound of a softly shutting door from the latter direction decided him. The place looked as when he left it a half hour before. Gnulemah's curtain had not been moved. The other door was closed; he ran up the steps between the granite sphinxes, and found it locked. Butting his shoulder against the panel with impatient force, the hinges broke from their rotten fastenings, and the door gave inwards. Balder stepped past it, and found himself in the sombre lamp-lit interior of the temple.

He could discern but little; the place seemed vast; the corners were veiled in profound shadow. At the farther end a huge lamp was suspended, by a chain from the roof, over a triangular altar of black marble. The architecture of the room was strange and massive as of Egyptian temples. Strong, dark colors met the eye on all sides; in the panels of the walls and distant ceiling fantastic devices showed obscurely forth. Nine mighty columns, of design like those in the doorway, were ranged along the walls, their capitals buried in the upward gloom.

Becoming used to the dusk, Balder now marked an array of colossal upright forms, alternating between the pillars. Their rough resemblance to human figures drew him towards one of them: it was an Egyptian sarcophagus covered with hieroglyphic inscriptions, and probably holding an immemorial mass of spiced flesh and rags. These silent relics of a prehistoric past seemed to be the only company present. In view of his uncle's well-known tastes, the nephew was not unprepared to meet these gentry.

But he was come to seek the living, not the dead. The figure that he had seen outside must be within these four walls, there being no other visible outlet besides the door through which Balder had entered. Was old Hiero Glyphic lurking in one of these darksome corners, or behind some thick-set column? The young man looked about him as sharply as he could, but nothing moved except the shadows thrown by the lamp, which was vibrating pendulumlike on its long chain.

He approached this lamp, his steps echoing on the floor of polished granite. What had set the thing swinging? It had a leisurely elliptical motion, as from a moderate push sideways. The lamp was wrought in bronze, antique of fashion and ornament. It had capacity for gallons of oil, and would burn for weeks without refilling. The altar beneath was a plain black marble prism, highly polished, resting upon a round base of alabaster. A handful of ashes crowned its top. Between the altar and the wall intervened a space of about seven feet.

The glare of the lamp had blinded Balder to what was beyond it; but, on stepping round it, he was confronted by an old-fashioned upright clock, such as were in vogue upon staircase-landings and in entrance-halls a hundred years ago. With its broad, white, dial-plate, high shoulders, and dark mahogany case, it looked not unlike a tall, flat-featured man, holding himself stiffly erect. But whether man or clock, it was lifeless; the hands were motionless,—there was no sound of human or mechanical heartbeat within though Balder held his yet panting breath to listen. Was it Time's coffin, wherein his corpse had lain still many a silent year,—only that years must stand still without Time to drive them on! But this still had had no part in the moving world,—knew naught of life and change, day and night. Here dwelt a moveless present,—a present at once past and to come, yet never here! No wonder the mummies felt at home! though even they could only partially appreciate the situation.

The clock was fastened against the wall. The longer Balder gazed at it, the more humanlike did it appear. Its face was ornamented with colored pictures of astronomical processes, sufficiently resembling a set of shadowy features, of a depressed and insignificant type. The mahogany case served for a close-fitting brown surtout, buttoned to the chin. The slow vibration of the lamp produced on the countenance the similitude of a periodically recurring grimace.

Not only did the clock look human, but—or so Balder fancied—it bore a grotesque and extravagant likeness to a certain elderly relative of his, whose portrait he had carried in an inner pocket of his haversack,—now in Long Island Sound. It reminded him, in a word, of poor old Uncle Hiero, whom he had—no, no!—who was alive and well, and was perhaps even now observing his dear nephew's perplexity, and maliciously chuckling over it!

The young man glanced uneasily over his shoulder, but all beyond the lamp was a gloomy blank, The same moment he trod upon some tough, thick substance, which yielded beneath his foot! Thoroughly startled, he jumped back. It lay near the foot of the clock. He stooped, picked it up, and held in his hands the well-known haversack, from which he had parted on board the "Empire State." How his heart beat as he examined it! It was stained and whitened with salt water, and the strap was broken in two. Opening it, there were his toilet articles and all his other treasures,—even the cherished miniature,—not much the worse for their wetting. So there could no longer be any doubt that his uncle had come back. Where was he?

That queer fancy about the clock stuck in Balder's head! Somehow or other it must be connected with Doctor Glyphic. The haversack, dropped at its foot, was direct evidence. Yet, did ever wise man harbor notion so irrational! Its manifest absurdity only excuse for thinking it.

With no declared object in view, Balder grasped the clock by its high shoulders and shook it, but with no result. He next struck the smartly with clenched fist: the blow sounded,—not hollow, but close and muffled! The case either solid, or filled with something that deadened the echo. Filled with what? who would think of putting anything in a clock? It was big enough to be sure, to hold a man, if he could find a way to get in!

The sequence of thoughts is often obscure, but Balder's next idea, wild as it was, could hardly be called incoherent. A man might be conceived to be in the clock; perhaps a man was in it; but if so, the man could be none other than Doctor Hiero Glyphic!

This conclusion once imagined, suspense was unendurable. The logician tried to open the front of the case, but it was riveted fast. With impetuous fingers he then wrenched at the disc. With a sound like a rusty screech, it came off in his hands. The lamp so flickered that Balder feared it was going out, and even at this epoch had to look round to reassure himself. Meanwhile, a pungent, but not unpleasant odor saluted his nostrils: he turned back to the clock,—a clock no longer!—and beheld the unmistakable lineaments of his worthy uncle peeping forth with half shut eyes from the place where the dial-plate had been.

The nephew dropped the dial-plate, and it was shattered on the granite floor. He was badly frightened. There was no delusion about the face,—it was a sufficiently peculiar one; and the miniature portrait, though doing the Doctor's beauty at least justice, was accurate enough to identify him by. This was no unsubstantial apparition,—no brain phantom, to waver and vanish, leaving only an uncomfortable doubt whether it had been at all. Stolid, undeniable matter was, peering phlegmatically between its wrinkled eyelids.

But admitting that now, at last, we have lighted upon the genuine and authentic Doctor Glyphic, why should the sight of him so oddly affect Balder Helwyse, whose avowed object in pulling off the dial-plate had been to justify a suspicion that Uncle Hiero was behind it? Why, moreover, did the young man not address his relative, congratulating himself upon their meeting, and rallying the old gentleman on his attempt to escape his nephew's affectionate solicitude? There had, indeed, been a misunderstanding at their last encounter, and Balder had so far forgotten himself as to throw Hiero into the sea; but it was the part of good-breeding, as well as of Christianity, to forget such errors, and heal the bruise with an extra application of balsamic verbiage.

Why so speechless, Balder? Do you wait for your host to speak first? Nay, never stand on ceremony. He is an eccentric recluse, unused to the ways of society, while a man of the world like you has at his tongue's tip a score of phrases just suited to the occasion. Speak up, therefore, in your most genial tone, and tell the Doctor how glad you are to find him in such wonderful preservation! Put him at his ease by feigning that his position appears to you the most natural in the world,—just what befits a gentleman of his years and honors! Flatter him, if only from self-interest, for he has a deep pocket, and may be induced to let you put a hand in it.

Not a word in response to all this eloquence, Balder? Positively your behavior appears rather curmudgeonly than heroic! You stand gazing at your relative with almost as much fixedness as he returns your stare withal. There is something odd about this.

What is that pungent odor? Is the Doctor a dandy, that he should use perfumes? And where did he get so peculiar a scent as this? It is commonly in vogue only at that particular toilet which no man ever performed for himself, but which never needs to be done twice,—a kind of toilet, by the way, especially prevalent amongst the ancient Egyptians. Since, then, Doctor Glyphic is so ardent an Egyptologist, perhaps we have hit upon the secret of his remarkable odoriferousness. But to shut one's self up in a box that looks so uncommonly like a coffin,—is not that carrying the antiquarian whim a trifle too far?

This face of his,—one fancies there is a curiously dry look about it! The unnaturally yellow skin resembles a piece of good-for-nothing wrinkled parchment. The lips partake of the prevailing sallow tint, and the mouth hangs a little awry. From the cloth in which the head is so elaborately bandaged up strays forth, here and there, an arid lock of hair. The lack of united expression in his features produces an effect seldom observable in a living face. The eyes are lustreless, and densely black; or possibly (the suspicion is a startling one) we are looking into empty eye-sockets! No eyes, no expression, parchment skin, swathed head, odor of myrrh and cassia, and, dominating all, this ghastly immobility! Has Doctor Glyphic even now escaped, leaving us to waste time and sentiment over some worn-out disguise of his? Nay, if he be not here, we need not seek him further. Having forsaken this, he can attain no other earthly hiding-place. We must pause here, and believe either that this dry time-husk is the very last of poor Hiero, or that a living being which once bore his name has vanished inward from our reach, and now treads a more real earth than any that time and space are sovereign over.

Balder (whose perceptions were unlimited by artistic requirements) probably needed no second glance to assure him that his uncle was a mummy of many years' standing. But no effort of mental gymnastics could explain him the fact. Were this real, then was his steamboat adventure a dream, the revelation of the ring a delusion, and his water-stained haversack a phantom. He wandered clewless in a maze of mystery. Nor was this the first paradox he had encountered since overleaping the brick wall. He began to question whether supernaturalism had not teen too hastily dismissed by lovers of wisdom!

Thus do the actors in the play of life plod from one to another scene, nor once rise to a height whence a glance might survey past and future. Memory and prophecy are twin sisters,—nay, they are essentially one muse, whom mankind worships on this side and slights on that. This is well, for had she but one aspect, the world would be either too confident or too helpless. But in reviewing a life, one is apt to make less than due allowance for the helplessness. Thus it is no prejudice to Balder's intellectual acumen that he failed for a moment to penetrate the thin disguises of events, and to perceive relations obvious to the comprehensive view of history. We will take advantage of his bewildered pause to draw attention to some matters heretofore neglected.

XXV.

The Happiness of Man.

When Manetho,—who shall no longer perplex us with his theft of a worthier man's name,—when Manetho felt himself worsted in the brief strenuous struggle, he tried to drag his antagonist overboard with him. But his convulsive fingers seized only the leathern strap of the haversack. Balder—his Berserker fury at white heat—flung the man with such terrible strength as drove him headlong over the taffrail like a billet of wood, the stout strap snapping like thread!

Manetho struck the water in sorry plight, breathless, bruised, half strangled. He sank to a chilly depth, but carried his wits down with him, and these brought him up again alive, however exhausted. Too weak to swim, he yet had strength left to keep afloat. But for the collision, he had drowned, after all!

The cool salt bath presently helped him to a little energy, and by the time the steamer was under way, he could think of striking out. It was with no small relief that he heard near voices sounding through the black fog. Partly by dint of feeble struggles, partly shouldered on by waves,—ready to save as to drown him,—he managed to accomplish the short distance to the schooner. With all his might he shouted for a rope, and amidst much yo-heave-ho-ing, cursing, and astonishment, was at length hauled aboard, the haversack in his grasp.

The skipper and his crew were kind to him; for men still have compassion upon one another, and give succor according to the need of the moment,—not to the balance of good and evil in the sufferer. The wind freshened, an impromptu, bowsprit was rigged, and the "Resurrection" limped towards New York. Manetho's partial stupor was relieved by hot grog and the cook's stove. He gave no further account of himself than that he had fallen overboard at the moment of collision; adding a request to be landed in New York, since he had left some valuable luggage on the steamer.

The skipper gave the stranger his own bunk, the off-watch turned in, and Manetho was left to himself. He lay for a long while thinking over what had happened. Bewitched by the spell of night, he had spoken to Helwyse things never before distinctly stated even to his own mind. The subtle, perverse devil who had discoursed so freely to his unknown hearer had scarcely been so unreserved to Manetho's private ear; and the devilish utterances had stirred up the latter not much less than the former.

Both men had been wrought, according to their diverse natures, to the pitch of frenzy. But similar crazy seizures had been incident to the Egyptian from boyhood. He had anxiously watched against them, and contrived various means to their mitigation,—the most successful being the music of his violin, which he seldom let beyond his reach. Yet, again and again would the fit steal a march on him. Hence, in part, his retired way of life, varied only by the brief journeys demanded by the twofold craving—for gambling and for news of Thor, who figured in his morbid imagination as the enemy of his soul!

The news never came, but all the more brooded Manetho over his hatred and his fancied wrongs. His mind had never been entirely sound, and years tinged it more and more deeply with insanity. His philosophy of life—obscure indeed if tried by sane standards—emits a dusky glimmer when read by this. He would creep through miles of subterranean passages to achieve an end which one glance above ground would have argued vain!

Lying on the bunk in the close cabin, lighted by a dirty lantern pendent from the roof, the Reverend Manetho began to fear that not his worst misfortune was the having been thrown overboard. At the moment when madness was smouldering to a blaze within him, the lantern flash had revealed to him the face which, for twenty years, he had seen in visions. Often had he rehearsed this meeting, varying his imaginary behavior to suit all conceivable moods and attitudes of his enemy, but never thinking to provide for perversity in himself! So far from veiling his designs with the soft-voiced cunning of his Oriental nature, he had been a wild beast! A misgiving haunted him, moreover, that he had babbled something in the false security of darkness, which might give Helwyse a clew to his secret.

But here Manetho asked himself a question that might have suggested itself before. Was it really his enemy, Thor Helwyse, whose face he had seen? or only some likeness of him?

Thor must be threescore years old by this,—the senior by ten years of Manetho himself; while his late antagonist had the strength and aspect of half that age. Yet how could he be mistaken in the face which had haunted him during more than the third part of his lifetime? He had recognized it on the instant!

"I will ask the haversack!" said he. He sat up, and, bracing himself against the roll of the vessel, he opened the bag and carefully examined its contents. In an inner pocket he found an old letter of Doctor Glyphic's to Thor; another from Thor to his son, dated three years back; and finally a diary kept by Balder Helwyse, which gave Manetho all the information he wanted.

He had so arranged matters that at Glyphic's death he had got the control of the money into his own hands, and had made such diligent use of it that enough was not now left to pay for his prosecution as a thief and forger. In fact, had Balder delayed his return another year, he would have found the enchanted castle in possession of the auctioneer; and as to the fate of its inhabitants, one does not like to speculate!

Having read the papers, Manetho replaced them, and next pulled out the miniature of Doctor Glyphic. He studied this for a long time. It was the portrait of a man to whom—so long as their earthly relations had continued—the Egyptian renegade had been faithful. Perhaps there was some secret germ of excellence in poor Hiero, unsuspected by the rest of the world, but revealed to Manetho, from whom in turn it had drawn the best virtues that his life had to show. Doctor Glyphic had never been a comfortable companion; but Manetho was always patient and honest with him. This integrity and forbearance were the more remarkable, since the Doctor seldom acknowledged a kindness, and knew so little of business that he might have been robbed of his fortune at any moment with impunity.

Either from physical exhaustion or for some worthier reason, the Egyptian cried over this miniature, as an affectionate girl might have cried over the portrait of her dead lover. For a time he was all tears and softness. His emotion had not the convulsiveness which, with men of his age, is apt to accompany the exhibition of much feeling. He wept with feminine fluency, nor did his tearfulness seem out of character. There was a great deal of the woman in him.

Having wept his fill, he tenderly wiped his eyes, and returned the picture to its receptacle; and first assuring himself that nothing else was concealed in the haversack, he shut it up and resumed his meditations.

It was the son, then, whom he had met,—and Thor was dead. Dead!—that was a hard fact for Manetho to swallow. His enemy had escaped him,—was dead! Through all the years of waiting, Manetho had not anticipated this. How should Thor die before revenge had been wreaked upon him?—But he was dead!

By degrees, however, his mind began to adjust itself to the situation. The son, at all events, was left him. He cuddled the thought, whispering to himself and slyly smiling. Did not the father live again in the son? he would lose nothing, therefore,—not lose, but gain! The seeming loss was a blessing in disguise. The son,—young, handsome, hot of blood! Already new schemes began to take shape in the Egyptian's brain. His dear revenge!—it should not starve, but feed on the fat of the land,—yea, be drunk with strong wine.

He lay hugging himself, his long narrow eyes gleaming, his full lips working together. He was revolving a devilish project,—the flintiest criminal might have shuddered at it. But there was nothing flinty nor unfeeling about Manetho. His emotions were alert and moist, his smile came and went, his heart beat full; he was now the girl listening to her lover's first passionate declaration!

He had gathered from Balder's diary that the young man was in search of his uncle, and had been on his way to the house at the time of their encounter. There was a chance that this unlucky episode might frighten him away. He no doubt supposed himself guilty of man-slaughter at least; how gladly would the clergyman have reassured him! And indeed there was no resentment in Manetho's heart because of his rough usage at Balder's hands. His purposes lay too deep to influence shallower moods. He presented a curious mixture of easy forgiveness and unmitigable malice.

The only other anxiety besetting him arose from the loss of the ring. He looked upon it as a talisman of excellent virtue, and moreover perceived that in case Balder should pick it up, it might become the means of identifying its owner and obstructing his plans. But these were mere contingencies. The probability was that young Helwyse would ultimately appear at his uncle's house, and would there be ensnared in the seductive meshes of Manetho's web. The ring was most likely at the bottom of the Sound. So, smiling his subtle feminine smile, the Egyptian fell asleep, to dream of the cordial welcome he would give his expected guest.

Towards midnight of the same day he approaches the house by way of the winding avenue, his violin-case safe in hand. He steps out joyfully beneath the wide-spread minuet of twinkling stars. On his way he comes to a moss-grown bench at the foot of a mighty elm,—the bench on which he sat with Helen during the stirring moments of their last interview. Manetho's soul overflows tonight with flattering hopes, and he has spare emotion for any demand. He drops on his knees beside this decayed old bench, and kisses it twice or thrice with tender vehemence; stretches out his arms to embrace the air, and ripples forth a half dozen sentences,—pleading, insinuating, passionate. He can love her again as much as ever, now that the wrong done him is on the eve of requital.

But his mood is no less fickle than melting. Already he is up and away, almost dancing along the shadowed, romantic tree-aisle, his eyes glistening black in the starlight,—no longer with a lover's luxurious sorrow, but with the happy anticipation of an artless child, promised a holiday and playthings. So lightsome and expansive is Manetho's heart, the hollow hemisphere of heaven seems none too roomy for it!

Evil as well as good knows its moments of bliss,—its hours! Hell is the heaven of devils, and they want no better. Often do the wages of sin come laden with a seeming blessing that those of virtue lack. The sinner looks upon Satan's face, and it is to him as the face of God!

But from the womb of this grim truth is born a noble consolation. Were hell mere torment, and joy in heaven only, where were the good man's merit? Only when the choice lies between two heavens—the selfish and the unselfish—is the battle worthy the fighting! No human soul dies from earth that attains not heaven,—that heaven which the heart chiefly sought while in this world; and herefrom is the genesis of virtue. Sin brings its self-inflicted penalties there as here; but hell is still the happiness of man, heaven of God!

Reaching the house, Manetho passed through the open door, crossed the hall with his customary noiselessness, and entered the conservatory. Despite the darkness, he was at once aware of the motionless group beneath the palm-trees. A stranger in the house was something so unprecedented that he could not repress a throb of alarm. Nurse looked up and beckoned him. Drawing near, he heard the long, deep breathing of the sleeper. With a sudden fore-glimpse of the truth, he knelt down, and bent over the upturned countenance.

Though the beard was close-shaven and the hair cropped short, there could be no doubt about the face. His guest had come before him, and was lying defenceless at his feet; but Manetho harbored no thought of violence. He pressed his slender hands together with an impulse of sympathy. "Poor fellow!" he whispered, "how he has suffered! How the horror of blood-guiltiness must have tortured him! The noble Helwyse hair,—all gone! Too dear a price to pay for the mere sacrifice of a human life! And pain and all might have been spared him,—poor fellow! poor fellow!" Manetho lacked but little of shedding true tears over the evidence of his dearest foe's useless dread and anguish. Did he wish Balder to bring undulled nerves to his own torture-chamber?

His lament over, Manetho turned to Nurse for such information regarding the guest's arrival and behavior as she might have to communicate. Of his own affair with Balder he made no mention. The conversation was carried on by signs, according to a code long since grown up between the two. When the tale was told, Nurse was despatched to make ready Helen's room for the newcomer, and thither did the two laboriously bear him, and laid him, still sleeping, on his mother's bed.

XXVI.

Music and Madness.

Before leaving Balder to his repose, Manetho paused to regain his breath, and to throw a glance round the room. It was a place he seldom visited. He had seen Helen's dead body lie on that bed, and the sight had bred in him an animosity against the chamber and everything it contained. After Doctor Glyphic's death he had gratified this feeling in a characteristic manner. Possessing a genius for drawing second only to that for music, he had exercised it on the walls of the room, originally modelled and tinted to represent a robin's egg. He mixed his colors with the bitter distillations of his heart, and created the beautiful but ill-omened vision which long afterwards so disquieted Balder.—

From the chamber he now repaired to the kitchen, which was in some respects the most attractive place in the house. The smoky ceiling; the cavernous cupboards opening into the walls; the stanch dressers, polished by use and mottled with many an ancient stain; the great black range, which would have cooked a meal for a troop of men-at-arms,—all spoke of homely comfort. Nurse had Manetho's meal ready for him, and, having set it out on the table, she retired to her position in the chimney-corner. The Egyptian's spare body was ordinarily nourished with little more than goes to the support of an Arab, and Nurse's monotonous life must have been unfavorable to large appetite. As for Gnulemah,—although young women are said to thrive and grow beautiful on a diet of morning dew, noonday sunshine, and evening mist,—it seems quite likely that she ate no less than the health and activity of a Diana might naturally require.

Manetho made a gleeful repast, and Nurse looked on from her corner, externally as unattractive-looking a woman as one would wish to see. Nevertheless, had she been made as some clocks are, with a plate of glass over her inner movements, she would have monopolized the clergyman's attention and impaired his appetite. He did not sit down to the table, but took up one viand after another, and ate as he walked to and fro the floor. Supper over, he crowned it with an unheard-of excess,—for Manetho was commonly a very temperate man. He brought from a cupboard a dusty bottle of priceless wine, which had once enriched the cellar of a king of Spain. Drawing the cork, he poured some of the golden liquor into a slender glass, while the spiritual aroma flowed invisible along the air, visiting every darksome nook, and even saluting Nurse, who had long been a stranger to any such delicate attention.

Manetho filled two glasses, and then beckoned Nurse to come from her corner, and drink with him. Forth she hobbled accordingly, looking more than usually ugly by reason of her surprise and embarrassment at the unexpected summons. Manetho, on the other hand, seemed to have cast aside his years, and to be once more the graceful, sinuous, courteous youth, whose long black eyes had, long ago, seen Salome's heart. With an elegant gesture he handed her the brimming wineglass, accompanying it with a smile which well-nigh shook it from between her fingers. He took up his own glass, and said,—

"I seldom drink wine, Nurse,—never, unless a lady, joins me! Once I drank with her whose chamber our guest now occupies; and once with another—" Manetho paused. "I never speak her name, Nurse; but we loved each other. I did not treat her well!" He murmured with a sigh, tears in his eyes. "Were she here tonight, at her feet would I sue for pardon,—the renewal of our love. By my soul!" he cried, suddenly, "I had thought to drink a far different toast; but let this glass be drained to the memory of the sweet moments she and I have known together! Drink!"

He tossed off the wine. But poor Nurse, strangely agitated, dropped hers on the floor; the precious liquor was spilled, and the glass shivered. She gazed beseechingly at Manetho. Could he not penetrate that mask to the face behind it? Is flesh so miserably opaque that no spark of the inwardly burning soul can make itself felt or seen without? Manetho saw only the broken glass and its wasted contents!

"You are as clumsy as you are ugly!" said he, "Go back to your corner. I must converse with my violin."

She returned heavily to her place, feeling the darker and colder because that wine had been spilled before she could raise it to her lips. One taste, she fancied, might have begun a transformation in her life! But we know not the weight of the chains we lay upon our limbs.

The Egyptian's buoyant humor had dismissed the whole matter in another moment. He opened his violin-case, lovingly caressing the instrument as he took it out. Then he tucked it fondly under his chin, and resumed his walking. The delicately potent wine warbled through his nerves, and tinted memory with imagination.

The bow, traversing the strings, drew forth from them a sweet and plaintive note, like the tender remonstrance of a neglected friend. No language says so much in so short space as music, nor will, till we banish those dead bones, consonants, and adopt the pure vowel speech of infants and angels.

"Ay, long have we been apart, my beloved one, and much have I needed thee!" murmured Manetho. "I yearned for thy soothing and refreshing voice; yea, death walked near me, because thou, my preserver, wast not by to guard me. But, rejoice! all is again well with us,—the hour of our triumph is near!"

The fine instrument responded, carolling forth an exquisite pæan,—an ascending scale, mounting to a breathless ecstasy, and falling in slower melody along gliding waves of fortunate sound. The player drank each perfect note, till his pulses beat in unison with the rhythm. His violin and he were wedded lovers since his youth, nor had discord ever come between them.

"Two little children weaving flower-chains for each other in the grass. I said, 'The one that first comes to me shall be mine!' And the little maiden arose, leaving her brother among the flowers. So one was taken and the other left. But, behold! the brother has come to play with his sister once more!"

Again the music—a divine philosopher's stone—touched the theme into fine-spun golden harmony. The dusky kitchen, with its one dull lamp glimmering on the table, broadened with marble floors, and sprang aloft in airy arches! Twinkling stars hung between the columns, burning with a fragrance like flowers. It was a summer morning, just before sunrise. The clear faces of children peeped from violet-strewn recesses where they had passed the night; and, as their sweet eyes met, they shouted for joy, and ran to embrace one another.

"Oh! my beloved," softly burst forth the Egyptian, "how blessed are we tonight!" He touched the strings to a measured tune, following with a minuet-step up and down the floor. A fantastic spectacle! for as he passed and repassed the lamp, an elastic shadow crept noiselessly behind him, dodged beneath his feet, and anon outstretched itself like a sudden pit yawning before him. "This night repays the dreary years that lie behind. How have I outlasted them! What had I fallen on the very threshold of requital?—all I had hoped and labored for, a failure!"

Here paused the tune and the dance, and arose a weird dirge of compassion over what might have been! So moving was it, the player himself was melted. His dark nature showed its fairest side,—sensitive refinement, grace of expression, flowing ease of manner. Quick was he in fancy, emotional, soft and strong, gentle and fiery. In this hour he bloomed, like some night-flowering plant, of perfume sweet but poisonous. This was Manetho's apogee!

Again his humor changed, and he became playful and frivolous. Had old Nurse in the corner been little more personable, he might have caught her round the waist, and forced her to tread a wild measure with him. But this unfolding of his faculties in the shower of good fortune had refined his æsthetic susceptibility. The withered, disfigured woman was no partner for him!

She sat, following, with the intentness of her single eye, his every motion, her head swaying in unconscious sympathy. Although her body sat so stiff and awkward in the chimney-seat, her spirit, inspired with the grace of love, was dancing with Manetho's. But the body kept its place, knowing that erelong he too must come to rest. In the light of a vivid recollection, the long tract between fades and foreshortens, till only the Then and the Now are notable. However, the light will pale, the dusty miles outstretch their length once more, and the pilgrim find himself wearier than ever.

But meanwhile the clergyman floats hither and thither like a wreath of black smoke blown about by a draught of air. One might have expected to see him all at once vanish up the wide-mouthed chimney. The music seems to emanate less from the instrument than from the player; it interprets and colors every motion and expression. His chanting and his playing answer and supplement each other, like strophe and antistrophe.

"Let me tell thee why I rejoice, that thy sympathy may increase my joy!

"A beautiful woman, young, a fountain of fresh life, an ivory vase filled with earthly flowers. The eye that gazes on her form is taken captive; yea, her face intoxicates the senses. But she is poisonous, a queen of death, and her feet walk towards destruction!

"Supple and strong is she as the serpent, quick and graceful as the panther. Food has she for nourishment, for the warming of the blood; exercises for the body, to keep her healthful and fair. Her triumph is in the flesh,—she finds it perfect. The flesh she deems divine,—the earth, a heaven!

"Books, the world of men,—she knows not: sees in herself Creation's cause and centre; in God, but the myriad reflex of her beauty. Self is her God, whom she worships in thunder and lightning, in sun and stars, in fire and water. Dreaming and waking are alike real to her: she knows not to divide truth from falsehood.

"Whom should she thank for health, for life and birth? She is born of the fire that burns in her own bosom. To her is nothing lawful nor unlawful. No tie binds her soul to salvation. A fair ship is she, but rudderless, and the wind blows on the rocks. Let God save her if He will—and can!"

The inspiration of the Arab improvisatore would have seemed

tame beside Manetho's nervous exaltation. Save for the tingling satire of the violin-strings, his rhapsody might easily have lapsed to madness. From this point, however, his rapture somewhat abated, and he began to descend towards prose, his music clothing him downwards.

"As for me, I have bowed down before her, pampering her insolent majesty, preserving her poison to rancor first in her father's heart. Of him, death robbed me; but the son,—the brother is left. Even death spared brother and sister to each other!

"A handsome man! worthy to stand by her. Never fairer couple sprang from one stem. They love each other,—and shall love!—more than ever brother and sister loved before. But they shall be bound by a tie so close that the mere tie of blood hangs loose beside it! Then shall night come down on them,—a night no rising sun shall ever chase away. In that; darkness will I speak—"

This devilish monologue ended abruptly here. The faithful instrument, whose responsive sympathy had failed him, jarringly snapped a string! A sting of anguish pricked through Manetho's every nerve. His fictitious buoyancy evaporated like steam,—he barely made shift to totter to a chair. Laying the violin with tremling hands on the table, his head dropped on his arms beside it; and there was a long, feverish silence.

At length he raised his haggard face, and, supporting it upon his hands, he gazed at the figure in the chimney-corner; and began, in a tone sullen and devoid of animation as November rain,—

"Why did you force yourself upon me?—not for Gnulemah's sake, I think. Not for money,—you had none. Not for love of me either, I fancy,—grisly harpy!

"Once I suspected you of being a spy. You walked among pitfalls then! But what spy would sit for eighteen years without speech or movement? You have been useful too. No one could have filled your place,—with your one eye and dumb mouth!

"Did you hate Thor? were you my secret ally against him? But how could you fathom my purposes enough even to help me? And what wrong has he done you terrible enough for such revenge as mine? What human being, except Manetho, could hold an unwavering purpose so many years? Have you never pitied or relented? Sometimes I have almost wavered myself!

"What name and history have you buried, and never shown me? Why have you spent your dumb life in this seclusion? You are a mystery,—yet a mystery of my own making! I might as wisely dissect my violin to find where lurks the music. A mass of wood and strings,—the music is from me!

"Have you a thought of preventing the scheme I spoke of tonight?" The Egyptian leaned far across the table, the better to scrutinize the unanswering woman's face. Her eye met his with a steady intelligence that disconcerted him.

"Are you a woman?" he muttered, drawing back, "and have you no pity on the children whom you nursed in their infancy?—not any pity! as implacable—almost more implacable than I? But think of her beauty and innocence,—for is she not innocent as yet? Would you see her forever ruined,—and stretch forth no saving hand?" Nurse moved her head up and down, as in slow, deliberate assent. Manetho, beholding the reflection in her of his own moral deformity, was filled with abhorrence!

"More hideous within than without,—you demon! come to haunt me and make me wicked as yourself. It was you snapped the chord of my music,—that better spirit which had till then saved me from your spells! My evil genius! I know you now, though never until this moment."

This madman was not the first sinner who, happening to catch an outside glimpse of his interior grime, has tried to cheat his scared conscience by an outcry of "Devil!—devil!" Is there not a touch of pathos in the vanity of the situation? For the cry is in part sincere; no man can be so wholly evil, while in this world, as quite to divorce the better angel from his soul. But alas! for the poor righteous indignation.

XXVII.

Peace and Good-Will.

Balder Helwyse, dumfounded before the revelation of the clock, might have stared himself into imbecility, had not he heard his name spoken in sweet human music, and, turning, beheld Gnulemah peeping through the doorway down the hall.

There was no great distance between them, yet she seemed immeasurable spaces away. Against the bright background of the conservatory her form stood dark, the outlines softened by semi-transparent edges of drapery. But the dull red lamplight lit duskily up the folds of her robe, her golden ornaments, and the black tarns, her eyes. She appeared to waver between the light of heaven and the lurid gloom of heaven's opposite.

Balder came hastily towards her, waving her back. He was superstitiously anxious that she should return unshadowed to the clear outer sunshine, instead of joining him in this tomb of dead bones and darkness. Darkness might indeed befriend his own imperfections; but should Gnulemah be dimmed to soothe his vanity?

Such emblematic fancies are common to lovers, whose ideal passion tends always to symbolism. But to those who have never loved, it will be enough to say that the young man felt an instinctive desire to spare Gnulemah the ugly spectacle in the clock, and was perhaps not unwilling to escape from it himself!

She awaited him, in the bright doorway, like an angel come to lead him to a better world. "Do not leave me any more!" she said, putting her hand in his. "You did not do the thing you thought. Let us be together, and dream no more such sadness!"

"Is her innocence strong enough to protect her against that sinful deluge of confession I poured out upon her?" thought Helwyse, glancing at her face. "Has it fallen from her harmless, like water from a bird's breast? And am I after all no murderer?"

Doubt nor accusation was in her eyes, but soft feminine faith. Her eyes,—rather than have lost the deep intelligence of their dark light, Balder would have consented to blotting from heaven its host of stars! Through them shone on him,—not justice, but the divine injustice of woman's love. That wondrous bond, more subtile than light, and more enduring than adamant, had leagued her to him. Consecrated by the blessing of her trust, he must not dare distrust himself. If the past were blindly wrong, she was the God-given clew to guide him right.

An unspeakable tenderness melted them both,—him for what he received, her for what she gave. The rich bud of their love bloomed at once in full, fragrant stateliness. Their hearts, left unprotected by their out-opened arms, demanded shelter, and found it in nestling on each other. Heaven touched earth in the tremulous, fiery calm of their meeting lips,—magnets whose currents flowed from the mysterious poles of humanity.

At such moments—the happiest life counts but few—angels draw near, but veil their happy eyes. Spirits of evil grind their teeth and frown; and, for one awful instant, perceive their own deformity!

Before yet that dear embrace had lasted an eternity, the man felt the woman shiver in his arms. The celestial heights and spaces dwindled, the angelic music fainted. Heaven rolled back and left them alone on earth. Manetho stood on the threshold between the sphinxes, wearing such a smile as God has never doomed us to see on a child's face!

To few men comes the opportunity of facing in this life those whom they believed they had put out of it. One might expect the palpable assurance of the victim's survival would electrify the fancied murderer. But to Balder's mind, his personal responsibility could not be thus lightened; and any emotion of selfish relief was therefore denied him. On the other hand, such inferences as he had been able to draw from things seen and heard were not to Manetho's advantage. While he could not but rejoice to have been spared actually hurrying a soul from the life of free will to an unchangeable eternity, yet his dominant instinct was to man himself for the hostile issues still to arise. He looked at the being through whom his own life had received so dark a stain with stern, keen eyes.

Gnulemah remained within the circle of her lover's arm. She seemed but little interested in Manetho's appearance, save in so far as he invaded the sanctity of her new immortal privilege. She had never known anxiety on his account; he had never appealed to her feeling for himself. If she loved him, it was with an affection unconscious because untried. She had shivered in Balder's embrace at the moment of the Egyptian's presence, but before having set eyes on him. Had the nearness of his discordant spirit—his familiar face unseen—made her conscious of an evil emanation from him, else unperceived?

Manetho, to do him justice, assumed anything but a hostile attitude. His pleasure at seeing the pair so well affected towards each other was plainly manifested. He clasped his hands together, then extended them with a gesture of benediction and greeting, and came forward. His swarthy face, narrowing from brow to chin, if it could not be frank and hearty, at least expressed a friendliness which it had been ungracious to mistrust.

"Yes, son of Thor, I live! God has been merciful to both of us. Let one who knew your father take your hand. Believe that whatever I have felt for him, I now feel for you,—and more!"

The speaker had cast aside the fashionable clothes which he was in the habit of wearing during his journeys abroad, probably with a view to guard against being conspicuous, and was clad in antique priestly costume. A curiously figured and embroidered robe fell to his feet, and was confined at the waist by a long girdle, which also passed round his shoulders, after the manner of a Jewish ephod. It invested him with a dignity of presence such as ordinary garments would not have suggested. This, combined with the unexpectedly pacific tone of his address (its somewhat fantastic formality suiting well with that of his appearance), was not without effect on Balder. He gave his hand with some cordiality.

"Yours, also?" continued the other, addressing Gnulemah with an involuntary deference that surprised her lover. She complied, as a princess to her subject. This incident seemed to indicate their position relatively to each other. Had the wily Egyptian played the slave so well, as finally in good earnest to have become one?

The three stood for a moment joined in a circle, through which what incongruous passions were circulating! But Gnulemah soon withdrew the hand held by Manetho, and sent it to seek the one clasped by Balder. The priest turned cold, and stepped back; and, after an appearance of mental struggle, said huskily,—

"Hiero is forgotten; you are all for the stranger!"

"You never told me who lived beyond the wall," returned Gnulemah, with simple dignity; and added, "You are no less to me than before, but Balder is—my love!" The last words came shyly from her lips, and she swayed gently, like a noble tree, towards him she named.

Manetho's lips worked against each other, and his body twitched. He was learning the difference between theory and practice,—dream and fact. His subtle schemes had been dramas enacted by variations of himself. No allowance had been made for the working of spirit on spirit; even his special part had been designed too narrowly, with but a single governing emotion, whereas he already found himself assailed by an anarchic host of them.

"Gnulemah!" he cried at length, "my study,—my thought,—my purpose,—body of my hopes and prayers!" He knelt and bowed himself at her feet, in the Oriental posture of worship, and went on with rising passion:—"My secrets have bloomed in thy beauty,—been music in thy voice,—darkened in thine eyes! O my flower—fascinating, terrible!—the time is ripe for the gathering, for the smelling of the perfume, for the kissing of the petals! I must yield thee up, O my idol! but in thy hand are my life and my reason,—yea, Gnulemah, thou art all I am!"

The tears, gestures, voice, with which Manetho thus delivered himself, shocked the Northern taste of Helwyse. Through the semi-scriptural, symbolic language, he fancied he could discern a basis of materialism so revolting that the man of the world—the lover now!—listened with shame and anger. Here was a professed worshipper of Gnulemah, who ascribed to her no nobler worth than to be the incarnation of his own desires and passions! It was abject self-idolatry, thought Balder, masquerading as a lofty form of idealization.

The priest's mind was in a more complex condition than Balder imagined. His absorption in Gnulemah, if only as she was the instrument of his dominant purpose, must have been complete; the success (as he deemed it) of his life was staked on her. But, in addition to this, the unhappy man had, unwittingly, and with the vehemence of his ill-ordered nature, grown to love the poison-draught brewed for his enemy! When the enemy's lips touched the cup, did Manetho first become aware that it brimmed with the brewer's own life-blood!

Yet it might have been foreseen. He loved her, not because she was identified with his aims, nor even because she was beautiful, but (and not inconsistently with his theoretical belief in her devilishness) because she was pure and true. Under the persuasion that he was influencing her nature in a manner only possible, if at all, to a moral and physical despot, he had himself been ruled by her stronger and loftier spirit. The transcendent cunning on which he had prided himself, as regarded his plan of educating Gnulemah, had amounted to little more than imbecile inaction.

As Manetho prostrated himself, and even touched the hem of Gnulemah's robe to his forehead, Balder looked to see her recoil; but she maintained a composure which argued her not unused to such homage. So much evil (albeit unintentionally) had the Egyptian done her, that she could suffer, while she slighted, his worship. Yet, in the height of her proud superiority to him, she turned with sweet submission to her lover, and, obedient to his whisper, gathered up her purple mantle and passed through the green conservatory to her own door, through which, with a backward parting glance at her master, she superbly vanished. Balder had disliked the scene throughout, yet his love was greater than before. An awe of the woman whose innate force could command a nature like this priest's seemed to give his passion for her a more vigorous fibre.

The two men were now left alone to come to what understanding they might. Manetho rose to his feet, obliquely eying Helwyse, and spoke with the manner and tone of true humility,—

"You have seen me in my weakness. I am but a broken man, Balder Helwyse."

"We had better speak the plain truth to each other," said Balder, after a pause. "You can have no cause to be friendly to me. I cannot extenuate what I did. I think I meant to kill you."

"You were not to blame!" exclaimed the other, vehemently, holding up his hands. "You had to deal with a madman!"

"It is a strange train of chances has brought us together again; it ought to be for some good end. I came here unawares, and, but for this ring, should not have known that we had met before."

"I lie under your suspicion on more accounts than one," observed Manetho, glancing in the other's face. "I have assumed your uncle's name, and the disposal of his property; and I have concealed his death; but you shall be satisfied on all points. The child, too, Gnulemah!—I have kept her from sight and knowledge of the world, but not without reason and purpose, as you shall hear. Ah! I am but a poor broken man, liable, as you have seen, to fits of madness and extravagance. You shall hear everything. And listen,—as a witness that I shall speak truth, I will say my say before the face of Hiero Glyphic yonder, and upon the steps of his altar! See, I desire neither to palliate nor falsify. Shall we go in?"

With some repugnance Helwyse followed the priestly figure through the low-browed door, He had seen too much of men to allow any instinctive aversion to influence him, in the absence of logical evidence. And this man's words sounded fair; his frank admission of occasional insanity accounted for many anomalies. Nevertheless, and apart from any question of personal danger, Balder felt ill at ease, like animals before a thunderstorm. As he sat down beside his companion on the steps of the black altar, and glanced up at the yellow visage that presided over it, he tried to quiet his mind in vain; even the thought of Gnulemah yielded a vague anxiety!

XXVIII.

Betrothal.

The ring, which Balder had taken off with the intention of returning it to its owner, still remained between his thumb and finger; and as he sat under the gloom of the altar, its excellent brilliancy caught his eye. He had never examined it minutely. It was pure as virtue, and possessed similar power to charm the dusky air into seven-hued beauty. A fountain of lustre continually welled up from its interior, like an exhaustless spring of wisdom. From amidst the strife of the little serpents it shone serenely forth, with, divine assurance of good,— eternal before the battle began, and immortal after it should cease. The light refreshed the somewhat jaded Helwyse, and during the ensuing interview he ever and anon renewed the draught.

But the Egyptian seemed to address a silent invocation to the mummy. The anti-spiritual kind of immortality belonging to mummies may have been congenial to Manetho's soul. Awful is that loneliness which even the prospect of death has deserted, and which must prolong itself throughout a lifeless and hopeless Forever! If Manetho could imagine any bond of relationship between this perennial death's-head and himself, no marvel that he cherished it jealously.

"You shall hear first about myself," said the priest; "yet, truly, I know not how to begin! No mind can know another, nor even its own essential secrets. My time has been full of visions and unrealities. I am the victim of a thing which, for lack of a better name, I call myself!"

"Not a rare sickness," remarked Balder.

"A ghost no spell can lay! It grasps the rudder, and steers towards gulfs the will abhors. A crew of unholy, mutinous impulses fling abroad words and thoughts unrecognizable. Not Manetho talked in the blackness of that night; but a devil, to whom I listened shuddering, unable to control him!"

"The Reverend Manetho Glyphie, my cousin by adoption,—and sometimes a devil!" muttered Balder, musingly. "I had forgotten him."

People are more prone to err in fancying themselves righteous, than the reverse; nevertheless, the course and limits of self-deception are indefinite. It is within possibility for a man to believe himself wicked, while his actual conduct is ridiculously blameless, even praise-worthy! Although intending to mislead Balder, Manetho's utterances were true to a degree unsuspected by himself. He was more true than had he tried to be so, because truth lay too profound for his recognition!

"A shallower man," he resumed, "would bear a grudge against the hand that clutched his throat; but I own no relationship to the madman you chastised. And there are deep reasons why I must set your father's son above all other men in my regard."

"My father seldom spoke of you, and never as of an especial friend," interposed the ingenuous Balder.

"He knew not my feeling towards him, nor would he have comprehended it. It is a thing I myself can scarce understand. To the outward eye there is juster cause for hatred than for love.

"I will speak openly to you what has hitherto lain between my heart and God. Before Thor saw your mother, I had loved her. My life's hope was to marry her. Thor came,—and my hope lingered and died. For it, was no resurrection." Here Manetho broke all at once into sobs, covering his face with his hands; and when he continued, his voice was softened with tears.

"Thor called her to him, and she gladly went. He stormed and carried with ease the fortress which, at best, I could hope only slowly to undermine. She loved him as women love a conqueror; she might have yielded me, at most, the grace of a condescending queen. I kept silence: to whom could I speak? I had felt great ambitions,—to become honored and famous,—to preach the gospel as it had not yet been preached,—all ambitions that a lover may feel. But the tree died for lack of nourishment. See what is left!"

He opened out his arms with a gesture wanting neither in pathos nor dignity. Balder could not but sympathize with what he felt to be a genuine emotion.

"Amidst the ruins of my Memphis, I kept silence. I hated—myself! for my powerlessness to keep her. In my hours of madness I hated her too, and him; but that was madness indeed! Deeper down was a sanity that loved him. Since he had made my love his, I must love him. So only might I still love her. The only beauty left my ruins was that!

"She died; and with her would have died all sanity,—all love, but that her children kept me back from worse ruin than was mine already. They were a link to bind me to the good. Now Thor is dead, but still his son—her son—survives. Hence is it that you are more to me than other men."

"Did Doctor Glyphic know nothing of this?"

"I never told him of either my hope or my despair. My beloved master! he lived and died without suspicion that I had striven to be a brother as well as son to him."

"When did he die?"

"Eighteen years ago," said Manetho, solemnly. "You are the first to whom his death has been revealed. Beloved master! have I not obeyed thy will?" And he looked up to his master's parchment visage.

"I discovered his death for myself, you know," observed Helwyse. "But it could not have been more than eighteen years since my father, then on the point of departure for Europe, saw Hiero Glyphic alive!"

"Yes, yes! Did he ever tell you what passed in that interview?" demanded Manetho, eagerly.

"Little more than a farewell, I think. There was some talk about the estate. At my uncle's death, the house was to come to you, the property to my father or his heirs. But neither expected at that time that it was to be their last meeting."

"Was no one mentioned beside Thor's children and myself?" asked the priest, looking askant at Balder as he spoke.

"No my uncle neither had nor expected children, as far as I know!"

"Thor did not see her,—Gnulemah?"

"Gnulemah?—how should he have seen her?" exclaimed Balder, in surprise.

"Then her mystery remains!" said Manetho, looking up.

He had perhaps doubted whether any suspicion of who Gnulemah really was had found its way to the young man's mind. The latter's reception of his question reassured him. There could be no risk in catering to his aroused curiosity. The account Manetho now gave was true, though falsehood lurked in the pauses.

"That day Thor came, I left the house early in the morning. It was night when I returned; and Thor was gone. The house was dark, and at first there was no sound. But presently I heard the voice of a child, murmuring and babbling baby words. I passed through the outer hall and the conservatory, and came to where we now are. The lamp was burning as it has burned ever since.

"I saw him lying on the altar steps,—lying so!" Marrying act to word, the Egyptian slid down and lay prostrate at the altar's foot. "He was dead and cold!" he added; and gave way to a shuddering outburst of grief.

Balder's nerves were a little staggered at this tale with its heightening of dramatic action and morbid circumstance; and he was silent until the actor (if such he were) was in some degree repossessed of himself. Then he asked,—

"What of the child?"

"I have named her Gnulemah. She played about the dead body, bright and careless as the flame of the lamp. Whence she came she could not tell, nor had I seen her before that day. It seemed that, at the moment my master's life burned out, hers flamed up; and since that day it has lighted and warmed my solitude."

"And Doctor Glyphic—"

"I embalmed him!" cried Manetho, clasping his hands in grotesque enthusiasm. "It was my privilege and my consolation to render his body immortal. In my grief I rejoiced at the opportunity of manifesting my devotion. Not the proudest of the Pharaohs was more sumptuously preserved than he! In that labor of love there was no cunning secret of the art that I did not employ. Night and day I worked alone; and while he lay in the long nitre bath, I watched or slept beside him. Then I enwound him thousand-fold in finest linen smeared with fragrant gum, and hid his beloved form in the coffin he had chosen long before."

"Did my uncle choose this form of burial?"

"He lived in hopes of it! It was his wish that his body might be disposed as became his name, and the passion that had ruled his life. Me only did he deem worthy of the task, and equal to it. Had I died before him, his fairest hope would have been blighted, his life a failure!"

"A dead failure, truly!" muttered Balder, impelled by the very grewsomeness of the subject to jest about it. "Was his loftiest aspiration to mummy and be mummied?—But yours was a dangerous office to fulfil, Cousin Manetho. Had the death got abroad, you might have been suspected of foul play!"

"The cause was worth the risk," replied the other, sententiously.

Helwyse shot a keen look at his companion, but could discern in him none of the common symptoms of guilt. The priest, however, was a mine of sunless riddles, one lode connecting with another; it was idle attempting to explore them all at once. So the young man recurred to that vein which was of most immediate interest to himself.

"Have you no knowledge concerns Gnulemah's origin?" he inquired.

Manetho laid his long brown hand on Balder's arm.

"If she be not Gnulemah, daughter of fire, it must rest with you to give her another name," said he.

"I care not who was her father or her mother," rejoined the lover, after a short silence; "Gnulemah is herself!"

The lithe fingers on his arm clutched it hard for a moment, and Manetho averted his face. When he turned again, his features seemed to express exultation, mingled with a sinister flavor of some darker emotion.

"Son of Thor, you have your father's frankness. Do you love her?"

"You saw that I loved her," returned Balder, his black eyes kindling somewhat intolerantly.

"If I can hasten by one hour the consummation of that love, my life will have been worth the living!"

"That's kindly spoken!" exclaimed Helwyse, heartily; and, opening his strong white hand, he took the narrow brown one into its grasp. He had not been prepared for so friendly a profession.

"When I have seen your soul tied to hers in a knot that even death may not loosen,—and if it be permitted me to tie the knot, I shall have drained the cup of earthly happiness!" He spoke with a deliberate intensity not altogether pleasant to the ear. He would not relinquish Balder's hand, as he continued in his high-strung vein,—

"I know at last for whom my flower has bloomed. Through the world, across seas, by strange accidents has Providence brought you safe to this spot; and has made you what you are, and her incomparable among women.—You love her with heart and soul, Balder Helwyse?"

"So that the world seems frail; and I—except for my love—insignificant!"

In the sudden emphasis of his question, Manetho had risen to his feet; and Balder likewise had started up, before giving his reply. As he spoke the words strongly forth, his swarthy companion seemed to catch them in the air, and breathe them in. Slowly an expression of joy, that could hardly be called a smile, welled forth from his long eyes, and forced its way, with dark persistency of glee, through all his face.

"By you only in the world would I have her loved!" he said; and repeated it more than once.

He remained a full minute leaning with one arm on the altar, his eyes abstracted. Then he said abruptly,—

"Why not be married soon?"

The lover looked up questioningly, a deep throb in his heart.

"Soon—soon!" reiterated Manetho. "Love is a thing of moments more than of years. I know it! Do you stand idle while Gnulemah awaits you? We may die tomorrow!"

"I have no right to hurry her," said Helwyse in a low voice. "She knows nothing of the world. I would marry her tomorrow—"

"Tomorrow! why not today? Why wait? that she may learn the falsehoods of society,—to flirt, dress, gossip, crave flattery? Why do you hesitate? Speak out, son of Thor!"

"I have spoken. Do you doubt me? Were it possible, she should be my wife this hour!"

"Oh!" murmured Manetho, the incisiveness of his manner melting away as suddenly as it came; "now have you proved your love. You shall be made one,—one!—today. Four-and-twenty years ago this day, I married your parents on this very spot. The anniversary shall become a double one!"

The black eyesockets of the mummy stared Balder in the face. But at a touch from Manetho, he turned, and saw Gnulemah, bright with beautiful enchantment, in the doorway.

"Yes, today!" he said impetuously.

"You shall wed her with that ring!" whispered the victorious tempter in his ear. "Go to her; tell her what marriage is! I will call you soon."

The lover went, and the woman, coming forward, sweetly met him halfway. But glancing back again before passing out, Balder saw that the priest had vanished; and the lamp, flickering above the mummy's dry features, wrought them into a shadowy semblance of emotion.

XXIX.

A Chamber of the Heart.

Manetho neither sank through the granite floor, nor ascended in the smoke of the lamp. He unlocked a door (to the panels of which the clock was affixed, and which it concealed) and let himself into his private study, a room scarce seven feet wide, though corresponding in length and height with the dimensions of the outer temple. Books and papers were kept here, and such other things of a private or valuable nature as Manetho wished should be inaccessible to outsiders. Against the wall opposite the door stood a heavy mahogany table; beside it, a deep-bottomed chair, in which the priest now sat down.

The room was destitute of windows, properly so called. The walls were full twenty feet high; and at a distance of some sixteen feet from the floor, a series of low horizontal apertures pierced the masonry, allowing the light of heaven to penetrate in an embarrassed manner, and hesitatingly to reveal the interior. Viewed from without, these narrow slits would be mistaken for mere architectural indentations. To the inhabitant they were of more importance, contracted though they were; and albeit one could not look out of them, they served as ventilators, and to distinguish between fine and cloudy weather.

In his earlier and more active days, Manetho had lived and worked throughout the whole extent of this study, and it had been kept clean and orderly to its remotest corner. But as years passed, and the range of his sympathies and activities narrowed, the ends of the room had gradually fallen into dusty neglect, till at length only the small space about the chair and table was left clear and available. The rest was impeded by books, instruments of science, and endless chaotic rubbish; while spiders had handed down their ever-broadening estates from father to child, through innumerable Araneidæan generations. A gray uniformity had thus come to overspread everything; and with the exceptions of a cracked celestial globe, and the end of a worm-eaten old ladder, there was nothing to catch the attention.

Here might the Egyptian indulge himself in whatever extravagances of word or act he chose, secure from sight or hearing; and here had he spent many an hour in such solitary exercises as no sane mind can conceive. To him the room was thick with associations. Here had he pursued his studies, or helped the Doctor in his erratic experiments and research; here, with Helen in his thoughts, he had shaped out a career,—not all of Christian humility and charity, perhaps, but at least unstained by positive sin, and not unmindful of domestic happiness. Here, again, had Salome visited him, bringing discord and delight in equal parts; for at times, with the strong heat of youth, he had vowed to love only her and to forsake ambition; and anon the bloodless counsels of worldly power and welfare banished her with a curse for having crossed his path. Head and heart were always at war in Manetho. The talismanic diamond flashed or waned, and fiercely wriggled the little fighting serpents.

At length Thor Helwyse's gauntlet was thrown into the ring; and peace—if still present to outward seeming—abode not in the feverish soul of the Egyptian. But it was his nature to dissemble. In this room he had often outwatched the night, chewing the cud of his wrongs, invoking vengeance upon the thwarter of his hopes, and swearing through his teeth to even the balance between them. The black serpent held the golden one helpless in his coils. The obtuse Doctor, blundering in at morning, would find his adopted son with pallid cheeks and glittering eyes, but ever ready with a smile and pleasant greeting, obedience and help. Hiero Glyphic, however wayward and cross-grained, never had cause to censure this creature of his,—to remind him that he might have been food for crocodiles.

Manetho's dissimulation was almost without flaw. Even Helen, whose fancy had played with him at first, but who in time had indolently yielded to the fascination exerted over her, and even gone so far as to permit his adulation, and accept in the ring the mystic pledge thereof (during all the countless ages of its experience it had never touched woman's hand before),—even she, when her lazy heart and overbearing spirit were at length aroused and quelled by the voice rather of a master than suitor, was deceived by forsaken Manetho's unruffled face, gentle voice, and downcast eyes. She told herself that his love had never dared be warmer than a kind of worship, like that of a pagan for his idol, apart from human passion; such, at all events, had been her understanding of his attentions. As to the ring, it had been tendered as an offering at the shrine of abstract womanhood; to return it too soon would imply a supposition of more personal sentiment. Neither must Thor see it, however; his rough sense would fail to appreciate her fine-drawn distinction. So she concealed it in her bosom, and Manetho's serpents were ever between Thor and his wife's heart. She was false both to husband and lover.

Great Thor, meanwhile, pitied the slender Egyptian, and in a kindly way despised him, with his supple manners, quiet words, and religious studies. To the young priest's timid yet earnest request for permission to pronounce the marriage-service of him and his bride, Thor assented with gruff heartiness.

"Marry us? Of course! marry us as fast as you can, if it gives you any pleasure, my friend of the crocodile. A good beginning for your ministerial career,—marrying a couple who love each other as much as Nell and I do. Eh, Nellie?"

The ceremony over, Manetho had retired to his study, and there passed the night,—their marriage-night! What words and tones, what twistings of face and body, did those passionless walls see and hear? How the smooth, studious, submissive priest yearned for power to work his will for one day! And as the cool, still morning sheared the lustre from his lamp-flame, how desolate he felt, with his hatred and despair and blaspheming rage! Evil passions are but poor company, in the early morning.

But was not Salome left him? The only sincerely tender words he had ever spoken to woman had been said to her: his humblest and happiest thoughts had been born of their early acquaintance,—before he had raised his eyes to the proud and languid mistress. Yet on her only did the evil passions of Manetho wreak themselves in harm and wrong; her only, on a later day, did he dastardly strike down. Poor Salome had given him her heart. These walls had seen their meetings.

Years afterwards, Manetho had here embalmed his foster-father: through long hours had he labored at his hateful task, with curious zest and conscientiousness. As regarded the strange place of sepulture, the Egyptian had perhaps imagined a symbolic fitness in enclosing his human immortal in the empty shell of time. Over this matter of Hiero Glyphic's death and burial, however, must ever brood a cloud of mystery. Undoubtedly Manetho loved the man,—but death was not always the worst of ills in Manetho's philosophy.

The clock had been affixed to the study door both as an additional concealment, and possibly as a congenial sentry over the interior associations. Since then the place had become the clergyman's almost daily resort. Pacing the contracted floor, sitting moodily in the chair,— many a brooding hour had gone over his barrenly busy head, and written its darkening record in his book of life. Here had been schemed that plan of revenge, whose insanity the insane schemer could not perceive. Nor could he understand that mightier powers than he could master worked against him, and even used his efforts to bring forth contrary results.

But not all hours had passed so. Spaces there had been wherein evil counsels had retired to a cloudy background, athwart which had brightened a rainbow, intangible, whose source was hidden, but whose colors were true before his eyes. The grace and aerial beauty of sunshine lightened through the rain,—the pleasing loveliness of essential life was projected on the gloom of evil imaginations. For Manetho's actual deeds were apt to be prompted by far gentler influences than governed his theories. The man was better than his mind: and goodness, perhaps, bears an absolute blessing; insomuch that the sinner, doing ignorant good, yet feels the benefit thereof; just as the rain, however dismal, cannot prevent the sun from making rainbows out of it.

On this particular morning Manetho sank into his deep-seated chair, and was quite still. A great part of what had hitherto made his daily life ended here. The activity of existence was over for him. Thought, feeling, hope, could live hereafter only as phantoms of memory. But to look back on evil done is not so pleasant as to plan it; the dead body of a foe moves us in another way than his living hostile person.

When, therefore, Manetho should have hurled to its mark the long-poised spear, he would have little to look forward to. That one moment of triumph must repay, both for what had been and was to come. Today of all his days, then, must each sense and faculty be in exquisite condition. Unseasonably enough, however, he found himself in a perversely dull and callous state. Could Providence so cajole him as to mar the only joyful hour of his life! Then better off than he were savages, who could destroy their recusant idols. But nothing short of spiritual suicide would have destroyed the idol of Manetho!

He was wearing today the same priestly robe which he had put on when, for the first and last time, he performed a ministerial duty. In this robe had he married Helen to Thor. Itself a precious relic of antiquity, it had once dignified the shoulders of a contemporary of Manetho's remotest ancestors. Old Hiero Glyphic had counted it amongst his chiefest treasures; and on his sister's wedding-day had produced it from its repository, insisting that the minister should wear it instead of the orthodox sacerdotal costume. Since then it had lain untouched till today.

Manetho brooded over the dim magnificence of its folds, sitting amidst the cobwebbed rubbish, a narrow glint of sunshine creeping slope-downwards from the crevice above his head. He smoothed the fabric abstractedly with his hand, recalling the thoughts and scenes of four-and-twenty years ago.

"I joined them in the holy bonds of matrimony,—read over them that service, those sacred words heavy with solemn benediction. Rich, smooth, softly modulated was my voice, missing not one just emphasis or melodious intonation. Ah! had they seen my soul. But my eyes were half closed like the crocodile's, yet never losing sight of the two I was uniting in sight of God and man. The Devil too was there. He turned the blessings my lips uttered into blighting curses, that fell on the happy couple like pestilential rain!

"Laughable! Covered head to foot with curses, and felt them not! All was smiles, blushes, happiness, forward-looking to a long, joyful future. They knelt before me; I uplifted my hands and invoked the last blessing,—the final curse! My heart burned, and the smoke of its fire enveloped bride and groom, fouling his yellow beard, and smirching her silvery veil; shutting out heaven from their prayers, and blackening their path before them. They neither felt nor knew. They kissed,—I saw their lips meet,—as Balder and Gnulemah today. Then I covered my face and seemed to be in prayer!

"Gnulemah,—I hate her!—yes, but hatred sometimes touches the heart like love. I love her!—to marry her? Woe to him who becomes her husband! As a daughter?—no daughter is she of mine!—I hate her, then.

"Why am I childless?—how would I have loved a child! I would have left all else to love my child! I would have been the one father in the world! My life should have been full of love as it has been of hate. Why did not God send me a wife and a daughter?"

Men's ears have grown deaf to any save the most commonplace oracles. But there is ever a warning voice for who will listen. One may object that its language is unknown, or its whisper inaudible; but to the question, "Whence your ignorance and deafness?" what shall be the answer?

In Manetho's case it appears to have been the venerable robe that took on itself the task of remonstrance.

"You are unreasonable, friend," it interposed with a gentle rustle. "Gnulemah, if not your daughter, might, however, have stood you in place of one; and she would have done you just as much good, in the way of softening and elevating your nature, as though she had been the issue of your own loins. You have turned the milk and honey of your life into gall and wormwood; and I wish I could feel sure that only you would get the benefit of it!"

The reproof had as well been spared; it is doubtful whether the culprit heard so much as a word of it. His reverie rambled on.

"Keen,—that Balder! he half suspects me. Had I not so hurried him to a conclusion, he would have questioned me too closely. He shall know all presently, even as I promised him!—shall hear a sounder guess at Gnulemah's genealogy than was made today.

"Do I love her?—only as the means to my end! The end once

gained, I shall hate her as I do him. But not yet,—and therefore must I love him as well as her. They shall be, today, my beloved children! Tomorrow,—how shall I endure till tomorrow,—all the night through? O Gnulemah!—

"They love each other well,—seem made to make each other happy; yet have they come together from the ends of the earth to be each other's curse! Only if I keep silence might it be otherwise, for love might tame the devil that I have bred in Gnulemah. Even now she seems more angel than devil!—Am I mad?"

He straightened himself in his chair, and glanced up towards the crevice whence slanted the dusty sunshine. The old robe took the opportunity to deliver its final warning.

"Not yet mad beyond remedy, Manetho; but you look up too seldom at the sunshine, and brood too often over your own dusty depths. You have had no consciously unselfish thought during the last quarter of a century. You eat, drink, and breathe only Manetho! This room is yours, because it is fullest of rubbish, and least looks out upon the glorious universe. Break down your walls! take broom in hand without delay! Proclaim at once the crime you meditate. Go! there is still sunshine in this dust-hole of yours, and more of heaven in every man than he himself dreams of. The sun is passing to the other side. Go while it shines!"

But Manetho's dull ears heard not; and the aged garment of truth spoke no more.

XXX.

Dandelions.

It seems a pity that, with all imagination at our service, we should have to confine our excursions within so narrow a domain as this of Hiero Glyphic's. One tires of the best society, uncondimented with an occasional foreign relish, even of doubtful digestibility. Barring this, it only remains to relieve somewhat the monotony of our food, by variety in the modes of dishing it up.

Balder had been no whit disconcerted at the priest's abrupt evanishment. The divine sphere of Gnulemah had touched him with its sweet magnetism, and he was sensible of little beyond it. Their hands greeted like life-long friends. Drawing hers within his arm, he still kept hold of it, and her rounded shoulder softly pressed his, as they loitered out between the impenetrable sphinxes. The conservatory, however beautiful in itself and by association, was too small to hold their hearts at this moment. They passed on, and through the columns of the Moorish portico, into the fervent noon sunshine.

Grasshoppers chirped; fine buzzing flies darted swift circles and lit again; birds giggled and gossiped, bobbing and swinging among swaying boughs. Battalions of vast green trees stood grand in shadow-lakes of cooler green, their myriad leaves twinkling light and dark. Tender gleams of river topped the enamelled bank,—the further shore a slumbering El Dorado. The trees in the distant orchard wore bridal veils, and even Gnulemah's breath was not much sweeter than theirs!

Emerging arm in arm on the enchanted lawn the lovers turned southwards up the winding avenue. The fragrance, the light and warmth, the bird and insect voices, imperfectly expressed their own heart-happiness. The living turf softly pressed up their feet. This was the fortunate hour that comes not twice. Happy those to whom it comes at all! To live was such full bliss, every new movement overflowed the cup. Joy was it to look on earth and sky; but to behold each other was heaven! More life in a moment such as this, than in twenty years of scheming more successful than Manetho's.

They followed the same path Helen had walked the eve of her death; and presently arrived at the old bench. Shadow and sunshine wrestled playfully over it, while the green blood of the leaves overhead glowed vividly against the blue. Around the bench the grass grew taller, as on a grave; and crisp lichens, gray and brown, overspread its surface. Man had neglected it so long that Nature, overcoming her diffidence towards his handiwork, had at length claimed it for her own.

The glade was full of great golden dandelions, whose soft yellow crowns were almost too heavy for the slender necks. The prince and princess of the fairytale paused here, recognizing the spot as the most beautiful on earth,—albeit only since their love's arrival. They seated themselves not on the bench, but on the yet more primitive grass beside it. They had not spoken as yet. Balder plucked some dandelions, and proceeded to twist them into a chain; and Gnulemah, after watching him for a while followed his example.

"You and I have sat on the grass and woven such chains before," asserted she at length. "When was it?"

"I haven't done such a thing since I was a child not much taller than a dandelion," returned Balder. He was not ethereal enough to follow Gnulemah in her apparently fanciful flight, else might he have lighted on a discovery to which all the good sense and logic in the world would not have brought him.

"Yes; we have made these chains before!" reiterated Gnulemah, looking at her companion in a preoccupied manner. "They were to have chained us together forever."

"We should have made them of stronger stuff then. But which of us broke the chain?"

"They took us away from each other, and it was never finished. Do you remember nothing?"

"The present is enough for me," said her lover; and he finished his necklace with a handsome clasp of blossoms, and threw it over her neck. She gave a low sigh of satisfaction.

"I have been waiting for it ever since that time! And here is mine for you."

Thus adorned by each other's hands, their love seemed greater than before, and they laughed from pure delight. Their bonds looked fragile; yet it would need a stronger wrench to part them than had they been cables of iron or gold, unsustained by the subtile might of love.

"Let us link them together," proposed Balder; and, loosening a link of his chain, he reunited it inside Gnulemah's. "We must keep together," he continued with a smile, "or the marriage-bonds will break."

"Is this marriage, Balder? to be tied together with flowers?"

"One part of marriage. It shows the world that we belong only to each other."

"How could they help knowing that,—for to whom else could we belong? besides, why should they know?"

"Because," answered Balder after some consideration, "the world is made in such a way, that unless we record all we do by some visible symbol, everything would get into confusion."

"No no," protested Gnulemah, earnestly. "Only God should know how we love. Must the world know our words and thoughts, and how we have sat beneath these trees?—Then let us not be married!"

They were leaning side to side against the bench, along whose edge Balder had stretched an arm to cushion Gnulemah's head. As he turned to look at her, a dash of sunlight was quivering on her clear smooth cheek, and another ventured to nestle warmly below the head of the guardian serpent on her bosom, for Gnulemah and the sun had been lovers long before Balder's appearance. Where breathed such another woman? From the low turban that pressed her hair to the bright sandals on her fine bronze feet, there was no fault, save her very uniqueness. She belonged not to this era, but to the Golden Age, past or to come. Could she ever be conformed to the world of today? Dared her lover assume the responsibility of revealing to this noble soul all the meanness, sophistries, little pleasures, and low aims of this imperfect age? Could he change the world to suit her needs? or endure to see her change to suit the world? Moreover, changing so much, might she not change towards him? The Balder she loved was a grander man than any Balder knew. Might she not learn to abhor the hand which should unveil to her the Gorgon features of fallen humanity?—Much has man lost in losing Paradise!

Contemplating Gnulemah's entrance into the outer world, Manetho had anticipated her ruin from the flowering of the evil seed which he believed himself to have planted in her. Might not the same result issue from a precisely opposite cause? The Arcadian fashion in which the lovers' passion had ripened must soon change forever. It was perilous to advance, but to retreat was impossible. Balder was at bay; had he loved Gnulemah less, he would have regretted Charon's ferry-boat. But his love was greater for the danger and difficulty wherewith it was fraught. He could not summon the millennium; well, he might improve himself.

"If I could but shut her glorious eyes to all the shabby littleness they will have to see, we might hazard the rest," he sighed to himself. "If the pure visions of her maiden years might veil from her those gross realities of everyday life! With what face shall I meet her glance after it has suffered the first shock?"

Meanwhile her last objection remained unanswered, and Balder, distrustful of his capacity, was inspired to seek inspiration from her he would instruct.

"Tell me how you love me, Gnulemah," said he.

She roused herself, and bending her face to his, breathlessly kissed his lips. Then she drooped her warm cheek on his shoulder, and whispered the rest:—

"My love is to be near you, and to breathe when breathe; it is love to become you, as water becomes wave. And love would make me sweet to you, as honey and music and flowers. I love to be needed by you, as you need food and drink and sleep; and my love will be loved, as God loves the world."

To the lover these sentences were tender and sublime poetry. The tears came to his eyes, hearing her speak out her loving soul so simply. He had travelled through the world, while she had lived her life between a wall and a precipice. But not the noisy, gaudy, gloomy crust which is fresh today, and tomorrow hardens, and the next day crumbles, is the world; but the fire-globe within: and Gnulemah was nearer that fire than Balder. There was puissance in her simplicity,—in her ignorance of that crust which he had so widely studied. Her knowledge was more profound than his, for she had never learned to stultify it with reasons.

"It is true,—God only can know our love," said Balder, and, having said it, he felt his mind clear and strengthen. For it is the acknowledgment of God that lends the deepest seeing to the eye, and tunes the universe to man; and Balder, at this moment of mingled love, humility, and fear, made and confessed that supreme discovery.—"Only He knows what our love is, but the marriage-rite informs the world that He knows it."

"But why must the world know?" persisted Gnulemah, still seeming to shrink at the idea.

"Because it is wholesome for all men to know that we have made God party to our union. That our love may be pure and immortal, we must look through each other to Him; the acknowledgment will keep others as well as ourselves from misusing love's happiness."

"Then, after we have knelt together before Him, we shall be no longer two, but one!" Gnulemah spoke, after some pause, in a full tone of joy; yet her voice shrank at the last, from the feeling that she had penetrated all at once to a holy place. A delicious fear seized her, and she clung to her lover so that he could perceive the tremor that agitated her.

No more was said. Their confidence was in each other; with Balder at her side, Gnulemah was fearful of the world no longer. But her visions were all spiritual; even the kisses on her lips were to her a sacred miracle! Love makes children of men and women,—shows them the wisdom of unreason and the value of soap-bubbles. These lovers must meet the world, but the light and freshness of the Golden Age should accompany them. The man held the maiden's hand, and so faced the future with a smile.

Few as were the hours since they first had seen each other, it seemed as though they could hardly know each other better; then why put off the consummation a single hour? Manetho had been right, and Balder marvelled at having required the spur. He knew of no material hindrances; unlimited resources would be his, and these would render easier Gnulemah's introduction to society. Perhaps (for doubtless Manetho would desire it) they might begin housekeeping in this very house, and thus, by gradual approaches, make their way to life's realities,—vulgarly so called!

At this moment, Balder's respect for wealth was many fold greater than ever it had been before. It should be the sword and shield wherewith he would protect the woman of his heart. Gnulemah was not of the kind who need the discipline of poverty; her beauty and goodness would be best nurtured beneath an affluent sun. Wants and inconveniences would rather pain and mystify than educate her. How good was that God who had vouchsafed not only the blessing, but the means of enjoying it!

God gave Balder Helwyse opportunity to prove the soundness of his faith. Labor and poverty awaited him; what else and worse let time show. In anguish, fear, and humiliation had his love been born, but the birth-pangs had been as brief as they were intense. A brave soul's metal is more severely tried by crawling years of monotonous effort, discord of must with wish, and secret self-suppression and misgiving. Happily life is so ordered that no blow can crush unless dealt from within, nor is any sunshine worth having that shines only from without.

Balder's eyes were softer than their wont, and there was a tender and sweet expression about his mouth. Never had life been so inestimable a blessing,—never had nature looked so divinely alive. He could imagine nothing gloomy or forbidding; in darkness's self he would have found germs of light. His love was a panoply against ill of mind or body. He thought he perceived, once for all, the insanity of selfishness and sin.

Suddenly he was conscious through Gnulemah of the same shiver that had visited her in the conservatory that morning. Looking round, he was startled to see, beyond the near benison of her sumptuous face, the tall form of the Egyptian priest. He was not a dozen yards away, advancing slowly towards them. Balder sprang up.

"Our chain,—you have broken it!" exclaimed Gnulemah. It was only a flower chain, but flowers are the bloom and luxury of life.

Manetho came up with a smile.

"Come, my children!" said he. "This chain would soon have faded and fallen apart of itself, but the chain I will forge you is stronger than time and weightier than dandelions. Come!"

Gnulemah picked up the broken links, and they followed him to the house.

XXXI.

Married.

The significant part of most life histories is the record of a few detached hours, the rest being consequence and preparation. Helwyse had lived in constant mental and physical activity from childhood up; but though he had speculated much, and ever sought to prove the truth by practice, yet he had failed to create adequate emergencies, and was like an untried sword, polished and keen, but lacking still the one stern proof of use.

Thus, although a man of the world, in a deeper sense he was untouched by it. He had been the sentimental spectator of a drama wherein some shadow of himself seemed to act. The mimic scenes had sometimes moved him to laughter or to tears, but he had never quite lost the suspicion of an unreality under all. The best end had been—in a large sense—beauty. Beauty of love, of goodness, of strength, of wisdom,—beauty of every kind and degree, but nothing better! Beauty was the end rather than the trait of all desirable things. To have power was beautiful, and beautiful was the death that opened the way to freer and wider power. Most beautiful was Almightiness; yet, lapsing thence, it was beautiful to begin the round again in fresh, new forms.

This kind of spider-webs cannot outlast the suns and snows. Personal passion disgusts one with brain-spun systems of the universe, and may even lead to a mistrust of mathematics! One feels the overwhelming power of other than intellectual interests; and discovers in himself a hitherto unsuspected universe, profound as the mystery of God, where the cockle-shell of mental attainments is lost like an asteroid in the abyss of space.

What is the mind?—A little window, through which to gaze out upon the vast heart-world: a window whose crooked and clouded pane we may diligently clean and enlarge day by day; but, too often, the deep view beyond is mistaken for a picture painted on the glass and limited by its sash! Let the window by all means expand till the darksome house be transformed to a crystal palace! but shall homage be paid the crystal? Of what value were its transparency, had God not built the heavens and the earth?—

Though Helwyse had failed to touch the core of life, and to recognize the awful truth of its mysteries, he had not been conscious of failure. On the contrary he had become disposed to the belief that he was a being apart from the mass of men and above them: one who could see round and through human plans and passions; could even be separate from himself, and yield to folly with one hand, while the other jotted down the moral of the spectacle. He was calm in the conviction that he could measure and calculate the universe, and draw its plan in his commonplace book. God was his elder brother,—himself in some distant but attainable condition. He matched finity against the Infinite, and thereby cast away man's dearest hope,—that of eternal progress towards the image of Divine perfection.

Once, however, the bow had smitten his heart-strings with a new result of sound, awakening fresh ideas of harmony. When Thor was swept to death by that Baltic wave, Balder leapt after him, hopeless to save, but without demur! The sea hurled him back alone. For many a month thereafter, strange lights and shadows flashed or gloomed across his sky, and sounds from unknown abysses disquieted him. But all was not quite enough; perhaps he was hewn from too stanch materials lightly to change. Yet the sudden shock of his loss left its mark: the props of self-confidence were a little unsettled; and the events whose course we have traced were therefore able to shake them down.

For Destiny rained her sharpest blows on Balder Helwyse all at once, and the attack marks the turning-point of his life. She chose her weapons wisely. He was beaten by tactics which a coarser and shallower nature would have slighted. He sustained the onslaught for the most part with outward composure,—but bleeding inwardly.

His had been a vast egoism, rooted in his nature and trained by his philosophy. It must die, if at all, violently, painfully, and—in silence. The truer and more constant the soul, the more complete the destruction of its idol. Character is not always the slow growth of years: often do the elements mingle long in formless solution; some sudden jar causes them to spring at once to the definite crystal. There had, hitherto, been a kind of impersonality about Balder, having its ultimate ground in his blindness to the immutable unity of God. But so soon as his eye became single, he stood pronounced in his individuality, less broadly indifferent than of yore, but organized and firm.

In this inert world the body pursues but imperfectly the processes of the soul. These three days had made small change in Helwyse's face. His expression was less serene than of yore, but pithier as well as more joyful. The humorous indifference had given place to a kindlier humanity. Gone was the glance half satiric, half sympathetic; but in its stead was something warmer and more earnest. For the charity of scepticism was substituted a sentiment less broad, but deeper and truer. It would need an insight supernaturally keen to detect thus early these alterations in the page of Balder's countenance; but their germs are there, to develop afterwards.

During this pause in our narrative, Helwyse was sitting at his chamber window, awaiting the summons to the ceremony. The afternoon was far advanced, and the landscape lay breathless beneath the golden burden of the lavish sun. The bridegroom rose to his feet; surely the bride must be ready! Was that strange old Nurse delaying her? Did she herself procrastinate? Balder was waxing impatient!

The clear outcry of the hoopoe startled the calm air, and that good little messenger came fluttering in haste to the window. Bound its neck was twined a golden dandelion,—Gnulemah's love-token! With a knowing upturn of its bright little eye, the bird submitted to being robbed of its decoration; then warbled a keen good-by, and flew away.

The lover behaved as foolishly towards the dandelion as a lover should. At last he drew the stem through the button-hole of his velveteen jacket, and was ready to answer in person the shy invitation it conveyed. The bride waited!

His hand was on the latch, when some one knocked. He threw open the door,—and had to look twice before recognizing Nurse. Her dingy anomalous drapery had been exchanged for another sort of costume. Her scars strove to be hidden beneath the yellow lace and crumpled feathers of an antique headdress. She wore a satin gown of an old fashion, whose pristine whiteness was much impaired by time. An aged fan, ragged, but of tasteful pattern, dangled at her wrist. She resembled some forgotten Ginevra, reappearing after an age's seclusion in the oaken chest. Her aspect was painfully repellent, the more for this pathetic attempt at good looks. The former unlovely garb had a sort of fitness to the blasted features; but so soon as she forsook that uncanny harmony and tried to be like other women, she became undesirably conspicuous.

"The bridesmaid!" came to Balder's lips,—but did not pass them. He would not hurt the poor creature's feelings by the betrayal of surprise or amusement. She was a woman,—and Gnulemah was no more. According to his love for his wife, must he be tender and gentle towards her sex.

When, therefore, Nurse gave him to understand that she was to marshal him to the altar, Balder, never more heroic than at that moment, offered her his arm, which she accepted with an air of scarecrow gentility. Either the change of costume had struck in, or it was the symbol of inward change. She seemed struggling against her torpor, her dimness and deadness. She tried, perhaps, to recall the day when that dress was first put on,—the day of Helen's marriage, when Salome had attended her mistress to the altar,—when she hoped before many weeks to stand at an altar on her own account.—Not yet, Salome, nor in this world. Perchance not in another; for they who maim their earthly lives may not enjoy in heaven the happiness whose seed was not planted here. The injury is justly irreparable; else had angels been immediately created.

But Salome was practising deception on herself. Airs and graces which might have suited a coquettish lady's-maid, but were in her a ghastly absurdity, did she revive and perpetrate. Struggling to repress the ugly truth, she was in continual dread of exposure. Fain would she dream for an hour of youth and beauty, knowing, yet veiling the knowledge, that it was a dream. Divining her desire, Balder helped out the masquerade as best he might. She was thankfully aware of his kindness, yet shunned acknowledgment, as a too bare betrayal of the cause of thanks.

As they passed a cracked cheval-glass in an intervening room, the bridesmaid stole a glance at her reflection, flirting her fan and giving an imposing whisk to the train of her gown. Helwyse, whom, three days before, this behavior would simply have amused, felt only pitying sympathy today. Gnulemah was always before him, and charmed his eyes and thoughts even to the hag on his arm. He brought himself to address courteous and pleasant remarks to his companion, and to meet unwincingly her one-eyed glance; and was as gallant as though her pretence had been truth.

On entering the conservatory, Nurse seemed as much agitated as though she, instead of Gnulemah, were to be chief actress in the coming ceremony. At the Sphinx door she relinquished Balder's arm, and, hurrying across the conservatory, vanished behind Gnulemah's curtain. As she passed out of sight she threw a parting glance over her shoulder. The action recalled Gnulemah's backward look of the day previous, when she had fled at the sound of the closing door. What ugly fatality suggested so fantastic a parallel between this creature and Balder's future wife!

He entered the temple, which glowed and sparkled like a sombre gem. Many-colored lamps were hung on wires passing round the hall from pillar to massive pillar. Their glare defined the strange character of the Egyptian architecture and ornament; nevertheless, the place looked less real and substantial than in the morning. It seemed the impalpable creation of an enchanter, which his wand would anon dissolve into air once more!

On each side the door sat a statue of polished red granite, with calm regular face and hands on knees. Helwyse, who had not observed them before, fancied them summoned as witnesses to the compact then to be solemnized. Doubtless they had witnessed ceremonies not less solemn or imposing.

On the black marble altar at the further end of the hall was burning some rich incense, whose perfumed smoke, clambering heavily upwards, mingled with that of the lamps beneath the ceiling. On the polished floor, in front, lay a rug of dark blue cloth, heavily bordered with gold; upon it were represented in conscientious profile a number of lank-limbed Egyptians performing some mystic rite. To the right of the altar stood the priest Manetho, apparently engaged in prayer. Balder spoke to him.

"This is more like a tomb than a wedding hall. Would not the conservatory have been more fitting?"

"Better make a tomb the starting-point of marriage than its goal!" smiled the holy man. "And is it not well that your posterity should begin from the spot which saw the union that gave you being? and beneath the eyes of him but for whom neither this hall nor we who here assemble would today have existed!" He pointed to the mummy of old Hiero Glyphic, the aspect of which might have left a bad taste in the mouth of Joy herself. Balder shrugged his shoulders.

"It matters little, perhaps, where the seed is sown, so that the flower reach the sunshine at last. But your mummy is an ill-favored wedding-guest, whatever honor we may owe the man who once lived in it. I would, not have Gnulemah—"

"Behold her!" interrupted Manetho, speaking as hough a handful of dust had suddenly got in his throat.

Yes, there she came, the old Nurse following her like a misshapen shadow. Daughter of sun and moon,—a modern Pandora endowed with the strength of a loftier nature! She was robed in creamy white; her pendants were woven pearls. Fine lines of virgin gold gleamed in her turban, and through her long veil, and along the folds of her girdle. But the serpent necklace had been replaced by the dandelion chain that Balder had made her. Her lips and cheeks were daintily aflame, and a tender fire flickered in her eyes, which saw only Balder. She was a bridal song such as had not been sung since Solomon.

As the two reached the altar, Salome stepped to one side, and Manetho's eye fell upon her; for a moment his gaze fixed, while a slight movement undulated through his body, as the wave travels along the cord. The old white dress, unseen for five-and-twenty years; some intangible trick of motion or attitude in the wearer; the occasion and circumstance recurring with such near similarity,—these and perhaps other trifles combined to recall long-vanished Salome. She had stood at that other wedding, just where Nurse was now,—bright, shapely, sparkling-eyed, full of love for him. What a grisly contrast was this!—Why had he thrown away that ardent, loving heart? How sweet and comfortable might life have been today, with Salome his wife, and sons and daughters at her side,—daughters beautiful as Gnulemah, sons tall as Balder! But Hatred had been his chosen mistress, and dismal was the progeny begotten on her! The pregnant existence that might have been his, and the scars and barrenness which had actually redounded to him, were symbolized in the remembered Salome and her of today.

The brief reminiscence passed, leaving Manetho face to face with his sacred duty. With the warning of the past in his ears and that of the future before his eyes, did he step unrelenting across the threshold of his crime? At all events he neither hesitated nor turned back. But there was no triumph in his eyes, and his tones and manner were heavy and mechanical; as though the Devil (having brought him thus far with his own consent and knowledge) had now to compel a frozen soul in a senseless body!

The service began, none the less hallowed for the lovers, because for Manetho it was the solemn perversion of a sacred ceremony. His voice labored through the perfumed air, and recoiled in broken echoes from gloomy corners and deep-tinted walls. The encircling lamps glowed in serried lines of various light; the fantastic incense-flame rustled softly on the altar. The four figures seemed a group of phantoms,—a momentary rich illusion of the eye. And save for their viewless souls, what were they more? Earth is a phantom; but what we cannot grasp is real and remains!—

The rite was over, the diamond gleamed from Gnulemah's finger, and the priest with uplifted hands had bade man not part whom God had united. Husband and wife gazed at each other with freshness and wonder in their eyes; as having expected to see some change, and anew delighted at finding more of themselves than ever!

Male and female pervades the universe, and marriage is the end and fulfilment of creation. God has builded the world of love and wisdom, woman and man; truly to live they must unite, she yielding herself to his form, he moulding himself of her substance. As love unquickened by wisdom is barren, and knowledge impotent unkindled by affection, so are the unmarried lifeless.

Ill and bitter was it, therefore, for Manetho and Salome, after the married ones had departed, taking their happiness with them. The priest's, eyes were dry and dull, as he leaned wearily against the smoking altar.

"You did not speak!" he said to the woman; "you saw her betrayed to ruin and pollution, and spoke not to save her!—Dumb? the dead might have moved their tongues in such need as this! She will abhor and curse me forever! may you share her curse weighted with mine!—O Gnulemah!"—

Salome cowered and trembled in her satin dress, beneath the burden of that heavy anathema. She had risen that day determined to reveal the secret of her life before night. She had been awaiting a favorable moment, but opportunity or decision still had failed her. Nevertheless, another morning should not find her the same nameless, forsaken creature that she was now.—Manetho had bowed his face upon the altar, and so remained without movement. With one hand fumbling at the bosom of her dress—(the scar of her lover's blow should be the talisman to recall his allegiance),—Salome made bold to approach him and timidly touch his arm.

"Unhand me! whatever you are,—devil! my time is not yet come!"

He raised a threatening arm, with a gleam of mad ferocity beneath his brows. But the woman did not shrink; the man was her god, and she preferred death at his hands to life without him. Ignorant of the cause of her firmness, it seemed to cow him. He slunk behind the altar, hurriedly unlocked the secret door, and let himself into the study. His haste had left the key in the lock outside. The door slammed together, the spring-bolt caught, and the swathed head of old Hiero Glyphic shook as though the cold of twenty winters had come on him at once.

XXXII.

Shut In.

Left alone, Salome was taken with a panic; she fancied herself deserted in a giant tomb, with dead men gathering about her. She herself was in truth the grisliest spectre there, in her white satin gown and feathers, and the horror of her hideous face. But she took to flight, and the key remained unnoticed in the lock.

We, however, must spend an hour with Manetho in his narrow and prisonlike retreat. There is less day and more night between these high-shouldered walls than elsewhere; for though the sun is scarce below the horizon, cobwebs seem to pervade the air, making the evening gray before its time. Yonder seated figure is the nucleus of the gloom. The room were less dark and oppressive, but for him!

Does he mean to spend the night here? He sits at ease, as one who, having labored the day long hard and honestly, finds repose at sundown grateful. Such calm of mind and body argues inward peace—or paralysis!

But Manetho has food for meditation, for his work is still incomplete. Ah, it has been but a sour and anxious work after all! when it is finished, let death come, since Death-in-life will be the sole alternative. Yet will death bring rest to your weariness, think you? Would not Death's eyes look kindlier on you, if you had used more worthily Death's brother,—Life? What would you give, Manetho, to see all that you have done undone? if to undo it were possible!

One picture is ever before you,—you see it wherever you look, and whether your eyes be shut or open,—two loving souls, standing hand in hand before you to be married. How happy they look! how nobly confident is their affection! with what clear freedom their eyes sound one another's depths! Neither cares to have a thought or feeling unshared by the other.—What have you done, Manetho?—shall the deed stand? O dark and distorted soul! the minutes are slipping fast away, and you are slipping with them to a black eternity. Will you stir hand nor foot to save yourself, to break your fall? not raise your voice, for once to speak the truth? Even yet the truth may save!—

The night of your life will this be, Manetho. Will you dream of those whose few hours of bliss will stamp Forever on the seal of your damnation? Think,—through what interminable æons the weight of their just curse will pile itself higher and heavier on your miserable soul! Fain would you doubt the truth of immortality: but the power of unbelief is gone; devillike, you believe and tremble. And where is the reward which should recompense you for this large outlay? Does the honey of your long-awaited triumph offend your lips like gall?—Then woe for him whose morning dreams of vengeance become realities in the evening!—

How stands it between you and Gnulemah, Manetho? She has never loved you ardently, perhaps; but how will you face her hatred? It is late to be asking such questions,—but has not her temperate affection been your most precious possession? have you not yearned and labored for it? have you not loved her with more than a father's tenderness? Under mask of planning her ruin, have not all the softer and better impulses of your nature found exercise and sustenance? Conceiving a devil, have you brought forth an angel, and unawares tasted angelic joy?—If this be true, Manetho, your guilty purpose towards her is not excused, but how much more awful becomes the contemplation of her fate! Rouse up! sluggard, rush forth! you may save her yet. Up! would you risk the salvation of three souls to glut a meaningless spite? You have been fighting shadows with a shadow. Up!—it is the last appeal.—

You stir,—get stiffly to your feet,—put hand to forehead,—stare around. The twilight has deepened apace; only by glancing upwards can you distinguish a definite light. You are uncertain and lethargic in your movements, as though the dawning in you of a worthy resolution had impaired the evil principle of your vitality. You are as a man nourished on poison, who suddenly tastes an antidote,—and finds it fatal!

You halt towards the door and put forth a hand to open it. You will save Gnulemah; her innocence will save her from the knowledge of her loss. As for Balder,—his suffering will satisfy a reasonable enemy. No wife, no fortune, the cup dashed from his lips just as the aroma was ravishing his nostrils!—O, enough! Open the door, therefore, and go forth.

In your magnanimity you feel for the key, but it is not in its accustomed place. Try your pockets; still in vain! Startled, you turn to the table, and feel carefully over it from end to end. You raise the heavy chair like a feather, and shake it bottom downwards. Nothing falls. You are down on your knees groping affrighted amongst the dust and rubbish of the floor. The key is lost! You spring up,—briskly enough now,—and stand with your long fingers working against one another, trying to think. That key,—where had you it last?—

A blank whirl is your memory,—nothing stands clearly out. How came you here? With whom did you speak just now? What was said?—Two persons there seemed to be, oddly combined in one,—most unfamiliar in their familiarity. Or was it your evil genius, Manetho? who by devilish artifice has at this last hour shut the door against your first good impulse; locked the door against soul and body; shut you in and carried off the key of your salvation.

Do not give way yet; review your situation carefully.—Your voice would be inaudible through these massive walls, were the listener but a yard away.—Be quick with your thinking, for the unmitigable minutes are dying fast and forever.—Were it known that you were here, could you be got out? No, for the secret of the door is known only to yourself. Those who once shared the knowledge with you are dead, or many years gone! Your evil genius no doubt knows it, and all your secrets; but dream not that she will liberate you. She has been awaiting this opportunity. You shall remain here tonight and many nights. Your bones shall lie gaunt on this cobwebbed floor. Only the daily sunbeam shall know of your tomb. And Gnulemah?...

Your knees falter beneath you, and you sink in wretched tears to the floor,—tears that bring no drop of comfort. To be shut up alone with a soul like yours, at the moment when the sin so long tampered with has escaped your control, and is pitilessly doing its devilish work on the other side your prison-walls, near, yet inaccessible,—who can measure the horror of it? Till now you have made your will the law of right and wrong, and read your life by no higher light than your own. You read it otherwise tonight, lying here helpless and alone. That lost key has unlocked the fair front of your complacency and revealed the wizened deformity behind it. You have been insane; but the anguish that would craze a sane man clears the mist from your reason. You behold the truth at last; but as the drowning man sees the ship pass on and leave him.

But we care not to watch too curiously the writhings of your imprisoned soul, Manetho; the less, because we doubt whether the agony will be of benefit to you. Forgiveness of enemies is perhaps beyond your scope; even your rage to save Gnulemah was kindled chiefly by your impotence to do so. God forbid we do you less than justice! but hope seems dim for such as you; nor will a deathbed repentance, however sincere, avail to wipe away the sins of a lifetime. Jealousy of Balder, rather than desire for Gnulemah's eternal weal, awoke your conscience. For the thought of their spending life in happy ignorance of their true relationship inflames—does not allay—your agony!

Your womanish outburst of despairing tears over, a hot fever of restlessness besets you. The space is narrow for disquiet such as yours,—you hunt up and down the strip of floor like a caged beast. No way out,—no way out!—Face to face with lingering death, why not hasten it? No moral scruple withholds you. Yet will you not die by your own hand. Through all your suffering you will cling to life and worship it. Never will you open your arms to death,—which seems to you no grave, compassionate angel, but a malignant fiend lying in ambush for your soul. And such a fiend will your death be; for to all men death is the reflection of their life in the mind's mirror.—Still to and fro you fare, a moving shadow through a narrow gloom, walled in with stone.

Awful is this unnatural sanity of intellect: it is like the calm in the whirlwind's centre, where the waves run higher though the air is deadly still, and the surly mariner wishes the mad wind back again.—To and fro you flit, goaded on and strengthened by untiring anguish. You are but the body of a man; your thought and emotion are abroad, haunting the unconscious, happy lovers!—

Suddenly you stop short in your blind walk, throw up your arms, and break into an irrepressible chuckle. Has your brain given way at last?—No, your laugh is the outcome of a genuine revulsion of feeling, intense but legitimate. What is the cause of it?—You plunge into the rubbish-heap at one end of the room, and grasp and draw forth the rickety old ladder which has been lying there these twenty years. You have seen it almost daily, poking out amidst the cobwebs, and probably for that very reason have so long failed to perceive that it was susceptible of a better use than to be food for worms. You set it upright against the wall; its top round falls three feet below the horizontal aperture. Enough, if you tread with care. Narrow, steep, and rickety is the path to deliverance; but up! for your time is short.

Upward, with cautious eagerness! The ladder is warped and rests unevenly, and once or twice a round cracks beneath the down-pressing foot; the thing is all unsound and might fall to pieces at any moment. However, the top is gained, and your nervous hands are on the sill at last. Easing yourself a little higher, you look forth on the world once more.

Not so late after all! Red still lingers along the western horizon, but against it is mounting and expanding a black cloud, glancing ever and anon with dangerous lightning. In a clear sky-lake above the cloud, steadily burns a planet. The gentle twilight rests lovingly on earth's warm bosom—

Hark! look! what moves yonder beneath the trees?—

Your parched, eager face strained forwards, your hungry eyes eating through the gloom,—see emerge from the avenue two figures, sauntering loverlike side to side! How forgetful of the world they seem! Little think they of you, of the rack on which you have been outstretched. But their hour has come. This moment shall be their last of peace,—their last of happy love.

—What sound was that?—Was it a yell of triumph,—a shout for help,—a scream of terror?—It does not come again; but the silence is more terrible than the cry.

XXXIII

The Black Cloud.

"Hiero,—it was his voice!" said Gnulemah. She looked in her lover's face, trusting to his wisdom and strength. She rested her courage on his, but her eyes stirred him like a trumpet-call. The burden of that cry had been calamity. Love is protean, makes but a step from dalliance to grandeur. Balder, no longer a sentimental bridegroom, stood forth ready, brief, energetic,—but more a lover than before!

The voice had at the first moment sounded startlingly clear, then it had seemed distant and muffled. As Helwyse swiftly skirted the granite wall of the temple, his mind was busy with conjecture; but he failed to hit upon any reasonable explanation. The cry had come from the direction of the temple, and had he known of the existence of the apertures through the masonry, he might partly have solved the mystery. As it was, he thought only of getting inside, feeling sure that, explainably or not, Manetho must be there.

In the oaken hall he met Nurse, who had also heard the cry, but knew not whence it proceeded.

"In the temple, I think," said Helwyse, answering her agitated gesture.

The clew was sufficient; she sped along towards the door whence she had so lately fled panic-stricken, Helwyse following. Beneath the solemn excitement and perplexity, lay warm and secure in his heart the thought of Gnulemah,—his wife. Blessed thought! which the whips and scorns of time should make but more tenderly dear and precious.

As he breathed the incense-laden air of the temple, Balder's face grew stern. At each step he thought to see death in some ghastly form. In the joy of this his marriage night he had wished all the world might have rejoiced with him; but already was calamity abroad. Birth and death, love and hate, happiness and woe, are borne on every human breath, and mingled with daily meat and drink. So be it!—They were parodies of humanity who should live on a purer diet or inhale a rarer atmosphere.

All the lights in the great hall, except the altar lamp, were burnt out, and the place was very dusky. Nurse went straight towards the secret door, looking neither to the right nor left; while Helwyse, who did not suspect its existence, was prying into each dark nook and corner. An inarticulate exclamation from the woman arrested him. She was standing behind the altar, close to the clock. As he approached she pointed to the wall. She had found the key in the lock, but dared not be first to brave the sight of what might be within. She appealed to the strength of the man, yet with a morbid jealousy of his precedence.

Helywse saw the key, and, turning it, the seeming-solid wall disclosed a door, opening outwards, a single slab of massive granite. Within all was dark, and there was no sound. Was anything there?

He looked round to address Nurse, but her appearance checked him. She was staring into the darkness; he could feel her one-eyed glance pass him, fastening on something beyond. He moved to let the lamplight enter the doorway; and then in the illuminated square that fell on the floor he saw Manetho's upturned face. The fallen priest lay with one arm doubled under him, the other thrown across his breast. Nurse stared at her broken idol, motionless, with stertorous breathing.

But was Manetho dead? Helwyse, the physician, stepped across the threshold, and stooped to examine the body. The dumb creature followed and lay down, animallike, close beside the deity of her worship. Presently the physician said,—

"There's life in him, but he's hurt internally. We must find a way to move him from here."

"Life!"—the woman heard, nor cared for more. Her dry fixedness gave way with a gasp, and she broke into hysteric tears, rocking herself backwards and forwards, crooning over the insensible body, or stooping to kiss it. She had no sense nor heed for the lover of her youth.

"Could such a creature have been his wife? even his mistress?" questioned Helwyse of himself. But he spoke out sharply:—

"You must stop this. He must be revived at once. Go and make ready a bed, and I will carry him to it."

As he spoke, a silent shadow fell across the body, and Gnulemah stood in the doorway. Balder's first impulse was to motion her away from a spectacle so unsuited to her eyes. But though the shadow made her face inscrutable, the lines of her figure spoke, and not of weak timidity or effeminate consternation. Womanly she was,—instinct with that tender, sensitive power, the marvellous gift of God to woman only, which almost moves the sick man to bless his sickness. A holy gift,—surely the immediate influx of Christ's spirit. Man knows it not, albeit when he and woman have become more closely united than now, he may attain to share the Divine prerogative. Study nor skill can counterfeit it; but in the true woman it is perfect at the first appeal as at the last.

"He shall have my bed," said this young goddess Isis; "it is ready, and my lamp is burning."

Balder stooped to uplift his insensible burden.

"O, not so!—more tenderly than that," she interposed, softly. A moment's hesitation, and then she unfastened the golden shoulder-clasp, and shook off her ample mantle. This was Manetho's litter.

"I will help you carry him.—Why do you weep, Nurse? he will awake, or Balder would have told us."

Never, since Diana stooped to earth to love Endymion, was seen a nobler sight than Gnulemah in her simple, clinging tunic, whose heavy golden hem kissed her polished knee, while her round and clear-cut arms were left bare. After the first glance, her lover lowered his eyes, lest he should forget all else in gazing at her. But the blood mounted silently to his cheeks and burned there. As for her,—she trusted Balder more freely than herself.

Manetho was laid gently on the broad robe, and so upraised and borne forwards; Balder at the head, Gnulemah at the foot. Heavy, heavy is a lifeless body; but the man had cause to wonder at the woman's fresh and easy strength. What a contrast was she to the disfigured creature who hobbled moaning beside the litter, the relaxed hand clutched in both hers, kissing it again and again with grotesque passion! Yet both were women, and loved as women love.

The granite statues sitting serene at the doorway maintained the stony calm which, only, deserves the name of supernatural. These passed, the flowery heat of the dim conservatory brought them to Gnulemah's room. The curtain was looped up and the passage clear. Thus first did the wedded pair enter what should have been their bridal chamber, and laid the lifeless body on the nuptial bed.

A fair, pure room; the clear walls frescoed with graceful wreaths of floating figures. In the eastern window, through which the earliest sun-beams loved to fall, stood an alabaster altar; on it a chain of faded dandelions. The bed was a lovely nest, the lines flowing in long curves,—a barge of Venus for lovers to voyage to heaven in. On a table near at hand lay some embroidered work at which Gnulemah's magic needle had been busy of late. Balder glanced at these things with a reverence almost timid; and, turning back to what lay so inert and doltish on the sacred bed, he could not but sigh.

Every means was employed to rally the Egyptian from his swoon. He bore no external marks of injury, but there could be no doubt that he had sustained a terrible shock, and possibly concussion of the brain; the amount of the internal damages could not yet be estimated.—Mean-while the black cloud from the west was muttering drowsily overhead, and an occasional lightning-flash dulled the mild radiance of the lamp.

As consciousness ebbed back to the patient, the storm increased, and the trembling roll of heavy thunder drowned the first gasps of returning life. Had that vast cloud come to shut out his soul from heaven, and was its mighty voice uttering the sentence of his condemnation? The air was thick with the inconsolable weeping of the rain, and gusty sighs of wind drove its cold teardrops against the window.

How was it with Manetho?—During the instant after the ladder had given way and he was rushing through the air and clutching vainly at the dark void, every faculty had violently expanded, so that he seemed to see and think at every pore. The next instant his rudely battered body refused to bear the soul's messages; light and knowledge sank into bottomless darkness!

By and by—for aught he knew it might have been an eternity—a brief gleam divided the night; then another, and others; he seemed to be moving through air, upborne on a cloud. He strove to open his eyes, and caught a glimpse of reeling walls,—of a figure,—figures. A deep rumbling sound was in his ears, as of the rolling together of chaotic rocks, gradually subsiding into stillness.

He felt no pain, only dreamy ease. He was resting softly on a bank of flowers, in the heart of a summer's day. He was filled with peace and love, and peace and love were around him. Some one was nestling beside him; was it not the woman,—the bright-eyed, smiling gypsy with whom he had plighted troth?—surely it was she.

"Salome,—Salome, are you here? Touch me,—lay your cheek by mine. So,—give me your hand. I love you, my pretty pet,—your Manetho loves you!"

The slow sentences ended. Nurse had laid her unsightly head beside his on the pillow, and the two were happy in each other. O piteous, revolting, solemn sight! Those faces, grief-smitten, old; long ago, in passionate and lawless youth, they had perchance lain thus and murmured loving words. And now for a moment they met and loved again,—while death knocked at their chamber door!

But Balder had perceived a startling significance in Manetho's words. He took Gnulemah by the hand and led her to the eastern window. A flash greeted them, creating a momentary world, which started from the womb of night, and vanished again before one could say "It is there!" Then followed a long-drawn, intermittent rumble, as if the fragments of the spectre world were tumbling avalanche-wise into chaos.

"I remember now about the dandelions," Balder said. "Was not Nurse with us then?"

"Yes," answered Gnulemah; "and it was she and Hiero who took me from you. But why does he call her Salome? and who is Manetho?"

Balder did not reply. He leant against the window-frame and gazed out into the black storm. Knowing what he now did, it required no great stretch of ingenuity to unravel Manetho's secret.—He turned to Gnulemah, and, taking her in his arms, kissed her with a defiant kind of ardor.

"What is it?" she whispered, clinging to him with a reflex of his own unspoken emotion.

"We are safe!—But that man shall not die without hearing the truth," he added, sternly.

Again there was a dazzling lightning-flash, and the thunder seemed to break at their very ears. By a quick, sinuous movement, Gnulemah freed herself from his arm and looked at him with her grand eyes,—night-black, lit each with a sparkling star. Her feminine intuition perceived a change in him, though she could not fathom its cause. It jarred the fineness of their mutual harmony.

"Our happiness should make others' greater," said she.

He looked into her eyes with a gaze so ardent that their lids drooped; and the tone of his answer, though loverlike, had more of masculine authority in it than she had yet heard from him.

"My darling, you do not know what wrong he has done you—and others. It is only justice that he should learn how God punishes such as he!"

"Will not God teach him?" said Gnulemah, trembling to oppose the man she loved, yet by love compelled to do so.

Balder paused, and looked towards the bed. There was a flickering smile on Manetho's face; he seemed to be reviving. His injuries were perhaps not fatal after all. Should he recover, he must sooner or later receive his so-called punishment; meanwhile, Balder was inclined to regard himself as the chosen minister of Divine justice. Why not speak now?

This was the second occasion that he had held Manetho in his power, at a time when the Egyptian had been attempting his destruction. In the previous encounter he had retaliated in kind. Would the bitter issue of that self-indulgence not make him wary now? Here was again the murderous lust of power, albeit disguised as love of justice. Had Balder's penitent suffering failed to teach him the truth of human brotherhood, and equality before God? Love, typified by Gnulemah, would fain dissuade him from his purpose: but love (as often happens when it stands in the way of harsh and ignoble impulses) appeared foolishly merciful.

Once again his glance met Gnulemah's,—lingered a moment,—and then turned away. It was for the last time. At that moment he was less noble than ever before. But the expression of her eyes he never forgot; the love, the entreaty, the grandeur,—the sorrow!—

He turned away and approached the bedside, while Gnulemah went to kneel at her maiden altar. Manetho's eyes were closed; his features wore a singularly childlike expression. In truth, he was but half himself; the shock he had sustained had paralyzed one part of his nature. The subtle, evil-plotting Egyptian was dormant; his brain interpreted nothing save the messages of the heart; only the affectionate, emotional Manetho was awake. The evil he had done and the misery of it were forgotten.—All this Balder divined; yet his assumption of godlike censorship would not permit him to relent. It is when man deems himself most secure that he falls, in a worse way than ever.

"Do you know me, Manetho?" demanded the young man.

The priest opened his eyes dreamily, and smiled, but made no further answer.

"I am Balder Helwyse,—the son of Thor," continued the other, speaking with incisive deliberation, better to touch the stunned man's apprehension, "I once had a twin sister. You believe that Gnulemah is she."

The priest's features were getting a bewildered, plaintive expression. Either he was beginning to comprehend the purport of Balder's words, or else the sternness of the latter's tone and glance agitated him.

Bader concentrated all his force into the utterance of the final sentences, vowing to himself that his fallen enemy should understand! Did he think of Gnulemah then? or of Salome—partly for whose; sake, he feigned, he had assumed the scourge?

"My sister died,—was burned to death before she was a year old. In trying to save her, the nurse almost lost her own life. On that same night, this nurse gave birth to a daughter,—whose name you have called Gnulemah. Salome is her mother. Who her father is, Manetho, you best know!"

The words were spoken,—but had the culprit heard them? Salome (who from the first had shrunk back to the head of the bed, beyond the possible range Manetho's vision) burst into confused hysteric cries. Gnulemah had risen from her altar and was looking at Balder: he felt her glance,—but though he told himself that he had done but justice, he dared not meet it!—He kept his eyes fastened on the pallid countenance of the Egyptian. The latter's breath came feebly and irregularly, but the anxious expression was gone, and there was again the flickering smile. All at once there was an odd, solemn change.—

The man was dying. Balder saw it,—saw that his enemy was

escaping him unpunished! There yet remained one stimulant that might rouse him, and in the passion of the moment this self-appointed lieutenant of the Almighty applied it.

"Come forward here, Salome!" cried he; "let him look on the face that his sins have given you. As there is a God in Heaven, your wrongs shall be set right!"

Salome moved to obey; but Gnulemah glided swiftly up and held her back. Balder stepped imperiously forward to enforce his will. Had he but answered his wife's eyes even then!—He came forward one step.

Then burst a thunderclap like the crashing together of heaven and earth! At the same instant a blinding, hot glare shut out all sight. Balder was hurled back against the wall, a shock like the touch of death in every nerve.

He staggered up, all unstrung, his teeth chattering. He saw,—not the lamp, flickering in the draught from the broken window,—not Manetho, lying motionless with the smile frozen on his lips,—not Salome, prostrate across the body of him she had worshipped.

He saw Gnulemah—his wife whom he loved—rise from the altar's step against which she had been thrown; stand with outstretched arms and blank, wide-open eyes; grope forwards with outstretched arms and uncertain feet; grope blindly this way and that, moaning,—

"Balder,—Balder,—where are you?"

Shivering and desperate,—not yet daring for his life to understand,—he came and stood before her, almost within reach of those groping hands.

"I am here,—look at me, Gnulemah!—I am here—your husband!"

There was a pause. The storm, having spent itself in that last burst, was rolling heavily away. There was silence in the nuptial chamber, infringed only by the breathing of the newly married lovers.

"I hear you, Balder," said Gnulemah at length, tremulously, while her blank eyes rested on his face, "but I cannot see you. My lamp must have gone out. Will not you light it for me?"—

Vengeance is mine, saith the Lord: I will repay!

The storm-cloud moved eastward and was dispersed. Black though had been its shadow, it endured but for a moment; the echo of its fury passed away, and its deadly thunderbolt left behind a purer atmosphere. So sweeps and rages over men's heads the storm of calamity; and so dissolves, though seeming for the time indissoluble.

But the distant planet comes forth serene from its brief eclipse, and as night deepens, bears its steady fire yet more aloft. Like God's love, its radiance embraces the world, yet forgets not the smallest flower nor grain of sand. From its high station it beholds the infinite day surround the night, and knows the good before and beyond the ill. Great is its hope, for causes are not hidden from its quiet eternal eye.

No journal of a life has been our tale; rather a glimpse of a beginning! We have traversed an alpine pass between the illimitable lands of Past and Future. We have felt the rock rugged beneath our feet; have seen the avalanche and mused beside the precipice, and have taken what relief we might in the scanty greensward, the few flowers, and the brief sunshine. Now, standing on the farewell promontory, let us question the magic mirror concerning the further road,—as, before, of that from the backward horizon hitherwards.

Mr. MacGentle's quiet little office: himself—more venerable by a year than when we saw him last—in his chair: opposite him, Dr. Balder Helwyse. The latter wears a thick yellow beard about six inches in length, is subdued in dress and manner, and his smile, though genial, has something of the sadness of autumn sunshine. The two have been conversing earnestly, and now there is a short silence.

"We must give up hoping it, then," says Mr. MacGentle at last, in a more than usually plaintive murmur. "It is hard,—very hard, dear Balder."

"Now that I know there is no hope, I can acknowledge the good even while I feel the hardship. Her dreams have been of a world such as no real existence could show; to have been awakened would permanently have saddened her, if no worse. But she is great enough to believe without seeing; and in the deepest sense, her belief is true. She still remains in that ideal fairyland in which I found her; and no doubt, as time goes on, her visions grow more beautiful!"

Thus speaks Balder Helwyse, in tones agreeably vigorous, though grave and low.

"Yes—yes; and perhaps, dear Balder, the denial of this one great boon may save her from much indefinite disquiet; and certainly, as you say, from the great danger of disappointment and its consequences. Yes,—and you may still keep her lamp alight, with a more lasting than Promethean fire!—But how is it with you, dear boy?"

"Let none who love me pray for my temporal prosperity," returns Helwyse, turning his strong, dark gaze on the other's aged eyes. "I have met with many worshippers of false gods, but none the germs of whose sin I found not in myself. The *I* to whom was confided this excellent instrument of faculties and senses is a poor, weak, selfish creature, who fancied his gifts argued the possession of the very merits whose lack they prove. God, in His infinite mercy, deals sternly with me; and I know how to thank Him!"—

Mr. MacGentle does not reply in words; but a grave smile glimmers in his faded eyes, and, smiling, he slowly shakes his venerable head.

One more brief glimpse, and then we are done.—

A pleasant parlor of southern aspect, looking through a deep bay-window over a spacious garden. Here sits a stalwart gentleman of middle age, with a little boy and girl on either knee, who play bo-peep with his wide-spreading yellow beard. How they all laugh! and what a pleasant laugh has the stalwart, dark-eyed gentleman,—so deep-toned and yet so boyish! But presently all three pause to take breath.

"Thor," then says the gentleman, "whose portrait did I tell you that was?" And he points to an oil-painting hanging over the piano.

"Grandpapa MacGentle, papa!"

"What did he do for all of us?"

As Master Thor hesitates a moment, the little golden-haired lady breaks in,—"*I* know, papa! He made uth rich, and gave uth our houthe, and he thaw me when I wath a wee, wee baby, and then he—he—"

"He went to Heaven, papa!" says Thor, recovering himself.

Hereupon there was a silence, because the two children, glancing up in their father's face, saw that it was grave and thoughtful.

But suddenly the little girl pricks up her small ears, and scrambles to the carpet, and sets off for the door at full speed, without a word. Thor is close behind, but just too late to be first in opening the door.

"Mamma! mamma!"

And Balder Helwyse springs up, and as she enters with the rejoicing children at each hand, he meets her with the thrilling smile which, in this world, she will never see!

THE END.

www.ingramcontent.com/pod-product-compliance
Lightning Source LLC
Chambersburg PA
CBHW030502260626
47157CB00005B/1604